# On the Scent

## ANGELA CAMPBELL

Harper*Impulse* an imprint of
HarperCollins*Publishers Ltd*
77–85 Fulham Palace Road
Hammersmith, London W6 8JB

www.harpercollins.co.uk

A Paperback Original 2013

First published in Great Britain in ebook format by HarperImpulse 2013

Copyright © Angela Campbell 2013

Cover Images © Shutterstock.com

Angela Campbell asserts the moral right to
be identified as the author of this work

A catalogue record for this book
is available from the British Library

ISBN: 978-0-00-755965-7

This novel is entirely a work of fiction.
The names, characters and incidents portrayed in it are
the work of the author's imagination. Any resemblance to
actual persons, living or dead, events or localities is
entirely coincidental.

Automatically produced by Atomik ePublisher from Easypress

*Thank you to my BFF, Cindy, for encouraging me to follow my dreams.*

*Thank you to my best friends in fur, Dusti, Valentino, Sunny and Ginger, for inspiring the characters who stole this story.*

*Thank you to my amazing critique partners, Jennifer, Pamela and Cynthia, and the many beta readers who offered me their time and feedback.*

*Finally, thank you to Charlotte Ledger for recognizing the potential in this story and helping bring me it to the world.*

*For the rest of you, remember to spay and neuter your pets. There are lots of homeless animals at shelters in need of good homes. Please consider adopting one!*

# *Chapter One*

"Check this out, bro." E.J. lowered his voice as he stepped closer. "There's a real *dog* out here to see you."

Zachary Collins paused mid pull-up and clenched his jaw. Dammit, didn't E.J. know *anything* about office etiquette? Last thing they needed was a complaint about rude employees to the Better Business Bureau.

"Not appropriate, E.J." Zach huffed as he lifted his chin up over the bar he'd mounted in the doorway to his office's private bathroom. His left arm began to tremble beneath the strain. "What's she want?"

*Nine.*

*Ten.*

*Done.*

He dropped to the floor, shook the slight tingle out of his left hand, and reached for the towel draped across his chair. E.J. leaned back against the closed door and shrugged. "Dunno. She just asked for you."

He'd known putting E.J. at the reception desk was a bad idea. The kid was too rough around the edges. Too ignorant of the job.

Wiping the sweat from his neck, Zach made his way to his desk. The security monitor on his computer screen showed him the side profile of a dark-haired woman sitting in the waiting room.

1

Dog? Not from what he could see.

As though she sensed she was being watched, she shifted and looked directly into the corner camera mounted in the lobby. She stared for a minute before she looked down at her hands, clenching and unclenching in her lap.

Shit.

It was *her*.

Zach swore and pounded a fist on his desk. He reached for his phone. "Isn't Brian around? Kellan?" He punched in his partner's extension, only to get Brian's voicemail.

"Sure, but—" Beside him, E.J. tugged at the necktie Zach had insisted he wear and shuffled on his feet. "The lady specifically asked for you and said she'd take her business elsewhere if you weren't available."

Slamming the phone back in the cradle, Zach stepped into the bathroom and splashed some water on his face before hurrying to change into his respectable white button-down shirt and black slacks. "Did she say why she wanted to see me?"

The young man scrunched his face. "Nah, man. Just said it was important."

*I'm-here-to-serve-you-papers important?* He hoped not.

"Is she alone?" He ran a hand through his thick hair. Not too damp.

"There ain't nobody with her, but—"

"Send her in."

Deodorant. Where the hell was his deodorant? He splashed on a dash of cologne instead and hurried to his desk.

Zach's name might headline the private security agency—hell, his name *was* the agency—but he took a hands-off approach to handling cases these days. He liked the easy ones. Ones that could be done behind a computer or with a phone call here and there. He'd lost his desire for adrenaline rushes six months ago, right after—

*No. Don't even think about it.*

He had no need for that shit anymore. He was strictly in business management now. Safe and easy. That was his new work mantra.

Unfortunately, this woman was not going to be safe and easy for him, and he didn't have to be psychic to know that.

Reaching for the bottle of antacids in his drawer, he popped one in his mouth. He kept them there for when the bill collectors came snooping around. Or fans, who hadn't forgotten him yet.

His door opened, and Zach blinked in surprise when a short, stubby-legged, long-snouted golden retriever with beady eyes came trotting into his office. Some kind of mixed breed, or maybe a genetic experiment.

A smile got the better of him. Now that was a cute mutt.

The dog slowly maneuvered its chunky body over to where Zach was standing, wrapped its front paws around Zach's leg and started humping.

"Hey!" Zach tried to jostle him off, but the little guy was stronger than he looked.

"Oh, geez, I'm so sorry." The woman appeared in the doorway, her green gaze wide. She clapped her hands and yelled, "Costello! Down, boy. Down!"

The dog immediately obeyed.

"I'm so sorry. He got away from me." She closed her eyes and shook her head. She grabbed the leash the dog had been trailing behind him. When she straightened, she held out her other hand. "My name is Hannah Dawson. Thank you for giving me a few minutes of your time, Mr. Collins."

His vision blurred as his heart thumped a wild beat against his chest.

Just. Stay. Calm.

It took all of Zach's training not to react as he accepted her handshake. His body jerked in surprise when a furry white and black head popped out of the bag beneath the woman's arm. The cat let loose a loud yowling meow and took a swipe at his hand.

What the—?

Hannah wrenched back. "Oh, no I am *so* sorry. I don't know what's got into them."

Uh…

"Abbott, behave." She zipped the top of the pink mesh bag, leaving a pair of yellow eyes peering at him from behind a see-through front. A growling sound came from the carrier when the woman sat it on the ground.

This was weird, and for Zach, that was saying a lot. In his five years of running Collins Security Firm, he'd never felt so caught off-guard by a situation.

"Miss Dawson?"

She looked at him and nodded.

"Perhaps we could reschedule this for another time when you can leave your—" Zach squinted down at the dog, who was panting happily with its tongue hanging out of its mouth "—pets at home?"

And he could arrange for Brian to meet with her instead. Sweat gathered at the back of his neck. He didn't need this. Not now. Not *her*.

"Oh, but I can't. I can't go anywhere without them. I can't even go to the bathroom on my own anymore." She threw up her hands and looked like she was near tears. "That's why I need your help. That's why I'm here."

She had no idea who he was.

Every muscle in Zach's body relaxed at that realization. Even so, he skimmed her profile to reassure himself she wasn't playing him for a fool. Not much had changed. She was in her early thirties, but she looked younger. Long, straight black hair, average height but slim. Well-dressed.

Why the hell was she here if she didn't know who he was?

She lifted her pretty face, and the vulnerability he saw in her glistening green eyes had him second-guessing his decision to send her away. This woman wasn't vindictive or crazy. She was desperate.

He cleared his throat. "Why don't you have a seat?"

Sinking into the chair across from his desk, Hannah buried her face in her hands and groaned. She spread her fingers and looked at him. "I seem like a freak, don't I?" Glancing around his office, she lowered her hand and began petting the dog. "I'm not crazy. I'm just…stressed."

Nodding, he sank into his cushy office chair. "Before you get too far, I should warn you that our prices aren't cheap. I offer a free consultation on referral, but—"

"I can pay for the consultation," she interjected. "And I can afford your services." She glanced down at the dog. "Actually, *they* can afford your services. They're the ones who will be hiring you."

Another one he hadn't heard before.

Before he could speak, she snatched the newspaper lying on his desk, turned to a page close to the front and pressed it down in front of him. She tapped the top headline.

*Secret heiress leaves $10 million to her cat, dog.*

"That's Abbott, the cat, and Costello is the dog." She gestured to each animal as she said their names. A picture of the dog and cat posing with an elderly woman accompanied the article. "And if you'd like to take a few minutes to read this, I don't mind waiting."

Zach picked up the newspaper and focused on the article, trying to keep his expression rigid, give nothing away. Not easy, since most of the information he read surprised the hell out of him. The elderly heiress had kept her fortune a secret, leaving a trust fund in her animals' names. A nurse who'd cared for Ellie Parham in her final years had been tasked with minding the ridiculously rich cat and dog.

He guessed the reason Hannah Dawson was here was because she'd become a target for every wacko and get-rich schemer in the region. Her coming to their agency today seemed like an awfully big coincidence, though. How much did she know? What had the old woman told her?

"If you don't mind my asking, Miss Dawson, why did you choose our firm?" He watched her expression for a nonverbal giveaway.

"I recognized your name. From your TV show," she clarified, although it wasn't necessary.

A surprising demographic of people watched reality television—especially the true crime channel that had aired *The Psychic Detective* until its cancellation six years ago. That this woman had seen his show both surprised and pissed him off. He didn't like to be reminded of his past.

Shit.

Ten million dollars. Left to a cat and dog. How could he not want a slice of that? There was a past due notice for the office's lease sitting on his desk right now that could be taken care of by the end of the week with profit from a client like Hannah. He could stop losing sleep for worry of not making payroll.

His mama's voice whispered through his mind in a childhood memory from Sunday school. *Whatsoever a man soweth, that shall he also reap, Zachary.*

If Hannah Dawson figured out the connection between them, she might pull her business, maybe file a lawsuit against him, expose the psychic detective for the sham he'd been. That was a headache he didn't need. The smart thing would be to refer her to another agency and cut ties now.

No.

They needed the money too much. It was a risk he'd have to take.

Zach held the folded newspaper up with one hand. "So you're the unnamed nurse mentioned in this article?" His glance fell to the pink carrier beside her. "And this is the richest cat and dog in America?"

"I think they might be the richest cat and dog in the world, but who knows?" She flashed an endearing smile as her fingers brushed through the dog's mane of fur. "In her will, Miss Parham named me as their caregiver and also left me a considerable amount of money. She knew I would take care of them—or die trying. It's that die trying part I'm a little worried about."

Zachary stood and perched on the edge of his desk before leaning forward. "I'm listening."

She took a deep breath. "Ellie passed away about nine months ago, but the newspaper didn't pick up on her will until four weeks ago. Some baseball player died, and a reporter came across Ellie's records in probate while researching that man's wealth. Anyway, people started calling Ellie's number and showing up at her place, looking for a handout, so I moved. Yesterday someone broke into my new house and tried to kidnap the boys. That person—"

He held up a hand. "The boys?"

"Sorry. That's what I call the cat and dog." She gave her dog a pat on the head before resting her hands in her lap. "Anyway, the person probably would've succeeded, but Costello is…quite heavy for such a short dog. Plus, he can be aggressive when he realizes something is wrong. He bit a piece of the man's pants off before I grabbed my baseball bat and chased the guy away."

"I see." She was beautiful *and* gutsy. He liked that. "How do you know they were there for the cat and dog?"

Her fingers tugged and pulled at each other. "He'd left a ransom note on the table. It said I would be contacted about paying one million to get the animals back alive." Her eyes glistened, but she blinked away the tears. "I called the police after making sure the boys were safe."

He frowned. "What'd they say?"

She shrugged. "Not much. I overheard one of the officers saying to the other one, 'What's the big deal? Nothing was taken. It's just a cat and dog. We've got better things to do with our time.'"

He rubbed at the tight muscles in his neck.

"Can you help me, Mr. Collins?"

Good question. Could he?

Hannah eased back in her chair and watched Zachary Collins closely, but if this sexy-as-sin man had known her late employer, he was doing a fine job of not giving the fact away.

His face still scrunched, he stood up and moved back to his chair. "Collins Security specializes in helping people safeguard their home. I can get one of my people to come out to your place, arrange an alarm system and teach you some safety precautions."

*Don't roll your eyes. Don't. Do. It. I mean, really.* As if she hadn't already tried all of that. "I came to your firm because I'm looking for more help than that." She bit her lip. "And because I would like to hire your services as a psychic."

There it was. The woman who thought all that supernatural mumbo jumbo was baloney wanted to hire a freaking psychic.

Good grief, had it really come to this?

She expected him to ask, "Why?" but Zachary simply sat back in his chair, rested one ankle on his opposite knee and created a triangle with his fingers. His penetrating gaze never wavered from hers.

"You want me to communicate with the animals?"

A rush of air escaped her lungs. She hadn't even realized she'd been holding her breath.

"Yes!" she exclaimed, wondering if she should tell him everything or stick to the story she'd rehearsed on the way over here. "Like I said, I'm familiar with the show you did several years ago, and even though your website didn't advertise your services as a psychic, I thought —"

"—that I could get inside their heads and tell you what they want from you? Are they happy? That kind of thing?" Not exactly, but she would use the excuse. Hannah nodded.

Lord, she almost hoped he wasn't psychic, or else he'd see right through her and know exactly why she was here.

Ellie's attorney had relayed to Hannah a cryptic message from the will. *These animals are the key to my past. Only they know the truth. When you're ready to hear it, they'll tell you.*

O-kay. Tell her what? Better yet, tell her *how*?

Mixed in with the instructions Ellie had left for Hannah had also been a brief scribbled note and a clipped article from a magazine. *When I die, hire this man to help you.* The torn and tattered old article had been a brief story previewing an upcoming season of *The Psychic Detective*. A publicity shot of Zachary Collins with his thick, dark hair, square-jawed masculinity, and eyes so blue they'd reminded her of the Georgia sky on a sunny day had taken up most of the page. His charisma in print had packed such a wallop, it was easy to understand why the man had been cast in his own TV show. Who the heck cared if he was psychic or a detective? The man was gorgeous.

Hannah had assumed he was only an actor, but Zachary Collins was a legit investigator. His website announced he'd opened an agency in Atlanta a little over five years ago. Licensed, bonded, and he'd come highly recommended by the Georgia Board of Private Detectives and Security Agencies when she'd called this morning.

Okay. Psychic plus detective. Hannah wasn't stupid. Ellie had obviously thought this guy could communicate with Abbott and Costello and—what? How had Ellie known Hannah would need protection? Because of the money?

"I was hoping you could use your, you know, psychic abilities or whatever it is you do, to help me talk to the boys. Is there anything they need to tell me?" She shrugged and tried to look sheepish as she waited to see if he'd pass her test and freak her the heck out by saying something along the lines of "Abbott said to tell you that Ellie had a detailed journal describing her life as a Mexican drug lord hidden in the floorboard of her bedroom."

Hannah needed that kind of proof to believe this guy could read minds, furry, human or otherwise.

His cobalt eyes captured hers, and *whoa mama*, she practically melted in the chair from the intensity of his stare. Tugging the collar of her shirt away from her neckline, she squirmed in her seat and looked away.

"I don't communicate with animals, Miss Dawson," he said. "My psychic abilities aren't specialized to pet readings."

"I understand that." She might as well be panning for gold when it came to figuring out why Ellie had wanted her to hire him—well, other than the old woman had lost her mind—but the only thing different about him from the other private investigators she'd researched was that he claimed to be psychic. "I'd hoped you might be persuaded to try, or perhaps you can recommend someone who does talk to animals? I've got the money. I can pay whatever it takes."

"I read people, not animals, but—" He seemed to hesitate. His eyes held hers. When he finally leaned forward and turned his gaze to the dog stretched out on his office floor, the tension she'd been feeling for the past few days loosened its grip on her muscles. "I sense that they're still grieving. They miss their former owner, but they are quite happy with you. I'd dare say grateful." He took a deep breath. "I'm afraid there's really not much else to tell you. Animals are pretty simple-minded creatures. People tend to think they're much smarter than they really are."

Oh, really? Hannah crossed her arms and studied him to see if he was feeding her a line of BS. Costello knew exactly when eight o'clock was each day without looking at a clock—it was his feeding time—and Abbott could open doors and cabinets like it was nothing.

Oh, no. This man was obviously a quack. Zachary Collins had one helluva poker face though. She snuck a look down at the bag containing the cat. Abbott had also awoken her when the person trying to kidnap Costello had been wrestling with the dog.

The cat's yellow eyes peered up at her with a sardonic expression. Almost as if the animal was thinking, *Are you buying this crap?*

She focused on Zachary again. "Are you sure?"

"Quite sure." Smiling, Zachary leaned forward. "As I said before, I have a couple of qualified men who can help you secure your home. If you're looking for a bodyguard to provide around-the-clock protection, I can arrange that, too."

Around-the-clock what? Lord have mercy, that sounded expensive.

Abbott's loud meow drew her attention. She straightened her shoulders and focused on the reason she was here. "They really aren't telling you anything else?" *Anything about Ellie I should know?*

Zachary seemed to stare at the wall, his eyes unfocused and glazed. "I'm sorry. Like I said…"

"Simple-minded. Right."

Well, crap. She was back in what-the-heck-do-I-do-now territory. How did a person find a legitimate psychic, if such a thing existed?

Costello made a low growling sound as he began to wiggle around on the carpet. The dog's stubby paw batted at her foot playfully. His tongue lolled to one side, and he panted. So maybe Zachary Collins had a point. Still, she'd thought it might be worth a try. She'd never felt so desperate for help in her entire life, and that was really saying something.

She felt so *alone* in all of this.

Someone had broken into her home, after all.

"Do you think I need a bodyguard?" The thought of someone following her around twenty-four hours a day kind of creeped her out.

"Do you live alone?"

"Yes."

"Are you involved with anyone?"

She felt her shoulders tense again. "No. Why?"

"Any friends who could stay with you?"

Her best friend might, but Hannah didn't want to inconvenience anyone, especially Sarah, who was studying hard to earn her IT certification. "No."

"Then I would say yes, at least for a temporary period, while you're still the focus of media attention." He reached for his phone and asked someone if Brian was available yet. After a brief exchange, he replaced the receiver. "I've requested my partner to come in and meet you. He's a former Marine as well as a trained police officer with a few years of experience on the force. If anyone can offer the protection you need, it's him."

The door opened and a good-looking, square-jawed man with a military cut poked his head in. "You wanted to see me, Zach?"

Zachary nodded, and Hannah stared when the other man's body came into full view. Muscular would have been an understatement. The burly man she assumed was Brian looked more suited to a gym than an office.

"Brian Burns, meet Hannah Dawson."

"Call me Hannah." Standing, she held her hand out to the man and was relieved when his grip didn't crush her fingers.

Zachary briefly explained the situation. "If you feel comfortable with Brian, we can arrange a trial period where he shadows you to make certain he's a good fit. He can also assess what your needs are while he's there."

"You won't even know I'm there." Brian half-smiled at her.

"Uh, okay." She crossed her arms again. "Is the trial period free?"

Zachary flexed his hands and exchanged looks with his partner. "The first day will be on us. After that, it's $200 an hour."

"An hour?" Talk about pricey.

Zachary shrugged. "For first-time clients with good credit, we do offer a slight discount that would bring it down to $175 an hour."

Better, but still pricey. It took Hannah a minute to remember that she could easily afford that now. Total craziness. She nodded. "Okay. I suppose that's alright. When can you start?" Maybe they weren't staffed with amazing psychics, but they seemed to be reputable security specialists. Right now she needed protection, for her and the animals.

"Give me an hour to get a bag packed." Brian reached for the door and, with a strange look in Zachary's direction, disappeared. Hannah returned her focus to the handsome man who, not least, made her secretly glad her dear friend Ellie had chosen this firm over all the others in Atlanta.

"While he's gone, we can take care of some paperwork, okay?"

She took a deep breath, grateful she wasn't being turned away. And a tad bit disappointed she wasn't going to be protected by *The Psychic Detective* himself.

# Chapter Two

Hannah peeked over her shoulder to make sure the guy who was going to be her shadow for a while had actually heeded her request and hadn't followed her inside. She punched in the security code to disable her new alarm.

His back was turned to her in the doorway, and he wasn't even looking inside. Wow. A man who actually did what she told him? Where had this mythological creature come from? "Just one more minute please."

Freeing the animals from their leash and bag, Hannah hurried to pick up the bras, socks and other laundry scattered throughout the living room. Not to mention the dirty plates, empty cups and candy wrappers. And cat and dog toys.

She normally wasn't a slob, but since moving, everything had been in chaos, including her mind. She seemed to prefer lounging on the sofa, watching old black and white movies that made her cry, and sharing buckets of ice cream with the boys to being her usual neat-freak, health-nut self.

*Girl, you have got to get it together.*

She eyed the still unpacked boxes with regret—she'd really had plenty of time to unpack by now, hadn't she?—and wrestled with two armfuls of clothes. It all went flying into the laundry room, barely missing the curious cat that had followed her. The door made a much louder sound than she expected when she slammed it shut. Hannah cringed, and Abbott shot her a dirty look once he stopped his mad dash down the hall to get away from her.

The noise caught Brian's attention, too, and Hannah smiled at him as she hurried back into the living room.

"Okay," she said. "All clear. I had to, um—" She jerked a thumb over her shoulder as she struggled for a reasonable excuse. "Clean up the mess Costello made before we left."

A strange whining sound came from the dog now sitting against her foot, and Hannah scanned down to see him looking up at her, his head cocked kind of funny. She squished her face up in apology and told him mentally, *Sorry, boy.* You know, just in case he'd understood her.

Brian reached down and gave the dog a friendly rub on the head. "Don't worry, fella. We're all a little messy sometimes."

But he was looking at Hannah when he said it.

Glancing around, he asked, "How did the intruder get in?"

She tucked her hands in the back pocket of her trousers and sighed. "The police seemed to think he disabled the security alarm first, then came in through the French doors in back."

"So he probably gained entry through the back yard," he concluded. "Is it fenced?"

"Of course."

Hannah hung back and watched as Brian inspected every window and door. He disappeared outside for a while, then returned holding a small piece of wire in a handkerchief.

"They were right about the security system, but they missed some evidence. Do you have a plastic bag?"

Seeing the piece of wire shot a zing of panic through her motionless body. This had really happened. Someone had actually been in her home. She really had beaten off a wannabe kidnapper with the old baseball bat she'd taken from Miss Parham's attic.

"You okay?" Brian asked, and she shook herself, feeling slightly dazed.

"There are some bags in the kitchen." Her fingers fumbled with opening the drawers, and Hannah swore under her breath. "The alarm company came out and repaired the alarm this morning, so it's okay, right?" When she passed the plastic bag to him, Brian wasn't smiling. "What?"

"I'll be honest with you, Miss Dawson."

"Hannah," she reminded him.

"Security alarms are great at scaring off amateurs, but against people who really know what they're doing, you're wasting your money." He looked sincere. "I'm not saying you shouldn't have one, but considering your situation, you really should take extra precautions."

She slid her hands into her back pockets again. "What kind of extra precautions?"

His stone-faced expression relaxed a bit. "Contacting us was a great start. I've got a few ideas we can work on—" He reached for the buzzing phone belted at his hip, frowned and told her, "I'm sorry. I need to take this."

Hannah leaned back against the counter and felt something furry press against her bare arm. Abbott, the darn cat, had jumped up on the counter again and rubbed his black and white head against her elbow. He circled around and got her from the other side too. She guessed that meant he forgave her for giving him a scare earlier, so she picked him up and gave him a proper petting in apology.

Honestly, she didn't know what she'd do without the cat and dog these days. Her little boys. She had a feeling she'd be ridiculously lonely without them.

They were her everything, which could mean only one thing.

She was a crazy cat lady. Well, crazy cat lady with a dog. Or maybe there was another name for her. Crazy…pet fanatic?

"Don't panic!" Brian exclaimed from the other room. Abbott tugged away, demanding to be set on the ground again, and darted into the living room. Hannah followed Abbott, and Costello followed Hannah.

One thing was immediately obvious. Her massive muscle of a bodyguard was weak on his feet. She hurried forward the same second he reached out a hand to steady himself against the back of the sofa, only to crumple to the floor anyway. He never let go of his phone, though, and as Hannah knelt beside him—his color was pale and the pulse at his wrist was unusually high—he told the person on the other end, "Don't worry. I'll be right there."

He pressed END on the phone and immediately began hyperventilating.

What the heck was going on?

Hannah checked his pulse again and then reached out to feel for his temperature. "Breathe slow," she told him. "Deep breaths. Release. Good."

Costello jumped up and began humping the leg that was sprawled out in front of Brian. "No." Hannah told the dog, shoving him away. "You're not helping."

The dog sat back so his chunky body was gathered around his back feet. She shot him an I-can't-believe-you look and shook her head, but the always-content canine opened his mouth and grinned.

"Are you having chest pains?" Hannah reached for Brian's phone and began dialing 911. "Nausea? How's your vision?"

Brian's hand reached out and stopped her. "No." He shook his head, looking dazed. A gleam of sweat glistened along his forehead. "I think maybe…panic attack?" He shook his head. "I've never had one before, but I've had friends who have." He reached for her shoulder and tried to press himself up.

"What happened?" Against her better judgment, she helped him rise to his feet.

His fingers were trembling when he reached for his phone again. "My wife's water just broke."

"Oh." As his words sank in, she felt him begin to tilt sideways and circled her arm around his back to keep him from falling again. Geez, the guy was heavy. *My wife's water just broke.* "Ooooh." She'd seen this before. First-time father. Panic attack.

Hannah had only worked in labor and delivery during her student nurse rotations, but she'd seen enough to know Brian wasn't the first tough guy to go down when labor began.

Brian stumbled around, and as his human crutch, Hannah stumbled around with him, the cat and dog dodging their footsteps. Hannah groaned. Where was a camera when you needed one? She didn't have a monitor handy, but she suspected Brian's blood pressure was dangerously low due to shock. She needed to get him seated and calm as soon as possible.

Propping her bodyguard against the wall, Hannah reached for her purse, hustled Abbot into his carrier and grabbed Costello's leash. Then she wrestled the three-ring circus out of her living room and into her car.

She prayed they'd all make it to the hospital in one piece.

Zach clenched his back teeth to keep from saying something that would land him in a lawsuit or worse. He leaned forward, rested his forearms on his desk and fisted his fingers.

"You want to tell me that again?" His voice was terse.

Kellan Murphy met his gaze unflinching across the desk. For the last three years, Zach and Brian had considered him their next-in-charge, the most dependable guy on their team, a leader for the others.

"You're quitting on us?" Zach clarified.

"I didn't say that." Red crept up Kellan's neck and colored his cheeks. He looked away. "I didn't mean for it to happen. I swear. It just happened. I thought you should know."

Zach didn't know how the hell sleeping with a client "just happened."

At least the other man hadn't sugar-coated things. Kellan had walked into his office, told him he'd gotten a job offer as a full-time bodyguard to their highest-paying client, an actress on a popular TV show filmed right outside of Atlanta. *And by the way, Zach, I've also been sleeping with her for the past few weeks.*

Zach popped another antacid into his mouth. This was exactly the kind of shit that had nearly tanked the agency. Regulars took a particular liking to one of their workers and stole them away along with the fees they'd been paying the firm directly. They'd lost good men and reliable income because their contracts hadn't incorporated the proper penalty fees.

Oh, yeah. They'd suffered a sharp learning curve that first year of business, but things had gotten better, much better, once they'd found their stride. They'd hired a whip smart manager to run the business side of things while they'd focused on getting the job done. Then bam. Things had started to go to hell in a handbasket again.

Zach had taken himself out of the field after what had happened in Kirkwood. Then Gillian, their business manager slash receptionist, had gotten pregnant and left them to be a stay-at-home mom. A national chain had moved into their turf, specializing in cyber security along with traditional private investigations, and Collins Security Firm had started losing business. Too much business.

The few savings Zach had from his time on TV had already gone into purchasing vehicles and equipment. If he couldn't somehow turn things around, and soon, they'd have to close the doors in three months, tops.

His attention swung back to Kellan. Sleeping with a client? The ex-cop should know better. It was career suicide. Eventually the actress would get tired of sleeping with him and fire his ass. Then where would he be?

"Does she understand we can sue her for hiring you away from us? It's in her contract, and yours." Zach reached into the bottom desk drawer where he kept his most important documents, including copies of the contracts with all of the firm's highest-paying clients. As soon as the drawer opened, his gaze fell on a file labeled DYLAN at the front. All it held was the birthday card he'd bought years ago but was too much of a coward to mail to his little brother—not that he even knew his brother's address anymore.

Another reminder of what an epic failure Zach was.

"Sue her?" Kellan sounded surprised. His face lost its color. "Are you gonna fire me?"

Zach was tempted, but he needed the asshole on staff too damn much. "I assumed you were quitting to take the job with your girlfriend. What would be the point of firing you?"

Shoving his brother's folder out of mind, he checked the actress's contract to make sure it was still valid for a while yet. Luckily, it was. Even if she broke it now, the agency would still get paid for another four months, plus a penalty fee. But then?

They were screwed. They needed to convince Kellan to stick around so she would, too.

Kellan shook his head. "I don't know what to do. I never thought I'd—" His words fell short as he turned and paced toward the opposite wall. Hands on his hips, he turned and faced the desk again. "I'm sorry, Zach."

"I think we need to revisit this conversation when Brian can be here, don't you? Dammit, Kellan." Zach pushed a hand through his hair. "I don't need this right now. Go do your job, and get out of my sight. We'll talk about this later."

Kellan hesitated, as if he wanted to stay and finish it now, but he must have sensed it wasn't a good time to push his luck. The office door shut behind the tall blond man, and Zach picked up his phone.

Instead of Brian's deep voice, a familiar feminine one answered his call. "Zachary! Oh, thank goodness. I was trying to find you in his contacts," Hannah said, and then in a calm voice informed him she was driving to the hospital with his partner passed out cold in the seat beside her. "Can you please check on his wife to make certain she's taken care of? Her water broke about ten minutes ago, and this guy is in no condition to go get her."

When Zach reached the hospital, Brian was waiting—in a wheelchair, no less—in a room with his wife, Jenny. Their newest client was nowhere in sight.

"The nurses told me Hannah left after they got me conscious," Brian muttered. "Damn, I owe that woman. Bigtime."

Zach tried calling the number for her he'd programmed into his phone earlier. She sent him to voicemail. Shit. This wasn't their day for retaining customers, was it?

"Maybe you could head over and check on her," Brian said. "Apologize for me."

Any other time, and he would have already been on his way. "No way, man. I've been looking forward to this. I want to be here when your kid is born. I'll go see Hannah later."

"At least see if Kellan can go keep an eye on her place in the meantime. Tell him to be discreet." Brian rubbed his forehead. "There was someone following her earlier. A black car. Tinted windows. Georgia license plate, but I didn't make the numbers."

Zach swore beneath his breath and punched in Kellan's number. His conversation with their next-in-charge was short and to the point. If Kellan didn't want to be sued for breach of contract, he'd get to Hannah's place pronto.

"Park across the street. Keep an eye on her house. I'll be there later. You see anything suspicious, call me. Got it?"

Three hours later, Brian's daughter was born, and damn if Zach didn't feel a swell of pride, looking at the tiny infant for the first time.

An unfamiliar emotion puffed out his chest when he peeked in on the nursery with Brian and saw little Jessica kicking her tiny feet against a pink blanket. He'd never been a kid kind of person, but he had a feeling that little squirt was gonna own his heart.

"Now that I know Jenny's fine and the baby's here, I need to get back over to Hannah's place," Brian said as they stood there. "I didn't tell her about the car following her." Brian rubbed the back of his neck. "She's not safe, and I owe her. I need to get back over there and—"

"You're not leaving this hospital." Zach pulled out his phone and began scrolling through his contacts. Kellan was due to bodyguard his actress girlfriend at a charity event tonight. What freelancers did they know? Who was available? "I'll put someone else on her."

"Who?" Brian held up his hands. "We're stretched too damn thin as it is." His glance strayed back to the crib that cradled his kid. "You should do it." Before Zach could manage a response, Brian stepped closer and lowered his voice. "Look, man, it's been six months. It's time for you to get back in the game."

"Not a good idea." Zach leaned in close. "Let's face it. I'm a better actor than a P.I. We don't need another screw up like what happened the last time I handled a job."

Brian scrunched his face in either disgust or disagreement. Maybe both. "You were an actor for fifteen minutes on some stupid reality show hardly anyone remembers. That's behind you. What's bringing this up now?"

Fifteen minutes? That barb stung. *The Psychic Detective* had lasted three seasons before Zach's conscience had gotten the best of him and he'd quit. The so-called psychic who'd replaced him hadn't lasted more than a year before viewership had dropped and the show had been cancelled.

People had liked him, dammit.

Zach opened his mouth to argue that perhaps if they'd taken advantage of that fact a little more, the firm wouldn't be in such a mess now, but he censored himself. The only time he and Brian had ever come to blows had been over Zach's television con. Brian had beat the shit out of Zach when he'd finished his tour of duty, returned to the states, and discovered Zach had been pretending to be psychic by using his eerie ability to pick up on the details others missed. Never mind his reasons for doing it. Brian hadn't cared.

Zach clenched his jaw and said nothing. Just looked at his best friend.

Brian lifted his chin and softened his tone. "Come on, man. You *do* have the background. You'd either be a Marine or a cop if it weren't for your arm." He flicked his fingers against Zach's left elbow. Zach instinctively massaged his forearm, remembering his basic training exercise gone bad. He'd been lucky some nerve damage was the only injury he'd gotten from the overturned vehicle. He kept it in check with medicine and exercise.

"Yeah, but I'm not a Marine, and I'm not a cop." *Thanks for rubbing it in, asshole.* His injury had prevented him from qualifying for either title.

"But you never gave up trying." Brian held up his hands, in full-on pep-talk mode now. "When I was stationed in Afghanistan, you were working your ass off at one of the best P.I. firms in Los Angeles. You were so good, a client recommended you to that TV producer. Hell, you've been a P.I. longer than me. So what if something bad happened on one case? It was just one case." When Zach stepped to move away, Brian grabbed his good arm and stilled him. He kept his voice low, but firm. "Point is, we need to help that woman, and you're more than capable. *I* need you to help that woman. Do it for me."

"You don't know what you're asking." Zach pulled his arm free. Brian hadn't been the one Ellie Parham had hired years ago to do the background check on the young woman she'd employed as a nurse. He had no idea the things Zach had done to meddle in Hannah's life after that. Zach would like to keep it that way.

Everything inside him was screaming for him to walk away. He couldn't say no to the only friend who'd stood by him.

"Fine. I'll do it." Zach cast one last glance toward the newborn in the nursery. "Just remember that I said this was a bad idea."

Twenty minutes later, Zach took a deep breath as he parked his SUV in front of the white-sided traditional home on the edge of one of Atlanta's nicer communities. He rarely came to Buckhead—too rich for his wallet—but he knew a woman who'd inherited ten million dollars could've picked a larger, newer, nicer house than this one-story ranch. He scanned the area, spotted an older woman walking her poodle along the sidewalk, watching him, and forced himself to get out of the car.

Brian was right. They needed to help Hannah Dawson. Maybe it was even meant for Zach to do penance by handling this case. Heaven help them both, but maybe it was.

He waved Kellan off and moved to press the doorbell. Sighing, he redirected his hand to push the hair away from his face instead.

This was gonna be awkward.

The echo of a dog's barking grew louder until he knew that chubby little mutt was right on the other side of the door. Zach blew out a breath and pressed the doorbell.

He heard movement on the other side followed by a quiet, "Hush, Costello." The chain rattled as the door opened against it, and he barely recognized the woman who peeked out at him. He saw enough to know she was now dressed in a pair of sweatpants, baggy shirt and bare feet. Her hair was yanked back in a ponytail, making her look years younger, too.

He felt his breath catch in his chest. He'd always enjoyed seeing her like this.

"Mr. Collins. Can I help you?"

The dog's long snout poked out from the bottom of the cracked door as if it thought it could squeeze its entire body through the tiny space.

Zach squared his shoulders and forced a smile. "Miss Dawson. May I come in?"

She sighed, but nodded. "Just give me a second." The door shut and the chain protested again as she unlatched it. The entrance cracked open. "Come in, and hurry."

She was bent over, holding the dog's collar as he stepped through the door. Zach made sure the cat was still inside—there it was, perched on the back of the sofa—and shut the door.

"Sorry. I wasn't expecting visitors."

The dog strained against her hold, and when she released him, he ran to Zach and jumped against his leg in greeting.

Hannah clapped and pointed at the ground. "Down, Costello." Her shoulders sank some. "I'm sorry. Ellie never had him trained. He's horribly disobedient." Seeing the dog sit, she walked toward the open kitchen, separated from the living room only by a large island. "Can I get you something to drink?"

Zach squinted down at the dog sitting on his left foot and looking up at him with a smelly, open-mouthed, tongue-hanging-to-the-side smile. "No thanks. I wanted to come by and apologize." He looked up to see her tugging a cookie sheet from the oven. The aroma of melted chocolate chips triggered his mouth to start watering. "And also to thank you for what you did today."

"How's Brian?"

"Holding up. His wife delivered a little girl. Seven pounds, eight ounces."

"No problems?"

"None."

"That's wonderful. What did they name her?"

"Jessica Marie."

"Pretty name." She checked the cookies to make sure they were done, and then she turned toward him and leaned against the counter. "I'm glad it ended well."

He took a deep breath. "I'm sorry Brian reacted that way. I assure you he has never fainted before, especially while on the job. We'd like to offer you a discount on our services for a month. Half off. It's the least we can do."

She looked away and her bottom lip disappeared between her teeth. She was hesitating. Why was she hesitating?

"Mr. Collins—"

"Call me Zach."

That seemed to give her more reason to pause. "I'm not certain your firm is the right one for me. Truthfully, I've decided I probably overreacted in coming to you."

"But you signed a contract."

"Yes, beginning with a trial day." She straightened. Her eyebrows pulled together, but her tone was polite when she told him, "I'm sure Brian would prefer to spend this time with his family anyway. Perhaps, in the future—"

"Someone was following you today."

"W-what?"

Ah, that had caught her attention. "Brian spotted the tail when you left our office." He gave her the vehicle description. "Have you noticed that car before?"

"I don't know." She sighed. "You know, maybe Brian was mistaken." But the expression on her face told him she was worried.

Why the hell was she being so stubborn? He blew a soft breath through his nose and said, "If it matters, I was also planning to take over your case personally."

"You were?"

Oh, it mattered, alright. He could tell by the way her eyes had sparked with interest. Why? *Because she thinks you're psychic, dumbass.*

Dammit. He did not want to lie to this woman, but what choice had she given him? They needed this paycheck, but more than that, his gut twisted at the idea of her being alone with only God-knows-who targeting her. He liked this woman. Always had. Hell, he *owed* her.

If he was careful with his wording, maybe that would excuse him from bending his ethics this one time. It was worth a shot. She might hate him when she discovered he'd twisted the truth, but at least she would be safe.

"I'd like to take over your case." He felt a heavy weight crush against his foot and realized the dog had decided to lie down against him. He gestured to the animal, swallowed, and prayed Brian wouldn't find out about this part. "And I will try my best to communicate with your cat and dog."

She crossed her arms and leaned her head a tad to the right while she considered it.

*Give her a reason to say yes.*

What did those stupid Facebook memes always suggest cats and dogs were thinking? Food. Something about food would seem real.

"Your cat would like a treat." He nodded toward the feline sitting on the floor behind her.

The cat perked up and shuffled its weight from paw to paw. As if Zach had said the magic word, the dog jumped to his feet and sat at attention.

*Bingo.*

Hannah uncrossed her arms. "You mentioned the T word.

Doesn't take a psychic to know that'll get a reaction."

Good point.

She turned and stretched up toward a cabinet. Zach used the opportunity to inspect his surroundings. Unopened boxes were strewn about the floor. Very few decorations were placed around the room. She wasn't giving him much to work with here.

A phone book was open on the sofa. He recognized the full-page ad of one the agency's biggest competitors. She was hiring someone else? Like hell.

What did he remember about her that he could use? His gaze landed on a familiar-looking DVD cover, half-buried beneath a few magazines on the coffee table behind him. He mentally snapped his fingers. When she faced him again, he gestured to the cat.

"He also wants to know when you're going to watch the short little man with the funny-looking hat and mustache again."

Her entire body froze as if he'd pressed a pause button on her. Slowly, she lifted her head and looked at him, wide-eyed. "What?"

"I'm feeling laughter and seeing —" He scrunched his eyebrows. "Is it Charlie Chaplin?"

The bag of treats fell from her fingers and hit the counter with a soft thud. She turned her attention to the cat, who was still staring at Zach—and swishing its tail like crazy.

"Okay, that's kinda creepy." She lifted the cat onto the island and gave it a few treats while she stroked its back. "I've got a new alarm. The police said they'd try to have a car patrol the area for a few days. I'm sorry, but my mind is made up." She rounded the island and stuck her hand out to him. "Thank you for your services, Mr. Collins."

A few minutes later, Zach stood on her doorstep, pissed at himself that he'd tried to con her with his psychic routine and angry at her because she hadn't taken the bait. Had he weirded her out, the way he was looking at her or something? He found her attractive, but getting involved with a client was the ultimate no-no in his book.

No, he knew he'd been careful not to give himself away on that front.

So what had happened? How did he fix this?

He scanned the neighborhood as he walked to his car, remembering Brian's words from the hospital.

*"I didn't tell Hannah, but there was someone following her today."*

He'd promised Brian he'd keep her safe.

And he'd blown it.

"What the hell do I do now?" Zach shook his head as he lifted his hand to start the ignition, but something—a gut feeling—gave him pause. The hair on the back of his neck tickled as it lifted. Goosebumps rose on his arms.

He felt like he was being watched.

# Chapter Three

Why the blazes was there a SUV in her driveway?

Hannah hesitated on the doorstep when she spotted the unfamiliar vehicle. She instinctively jerked Costello's leash to rein him in, but he pulled ahead with the strength of a freight train.

*Never mind calling the cops, Costello. For all we know there's a knife-wielding maniac waiting to jump out and grab us, but go on. Trudge ahead. I'm right behind you.*

She stumbled along after him as Costello yanked over to the grass and hiked his leg. She kept her gaze on the car, trying to decipher the huddled figure slumped behind the steering wheel and leaning against the truck's window.

Was that Zachary Collins?

Surely he hadn't stayed here all night. Why would he have?

She led Costello closer. Yep, it was Zach alright. When she tapped on the driver's side window, the man gave a start.

"Shit," he muttered, loud enough for her to hear through the glass.

He blinked several times as he glanced around. He reached forward, toyed with the ignition and rolled the power window down.

"Everything okay?" she asked, wondering if he had some weird health problem that had caused him to pass out in her driveway.

"Fine." He ran a hand over his face and nodded. "Good morning."

Costello jerked forward and almost tugged her down. She caught herself with one foot braced in front of the other. "Good morning."

"This probably seems kind of strange." His lips curved up in a boyish grin. "I didn't plan to fall asleep in your driveway. Sorry." He took a look at his watch. "I must have nodded off a half hour ago."

Only a half hour ago?

His eyes were blood-shot. Geez. Did the guy have a drinking problem? Drugs? Narcolepsy?

She said nothing, just played tug of war with Costello's leash and waited for Zach to either explain himself or leave.

It had been hard enough sending him away last night. There was something about Zach that drew her to him the way Costello was drawn to human legs, and she'd been worried she was making the wrong decision again.

Zach oozed charisma. She was attracted to him in a way she didn't want to be, and she didn't trust him for that reason alone. Smooth-talking, handsome men—especially those who'd been on TV—had a reputation for inflated egos. Only cared about themselves. Been there. Done that. Once was a mistake. Twice was a choice, and she'd be darned if she made the same one again.

She took a deep breath and reminded herself she had a representative from another private security firm coming over this afternoon. Besides, she'd finally broken down and told Sarah everything, and her best friend was now hell-bent on coming over to assess the situation herself. And if Hannah knew Sarah, her friend would be bringing at least one of her very huge, very intimidating brothers with her as a precaution.

Zach pulled the key from his ignition and opened the door. "Mind if I use your restroom?"

She stepped back and shrugged. "Of course not." She tilted her head toward the dog that was now munching on grass. She reached for the house key that was attached at her neck by a lanyard. "I've got to take him for our morning walk. Let yourself in. Please make sure Abbott doesn't get out."

He looked at her hand, but he didn't take the key. "How about I walk with you first? There's something I'd like to discuss."

What the hell? Getting away from him obviously wasn't going to be as easy as she'd hoped. And why did she feel so guilty about calling one of his competitors?

"Okay." She sighed and allowed the forty-pound dog to lead the way. As soon as Costello realized she wasn't holding him back, he stopped trying to drag her behind him like a ragdoll. Slowing her steps, Hannah spared a quick look at the disheveled man beside her.

A morning beard darkened his chin, and his hair was ruffled.

Whew. He was hot. Sexy.

Trouble.

"Are you going to tell me why you spent the night in my driveway?" She focused on Costello, who'd slowed down and was backing up to do his morning business on her neighbor's lawn. Hannah snatched a small bag out of her pocket and waited for the dog to finish, and the man to answer.

Zach scanned the street in front of them with hawk-eye precision. "Someone was following you yesterday. Last night your house was being watched."

Worry zinged through her brain until she shook herself free of the useless emotion. Had someone been following her, or had Zach invented it as a convenient excuse to scare her into retaining his services? She opted to believe the second, if only because the alternative was too terrifying.

She turned to him and forced a smile. "Thank you for staying, but I did make it clear your services aren't required."

"I'm not kidding, Hannah."

"Neither am I."

His fingers gripped her arm, forcing her to turn and look at him. "You could be in real danger. Let me help you."

"How do you know my house was being watched?" Costello hauled on the leash, demanding to be walked, so she gave in and hoped Zach would follow. "Did you actually see someone? What did they look like?"

He ran a hand through his hair as he casually matched her pace. His jaw clenched. "I didn't see anyone. I felt it."

"Like a psychic thing?"

He shook his head. "Call it a gut reaction. I've been doing this a long time. Trust me, I know when my instincts are dead on, and I know when I'm being watched."

Hannah had no idea how his psychic abilities worked—or if he was even psychic, for that matter—but she could hear the sincerity in his voice.

His fingers gripped her upper arm tight again, bringing her to another stop. His wide-eyed expression was serious—and a little alarming. "Who's watching the cat?"

"No one," she admitted. "I—" She stopped her words when Zach yanked the lanyard from her hand and sprinted back the way they came. Costello bounded after him, jerking her arm almost out of its socket and nearly dragging her to the ground. "Wait a minute!"

Then she remembered Zach's question, and she ran like hell to catch up to him, too.

His gut churned in a familiar way that told Zach something bad was about to happen. He might not be psychic, but he hadn't been lying when he told Hannah his instincts rarely led him wrong.

A few minutes ago, the thought to trigger that gut churning had been, *the damn cat is a sitting duck right now.*

He didn't see anything suspicious as he hurried up the steps to Hannah's house, but he still opened the front door carefully.

The house was eerily quiet. He scanned the room and saw nothing unusual—not even the cat. He took a step inside, and that's when it hit him. The pungent smell of cigarette smoke lingered in the air, as if someone who smoked often had been in the room.

"What on earth?" Hannah said, coming up behind him fast.

The dog's paws shoved against the back of his knees, and Zach almost fell face-first into the carpet. He stumbled forward and caught himself against the wall as Costello raced around him and bounced into the room.

He was gonna kill that damn dog.

He held out an arm to prevent Hannah from moving further inside and asked in a whisper, "Do you smoke?" But he already knew the answer.

"No."

The look of distaste on her face turned to something else as her nostrils flared and caught the same scent his had. She paled, and her fingers gripped the leather jacket covering his arm.

"Grab your cell phone and call the police. Go to a neighbor's house and wait on their porch." He pulled away from her and inched forward, wishing like hell he was carrying his gun or some other weapon. A single vase sat on the bookshelf, so he grabbed it, glad to feel that it was heavy and could do some damage if needed. His attention caught on Costello, who sniffed the air and headed down the hall toward what Zach assumed were the bedrooms. He kept a good pace behind the dog, just in case.

The mutt growled and dashed into the open doorway of one of the rooms. Zach waited for an intruder to run out, but then the dog's whimper ripped the silence.

"Dammit." He moved to charge forward and—

Someone rushed him from the side. Zach had enough time

to see the bat swinging toward him before it felt like his brain exploded inside his skull. His teeth rattled as he hit the floor. The metallic taste of blood coated his tongue as everything threatened to fade to black.

*Slurp. Slurp. Slurp.*

The strange sound brought him back toward consciousness. Zach swallowed, tasted his own blood and nearly gagged. He blinked and saw a furry black and white cat standing too close to his face, licking its paw over and over again. He jerked sideways in surprise, making stars swim in his vision and a groan escape his mouth.

*What the hell is his problem? It's not like I did this to him.*

The thought—more like a strong feeling than words—seemed oddly foreign to Zach. He felt pressure on his leg and looked down to see the damn dog going to town with a fury.

*Gotta help him. Gotta help him. Gotta show him who's boss. Gotta help him.*

Again with the strange thought-feeling. Zach groaned and dropped his head back down, jarred his teeth.

He heard more licking and turned his head to see the cat's tongue still taking long swipes at its paw.

*Dirty paw.*

*Hungry.*

*When's dinner?*

Was the cat actually talking or—?

"Gnn-mmmm," Zach groaned.

A second later, black engulfed him.

He should have come out by now.

Hannah shifted her weight from foot to foot as she debated going inside. She'd done as Zachary asked and called the police and was still holding on the line with the dispatcher, who annoyingly kept asking her for updates she couldn't give. She couldn't see or hear anything from where she stood on her absent neighbor's front porch.

"It will just be a few more minutes," the woman on the other end kept saying.

It had already been seven minutes.

"Screw this," she told the dispatcher. "I'm going inside."

"I wouldn't advise that, Miss Dawson. Stay—" The voice ended when Hannah moved forward and a double beep informed her she'd lost the call. Well, crap. She shoved the phone in her pocket and hurried across her lawn.

The smell of cigarette smoke wasn't as strong as it had been when she'd stepped inside earlier. She listened, heard absolutely nothing aside from the tick-tock of the clock above the mantle, and slowly moved forward.

She tried to remember where she'd put the baseball bat she'd been keeping close for comfort's sake. Bedroom. Damn. What else could she use for a weapon? Another vase? They were in a box somewhere. She really needed to unpack soon.

"Mreow."

The cat's call echoed through the living room seconds before Abbot's black and white body sauntered into view. He sat down, looked at her and meowed again. Then he rolled onto his side and gave her a sleepy-eyed look.

"Zach?" Her voice sounded loud, but she wasn't sure if it was because of the silence or because she'd spoken higher than she'd planned.

Hannah hurried toward the cat, scooped him up and stared down the empty hallway.

"Costello?" She whispered loudly.

The dog's head peeked out of a doorway. His beady eyes met hers, he barked and then he disappeared with a bunny-hop motion back into the room.

The curtains swayed in a breeze when she entered the area she had planned for an office. Her gaze landed on Zach's motionless body in the floor. Costello was busy humping one of the private detective's legs.

"Costello. No!"

Zach's chest barely rose and fell on shallow breaths. Her nurse training kicked in, and she bent to check for a pulse, trying to find evidence of what had caused the injury. A trickle of blood was drying below his nose. His pulse was steady.

"Zach, can you hear me?"

A low groan rumbled through his chest.

Abbot sat down on the other side of Zach's head and seemed fascinated by Hannah's actions as she used trembling fingers to lift his eyelids and check his pupil dilation. She reached for her phone, intending to dial 911 again, but the sound of a police car's siren in the distance stilled her.

She took a deep breath and caressed Zach's face. *I'm sorry. So sorry.* Someone had been in her home again. Someone had done this to him. She felt so violated and scared and angry. Angry at herself for not listening to him earlier. He'd been right.

The person doing this was dangerous, and worse, they didn't seem likely to give up anytime soon.

# *Chapter Four*

Sarah Taylor glared from across the room. "And *why* didn't you tell me any of this sooner?"

Hannah shrank deeper into the corner of her new sofa and watched her best friend pace a line in the living room rug. Sarah's ebony skin didn't turn red in anger the way hers did, but Sarah had other tells Hannah had picked up on throughout the years. Hannah knew her usually calm and quiet best friend was *livid*.

Well, at least she hadn't brought one of her brothers with her. Then Hannah would be defending herself against two of the Taylors. Heaven help her.

"I told you," Hannah said. "I didn't want to distract you from your schoolwork. You work a full-time job, and your mother is sick with cancer. The last thing you need to worry about is me."

"I *know* you didn't say that Hannah Michelle Dawson." Sarah stopped pacing and pointed an accusing finger at her. "You are practically my sister, and you know you can come stay with us. We could have been watching out for you."

Hannah grabbed the pillow beside her and hugged it. Batting her eyelashes, she feigned a proper British accent. "If you would be so polite as to grace me with your forgiveness, I'd be ever so grateful." Sarah could never resist the British accent.

"Don't even try it." Her friend's thinned lips twitched as she held up a hand in warning and spun away.

"Do you like crumpets?" Hannah batted her eyelashes. "I'll make you crumpets if you forgive me."

Glancing back at the sofa, Sarah rolled her eyes and relented with a smile. "Fine." She crossed her arms. "I forgive you, but only if you come stay with us."

Dropping the accent, Hannah groaned. "Come on, Sarah. You and I both know you and your mom have this weird phobia about cats. That's why Abbot is locked in the other room right now. I can't bring him into your house. It wouldn't be fair to any of you."

"I don't understand why you don't get rid of that thing anyway." A feigned shudder jiggled Sarah's shoulders. "Creepy-as-hell cat."

Gritting her teeth, Hannah moved to her feet. Every few minutes she felt the need to check on that so-called creepy-as-hell cat to make sure no one else had climbed in the window and tried to snatch him again.

"Besides the fact I love and adore Abbot, you know why." Hannah paused on her way to the bedroom to peek out the front window curtain. "Remember the money that paid off your mother's medical bills? Remember that money I gave you to pay for this semester's tuition? That's why."

"*Loaned* me," Sarah corrected, padding close behind her with Costello bringing up the rear. Hannah opened the bedroom door and spotted Abbot twisted in an unnatural kitty position in his fluffy bed, deep asleep.

A sigh of relief escaped her parted lips as she closed the door.

How was she ever going to get a decent night's sleep again, with her constant guarding over the two animals in her care?

"I'm gonna call Jeremy so he can come and stay with you." Sarah pulled out her cell phone. "The boy's crazy as hell, but he doesn't mind cats or dogs."

The mention of Sarah's youngest brother nearly tore a groan

from Hannah. She grappled with her friend's hand before Sarah could complete the dial. "Jeremy is in high school."

"So?"

"Sarah, I'm a 30-year-old single woman who just moved into this neighborhood." She shook her head. "I love your brothers like my own, but all my new neighbors will see is that a 15-year-old boy keeps coming and going from my house. *Awkward*." She let the word roll out in two syllables. "Besides, if anything happened to him, do you know what that would do to your mom?"

"Ugh. You are such a party pooper." Groaning, Sarah twirled, and her long, black hair swished around her shoulders. Her pretty features appeared drawn tight, and Hannah worried her friend hadn't been taking care of herself very well. Lord knew she had plenty to cause her stress. Sarah plopped onto the sofa, arms crossed, her hazel eyes sparkling with determination. "Fine. I'll stay."

Hannah closed her eyes and prayed for strength. She rarely won arguments with any of the Taylors, but she absolutely could not allow her friend to stay here. She refused to burden Sarah any more than she already was.

"If you stay, we'll both gain ten pounds from eating ice cream and get no sleep because we'll be watching your DVDs of *Downton Abbey* all night. You, my friend, have exams coming up. Get your butt home and study." Hannah moved toward the kitchen to grab a diet soda—maybe the caffeine would help keep her alert—and chewed her bottom lip as she came to terms with the decision she'd already made. "Besides, I've hired Zachary Collins' agency for protection. There is no need for you or anyone else to stay here."

"Yeah, because they're obviously doing a top-notch job so far." Sarah snorted. "How old is that kid guarding your house anyway? Sixteen?"

"E.J. is at least in his twenties, and he's been nothing but professional." Hannah closed the refrigerator and turned to face her friend. A zing of irritation on Zach's behalf triggered her temper. "Zach refused to leave the other night because he thought I was being watched. If he hadn't been here yesterday morning—" She didn't like to think what could have happened. She waved a dismissive hand. "Besides, they moved me to a hotel last night and made sure the house was safe to come back to. They've been keeping us safe, Sarah."

Her friend held up her hand. "Fine, but don't expect me to believe Zachary Collins is doing this out of the goodness of his heart. I'm sure he only sees dollar signs when he looks at you, Hannah."

"It's not like that." She frowned. "You don't even know him."

"I'm just sayin' be careful." Sarah sprang up from the sofa and joined her at the kitchen island. Sarah leaned against it and wiggled her eyebrows. "So, what's he like in person? I've only seen his show a few times."

"He's...good. I think he's good at what he does."

"Gay?"

"Sarah." Hannah couldn't keep the amusement out of her voice.

"What? He was on TV. You have to wonder."

"I don't think he's gay." Although she didn't have much to base that on. Wishful thinking probably.

Sarah's smile grew lascivious. "Is he as hot as he seems on TV?"

Hannah sighed dramatically. "Hotter. Much hotter."

Sarah snuck some pieces of popcorn from the bowl Hannah had left sitting there...had it been three days ago? Geesh. She really needed to clean. "What about the other bodyguards?"

Hannah gave her a quick run-down of the men she'd met so far, and Sarah released a long breath, picked off one last piece of popcorn and then pinned her with a look. "Promise me you'll be careful with him."

"With Zach?"

"You're beautiful. You have millions of dollars at your disposal." Sarah lifted her chin. "I don't want to see you get into another situation like you did with Eric. That's all."

Every muscle in Hannah's body snapped into painful awareness at the name. Sarah had always had a tendency to jump to conclusions that made absolutely no sense, but how she could compare hiring Zachary Collins to protect her with what had happened with Eric was beyond comprehension. "You're nuts. The two situations are nothing alike."

Sarah arched a brow. "He's gorgeous and exactly your type. I don't want him to take advantage of you because he wants your money. You've got to think about things like this now, Hannah. People are going to try to use you."

Hannah scoffed. She should have never told Sarah that Zach was even hotter in person. "I'm not stupid, you know. I know I have to be careful." She ticked off points with her finger. "I checked with the Better Business Bureau. No unresolved complaints against them. I had Mr. Russell check to make sure they were properly licensed." Ellie's attorney—now her attorney—had been a godsend. "And Brian gave me references from some of their past clients. I called and confirmed that these guys know what they're doing."

They stared at each other for several seconds.

"Alright then." Her friend heaved a reluctant sigh of surrender and reached for her purse. "If you didn't have a bigger, stronger bodyguard coming to take over for that puny guy on the porch, my rear would be planted on that sofa all night."

"E.J. is hardly puny."

Another snort. "He looks like a thug."

"Sarah."

Sarah threw up a hand. "Just sayin'. Know what he said to me when I walked up?"

Hannah shrugged.

"He got out of his car, ran over to me and said—" Sarah mimicked a gangsta's voice and gave Hannah a salacious look up and down her body. "'How ya doin', baby? Come 'ere often?'" She returned to her normal voice and stance. "Like I said. He's how old? Sixteen? My youngest brother doesn't act that way."

But Hannah couldn't conjure up any more defense. Her mind felt fractured. All because it was hanging on one stupid little word: Eric.

Would she ever reach a point where the mere mention of his name didn't feel like a stab to the heart? She hoped so. It had been almost four years. Why did his memory still have the power to wound her?

Sarah hesitated in the doorway before leaving. "Han?"

She looked at her friend.

"Sorry I mentioned the creep earlier. I've been under a lot of stress and I'm PMSing and worried and—" Her expression softened. "That's still no excuse. I'm sorry."

A shrug lifted Hannah's shoulders in response. "It happens."

They shared a hug. "Call me if you need me." Sarah drew back and pushed a strand of hair away from Hannah's face. "Remember. 'The Bodyguard' might have been an okay movie, but they didn't end up together. Know what I'm sayin'?"

"Good grief." She shoved her friend out the door. "Take your overactive imagination and get out of here."

As she watched Sarah climb into her car, Hannah's gaze drifted to the vehicle still sitting in her driveway. Zach's SUV. Was he out of the hospital yet?

And did he hate her for not listening to him?

"You left her alone?" Zach bit back a painful groan as he slid his arm into his jacket. Every movement of his body seemed to stir the tiny imp that was driving nails into his skull.

"Her friend was there," Brian said, reaching awkwardly to help his partner stand from the hospital bed. "And E.J. is keeping an eye on her. I figured the kid could handle that."

"What about the cops?"

Detective Ryan with the Atlanta Police Department had stopped by earlier to ask Zach some questions. It had been a humiliating experience, starting with the detective's comment, "Hey, weren't you the P.I. that was involved in that Kirkwood case—what?—about six months ago?"

Brian had stepped in before Zach could respond, which had pissed him the hell off. He was a big boy and capable of responding on his own, dammit.

"Nasty business. Sorry for the way it ended." The detective had given Zach a curious look before moving on to Hannah's situation.

He hadn't instilled much confidence with his departing words. "We'll have a patrol go by Miss Dawson's more often. In the meantime, we've advised her to consider an alarm system and maintain her private security."

Brian opened the door. "You know how it is, Zach. The APD is overloaded with cases. Sure, they take robbery seriously, but they give priority to cases they have leads on."

"You mean the fact someone tried to kill me inside her house didn't give them proper cause to station a patrol there twenty-four seven?" Damn cops.

The idea of Hannah being left unprotected made him feel edgy.

When he'd been parked in front of her house all night, keeping an eye out for trouble, Zach had spent half that time thinking about her. Why had she sought him out, only to turn him away the next day? His gut told him she was keeping something from him. But what, and why? He'd also noticed the way she looked at him when she didn't think he was watching. Maybe he was arrogant, but he could tell when a woman found him attractive.

At least they were even on that score.

This woman posed a serious threat to his vow never to fall for a client.

"The cops are doing what they can," Brian said, bringing him back to the conversation.

Zach took a few steps, felt the room spin around him, used the wall as a guide, and forced himself to keep moving. As he'd hoped, the weird sensation faded as quickly as it had come. Concussion. Wasn't the first time he'd had one, but it was definitely the worst.

"The cops advised her to leave the house. We arranged a hotel for her last night." Brian opened the door to the hospital room. "Do you know how damned hard it is to find a hotel willing to take both a cat and a dog? It's ridiculous."

Zach could only imagine.

"So she's at a hotel? Good."

"*Was* at a hotel," Brian corrected. "When I called her earlier, she'd already checked out and was back home."

Zach swore beneath his breath. She was going to have to learn to listen to them if she wanted to stay safe.

"As soon as I get you home, I'm going to head back over there. She'll be fine." Brian squeezed Zach's shoulder.

"Does that mean you convinced her to keep her contract with us?"

Brian smiled a bit sheepish. "I didn't have to do much convincing. I think she feels guilty about you getting hurt. Plus, she's scared. Can't say I blame her."

Zach shook his head. "Why would someone try so damn hard to kidnap a cat and a dog?"

"Ten million dollars isn't motive enough for you?"

Not really.

Zach had a feeling the reason went deeper than that. He had

no idea why he felt that way. He just did.

"No. Call it a hunch." He reached for the keys he'd put in his pocket, then realized he didn't have his car.

"No driving for at least another twenty-four hours," Brian chided, guiding him toward the parking lot. He waited until Zach was seated in his truck to say, "Maybe you were right. Maybe it's too soon for you to take another case."

"I'm fine," Zach growled.

Brian held up his hands. "I know she hired us, but we do need to consider another possibility here." He gave Zach a sideways look as he buckled his seatbelt. "What happens to the money if the cat and dog get killed? Does it all go to Hannah, and if so, that's one helluva motive right there."

The jolt of anger he felt at that suggestion was immediate. "She wouldn't do that."

"How do you know? I mean, what the hell do we really know about her? You have to admit. Greed makes people do some crazy shit. She could think hiring us gives her a cover."

Zach glared at Brian until he realized his friend hadn't intended the comment as a jab against Zach's own character. He tugged at his seatbelt and buckled up. "I already asked E.J. to do some digging on that front. Don't worry. I still remember how to do my job."

Besides, Hannah could get rid of the cat and dog easy enough. There were no other heirs to hold her accountable.

He reached for his phone and dialed E.J. They'd taken him in four months ago as a favor to E.J.'s grandfather. The kid had gotten mixed up with a gang but hadn't been in so deep he couldn't get out. Brian thought he'd shown potential, and he worked for peanuts. Right now, Zach wasn't above using him as a spotter on this case.

"Did you find anything on those background checks?" Zach asked when E.J. answered.

"Hey, man, you alright?" E.J. asked. "Brian said somebody put you down good."

He clenched his jaw, felt a shot of pain at his temple and sighed. "I'm fine. Tell me what you found."

"Hold on. I got my notes right here. I think I found something good, too." The sound of papers being rustled filled the slight pause in conversation. "Ellie Parham is the lady who left the money to Hannah, but funny thing is, Ellie Parham didn't exist before thirty years ago."

"What do you mean?"

"I mean there is no Ellie Parham of that age or race anywhere in the system before 1983. No social security number. No driver's license. No address. No employment records. Nothing, not even a birth certificate I can find."

"That's impossible. Maybe she was married." Or maybe the kid hadn't done something right.

"Already checked, and before you start thinking I screwed up, Kellan did a search too and came up empty. The lady didn't exist, boss. Hannah said Miss Parham told her she'd never been married, and I called the broad's lawyer. He seemed kind of shifty about it, like he knew more than he was telling, but he swore she hadn't mentioned being divorced or widowed either."

Interesting.

"What about her will? Who gets the money if something happens to the cat and dog?"

"Hannah does."

Zach refused to think that meant anything. "What if something happens to all three of them? Who gets the money then?"

The sound of papers shuffling again filled the line. "It all goes to charity."

Zach rubbed at his forehead, not liking that answer. That answer left them without another obvious suspect. "What about Hannah?

Did you run a background check on her?"

"No criminal record. Never been married. No kids. Went to nursing school at Emory. Worked five years at Saint Joseph's before going to work for a homecare service. That's how she met the old lady. She worked as a part-time nurse for a few different clients for about a year before moving in with Parham and working for the old lady full-time."

"Anything else?"

"Just basic background stuff." E.J. rattled off details Zach already knew. Hannah's birth mother had been a college exchange student from Ireland who stayed here after getting pregnant. Father unknown. Hannah had been twelve when her mother died. She was in and out of foster homes after that.

Zach listened. He already knew Hannah's background, but there was a gap he didn't know—spanning the last four years.

"Is that all you could find?"

"You want me to dig deeper?"

"Yes." A nudge at the edge of his conscience almost had Zach taking back the word. *Are your reasons for wanting to know personal or professional?*

He told his conscience to shut the hell up.

"Find out what her finances were before she got lucky and inherited a rich cat and dog. Find out if there are any ex-boyfriends who might want to cause her trouble and see what you can find on them." He looked away from Brian and lowered his voice as he lied through his teeth. "She mentioned a guy—Eric Meester. M-E-E-S-T-E-R. See what you can turn up on him."

Ending his call with E.J., Zach glanced at Brian in the driver's seat. "Why are we driving toward your place?"

Brian didn't say a word. His sunglass-covered gaze briefly turned toward him. His mouth was pursed in stubborn conviction.

"Take me to get my car," Zach ordered.

"You need to rest. You can get your car tomorrow." Brian's fingers gripped the steering wheel so tightly it squeaked. "You can help Jenny with Jessica while I'm gone, but you need to rest your head a while longer."

"I've been resting. I want back on this case. *Now.*"

"Why? Because of the money?"

A rush of frustrated air blew through Zach's nostrils. He pointed at his face where a nasty bruise had already begun forming. "Because someone made this personal."

This wasn't going to be as easy as he'd hoped.

Driving past the police car that had been crawling through the neighborhood at different times over the last 24 hours, the man lifted a hand and waved so as not to seem too suspicious. His skin itched beneath the fake beard, and his head was sweating under the baseball cap. Behind cheap sunglasses, he did a quick survey of the situation.

They'd been so close to getting what they wanted yesterday before that idiot had interrupted them. The cat had been within arm's reach and everything.

Zachary Collins. Yeah, he knew who the guy was. He'd done some research on the private investigator Hannah Dawson had hired yesterday. The guy's agency had a solid reputation. Might be trouble.

In his rearview, he watched Collins and another guy approach in a SUV and pull into the driveway.

*No opportunity. Gonna have to wait a little bit longer.*

As if he hadn't been waiting long enough.

His phone rang, and he answered it. "This is Fox. What do you got for me?" Fox wasn't his real name, but he'd adopted it after getting out of prison.

"I talked to the buyer and explained you were now in charge.

We still have to deliver the product by the third."

That was three weeks away. Should give them plenty of time.

"Good job," he told his newest partner. Too bad their partnership would be short-lived. He'd learned his lesson a long time ago. Partners were a liability. He'd disposed of one last night. Taken control since the old man wasn't doing what needed to be done.

Once he had what he needed to make the drop, he'd tie up the rest of the loose ends, including his new prodigy. Then he'd find another. That's what the old man had taught him. Take a job. Get the product. Keep moving.

In the meantime, he needed to regroup and come up with another plan.

That cat and dog were his. It was only a matter of time.

# Chapter Five

Hannah sank into the chair across from Zach and tried not to stare at the purple bruise beside his right eye. Butterfly bandages kept a gash closed above his eyebrow, reminding her of a boxer who'd fought one too many rounds. Guilt caused her face to warm.

"Are you sure you're okay?"

"I'll live," he said, leaning forward. "I was worried about you."

"You were?" His words induced an irrational, tiny shimmer of pleasure through her chest. Ridiculous. Of course he was worried about her. She was paying him to worry about her. She glanced at the man standing, arms crossed, beside Zach. Geez, Brian certainly could look intimidating. "You shouldn't have. Brian looked after us—along with E.J."

She'd been under someone's supervision since the ambulance had taken Zach away yesterday. She supposed she'd pay for that now that she'd officially hired them all to protect her and the boys. *Don't panic at the cost. Remember. You can afford it now.*

She released a slow breath of air at the surreal thought.

Zach glanced up at Brian, and a tense look passed between them before he spoke again. "We would have preferred for you to stay at the hotel a little longer. It's bound to be safer there until we can determine who broke in here." His blue gaze met hers again. "Did you see anyone before the police arrived? Maybe they tried to run out the back door after they knocked me out."

She shook her head. "When I found you, the person was gone. The window was open, so I assumed they left that way."

"You're certain nothing was taken?"

"Positive. Brian helped me do an inventory."

A glimpse of white and black movement alerted her to the fact Abbott had decided to join the conversation. Costello was already lying at Zach's feet, glancing back and forth as if the dog was following the conversation, too.

Zach's eyebrows drew together and he glanced down at the approaching cat with a strange expression. "Uh, so you didn't—" He shifted in his seat. "I'm sorry, did you say something?"

She had to do a mental backtrack. "Only that nothing was missing."

"Right." He looked down at the cat again and shook his head. "Sorry."

Brian stepped over to the window, pressed the curtain aside and glanced out. "The alarm was disabled again. We're dealing with someone who knows what he's doing." He moved back to Zach's side. "I believe it's the same person who broke in the first time. Now the question we need to answer is why are they so persistent? What do they want?"

Zach gestured toward Abbott, who was busy licking his paw. "The person was trying to get the cat when I interrupted. I know there was also someone else in the room." His finger brushed the injured side of his face. "We're dealing with at least two suspects."

"We have to assume they're dangerous, and they'll try again," Brian said. "Hannah, I really wish you would take our advice and let us put you somewhere safe."

Zach suddenly shot to his feet. "Did you hear that?"

She blinked and shrugged. "Yes, I heard what he said." She took a deep breath. "I'm sorry, but my life has been disrupted enough lately. I don't want to be relocated. This is my home now, and I—"

"Not that." Zach held out his hand and glanced around. "Did you hear someone say 'I want tuna for dinner'?"

A slow smile curved her lips. Was he pulling her leg or what? "I didn't hear anyone say that." She looked at the cat who'd decided to sprawl out on the rug and swish his tail. "But tuna is always Abbott's food of choice."

If Zach wanted her to think he was communicating with her animals, he really needed to come up with something more impressive. Sure, he'd spooked her the other night by knowing she had a Charlie Chaplin movie marathon planned. Only Abbott and Costello would have known how often she watched the silent film star's movies. She tried to meet Zach's gaze to determine if he was conning her or not, but his face was white and he kept looking around the room.

Brian reached over and put a hand on his friend's shoulder, and Zach jumped at the contact. "Zach, you okay, man? I told you it was too soon for you to jump back into work."

Hannah moved to her feet. "Are you dizzy? Nauseated?"

He backed away from her, which caused him to fall back onto the sofa. Costello jumped up and began humping Zach's left leg. He tried to jiggle the dog away, his eyes wide as he uttered a guttural, "Ahhhhh. No. No. You are not the boss of me. Stop saying that, dammit."

The dog sat back on its haunches and panted happily in response.

Hannah stood speechless, shifting her attention between the man and the animal. Even Brian seemed at a loss for words, until he cleared his throat and said, "I'm sorry, Hannah. He took quite a hit, and he's obviously not well enough to be here. I'm gonna take him home, and then I'll be back." He reached down to help his friend to his feet.

Zach ran a hand through his hair. "Yeah, I'm sorry. I must be worse off than I thought." His throat moved against a hard swallow before he met her gaze again. "I'll be back tomorrow. Brian or E.J. will stand guard until then, alright?"

She nodded and watched as Brian guided him out the door. The shorter of the two men turned and told her, "I'll be back in about half an hour after I drop Zach off at my place. Lock the door. Call me if you need me."

Closing the door behind them, Hannah sighed and looked at the two animals at her feet, demanding attention. "Did you guys say something to that man?"

All she got in response was a soft meow and heavy panting.

He was losing his friggin' mind. That was all there was to it.

Zach splashed his face with water from the bathroom sink and then blinked at himself in the mirror. He'd taken a painkiller and spent the past several hours out cold.

He knew he had a concussion, but seriously? He was nuts to even consider that the weird feelings and voices he'd heard at Hannah's had belonged to the cat and dog.

He needed to get his head back in the game and get over there. It wouldn't do him or anyone else any good if he started psyching himself out now.

The mouth-watering aroma of bacon teased his nostrils, and he found Brian's wife at the stove cooking. A stab of guilt speared his chest when he saw the dark circles under her eyes when she looked up at him. Jenny hadn't been home from the hospital a day, and here she was, taking care of him and a new baby while her husband was working a case Zach should have been handling.

He hurried to take the spatula from her grip. "What do you think you're doing, young lady?" He guided her over to a chair and urged her to sit. "You shouldn't be up and cooking yet."

Jenny yawned. "What else would I be doing? I've got to eat."

"Resting," he pointed out, and waved the spatula toward her bedroom. "You could have woken me and I would have gotten you breakfast."

"I'm not an invalid, Zach." She rested her elbow on the table and lowered her chin to her hand. "But I am damn tired. How about you? How's the head?" She eyed his arm. "Oh, Zach, you didn't hurt your arm, did you?"

He flexed his hand for her benefit. There was usually a dull pain in that arm, but no, he hadn't injured it yesterday.

"All good." He flipped the bacon onto a plate and tended to a pan of scrambled eggs. "As soon as I get some food into you, I'll go get your husband so he can take care of you. Don't worry. He'll be home for the next week at least."

"We can't afford for him to miss work, Zach."

He pointed the spatula at her. "Don't worry about that. I've got it covered. He's got paid leave for as long as he needs it."

"You sure?" Jenny's hazel gaze softened with hope. She knew how dire the agency's finances had been, and like Brian, had probably lost her own fair amount of sleep over the dilemma. But neither of their parents were in the picture to help, financially or otherwise. They were also too damn proud to ask for help from their friends. Zach would have to rally the troops into action. A little help with meals. Some babysitting duties. Clothes and toy donations. Whatever it took.

"Positive." He arranged a plate full of food in front of her before moving to the fridge to get her some orange juice. "How is my baby niece doing anyway?"

A happy grin tugged the edges of Jenny's mouth. "She's amazing. I still can't believe she's here."

"Of course she's amazing." He snagged a couple of pieces of bacon and thrust them into his mouth. "Can I go peek in at her?"

"Sure." She waved her fork at him. "Please don't wake her up. I was hoping to get a nap in after breakfast."

Baby Jessica was sound asleep when Zach looked into the crib he'd helped Brian assemble a month or so ago. He took a deep breath and released it, glad things felt normal again.

He had no idea what the hell had happened to him at Hannah's place last night. Maybe he was finally losing it. He could've sworn there'd been other people in the room with them, jabbering random things about food and going for a walk and the best windows with a view.

He'd had the crazy idea the cat had been talking to him.

Absurd.

The baby in the crib released a slight coo, and Zach reached in to tug the collar of her onesie up higher. Baby Jessica's eyes slowly opened and met his, but the kid didn't make a sound. She stared up at him with her big, blueish-gray eyes, so much like her father's. Her mouth made an O shape.

He hadn't been around a baby since his little brother Dylan, a helluva long time ago. *Dylan*. Did his brother have any kids yet? A bitter laugh escaped his control. Wouldn't that be something, if he were already an uncle, a *real* one, and didn't even know it.

"Hey, kiddo. Go back to sleep. Uncle Zach didn't mean to wake you up," he whispered.

A weird feeling gripped his gut.

It was quickly followed by the sensation of intense hunger, so strong it sent a bolt of pain through his belly.

The sound of Jessica's cry shattered the silence. She flung her tiny, clenched fists to the side and then quickly brought them back to her middle again. Jenny appeared in the doorway and scooped the infant up. "Uh oh. Somebody's hungry." Turning around to face him, she added, "Some privacy, please?"

He shut the door behind him, and not even a minute later, the hunger chewing at his insides began to dissipate.

Nah, it couldn't be.

He shook his head. No friggin' way.

A chuckle shook his chest. He'd better watch himself. He was starting to buy his own con.

# Chapter Six

It was official. This isolation was making Hannah nutso.

She'd had spent the past hour having a mostly one-sided conversation with her dog—in British. Well, with a British accent on her part. In her defense, she was pretty sure Costello had mumbled an uh-huh sound when she'd asked, "Aren't these candles just the dog's bollocks?"

She really needed to stop watching every version of *Pride and Prejudice* in her DVD collection when the classic film channel started showing weird stuff, which happened without fail every morning around two o'clock. And no more online streaming *Doctor Who*. It was making her wonky.

"Maybe I should have moved to London like Sarah suggested. What do you think, Costello? Would you like to live in England? I think you have some corgi in you, and we all know the Queen loves corgis."

The dog made a whiney-growling sound, rolled onto his side and covered his eyes with one stubby leg. She'd take that as *You're a completely nutter, woman. Leave me alone.*

Sighing, Hannah stepped away from the bookshelf and made sure the three baby blue candles she'd found in a box were positioned in a way that didn't clutter the thing, but ah, who was she kidding? She didn't own enough of anything to clutter a house of this size. It had been whimsical of her to buy this place in such a ridiculously wealthy neighborhood, but she'd wanted to start fresh somewhere memories couldn't haunt her—without leaving the city she loved.

When she'd lived in a dorm at college, she'd had so little space and money, she'd never bothered to decorate with more than a few posters or torn pages from a magazine. Her first apartment had been shared with two roommates, and she'd spent so little time there, she'd never seen the point. With Eric, she—

No. Don't go there. Don't think about him.

She sighed and rerouted her thoughts. When she'd moved in as Ellie's caretaker, she'd never felt right about trying to mix her own personal style with the older woman's outdated décor.

She'd lived there, but it hadn't been her home. She'd never really had a home, until now.

As soon as she'd seen this house—built in the 1930s and in need of a few repairs—she'd liked the idea of patching it up and making it *hers*. Maybe someday she'd have her own family, enough kids to fill the four bedrooms.

Hannah knelt beside one of the boxes filled with items from Ellie's house she either needed to sell, donate or put away and discovered a bunch of knickknacks she didn't remember packing. Ellie had owned a lot of knickknacks that seemed cruel to discard now without closer inspection. The older woman had spent almost ninety years collecting the things. The least Hannah could do was make sure they went to a home with someone who appreciated them.

She fingered a porcelain figurine of a white cat and shook her head. So far, she'd found at least one other box filled with similar figures. She felt the sting of tears behind her eyes. "Ellie did love animals, didn't she?"

Hearing her voice, Costello picked up the chew toy he'd been playing with and wandered closer, plopping down a few feet away before returning his focus to mauling the fuzzy goat.

She missed the older woman so much. Hannah hadn't realized how much she'd come to care for Ellie Parham until the woman had been gone. It was hard to believe her friend had been dead almost a year.

When Ellie's dog Fairbanks had passed away a few weeks after Hannah had moved in with her, Ellie had said, "Let's go save another life. This time the lucky critter will have two moms. Trust me. Whoever said money can't buy happiness has never paid a shelter fee."

They'd come home with not only a puppy, but a kitten, too. Hannah had always thought of Abbott and Costello as partially hers from that day forward. Even without the inheritance, Hannah would have taken care of the boys. Ellie had known that.

Blinking away the emotion that particular memory caused, Hannah closed the box and slid it toward the ones she'd marked "Garage." She twisted and turned to inspect a bigger box, only to squeal when Abbott sprang out of nowhere and landed in it before she could look inside. Crazy cat. Hannah would have made a lot more progress unpacking if Abbott stopped jumping into and making a bed inside of every box she opened.

The sound of the doorbell startled all three of them. Hannah jumped. Costello clambered to his feet barking, and Abbott darted out of the box and under the nearby sofa for safety.

She glanced at the clock she'd recently sat on the mantle. Almost ten. Brian had said he would be changing shifts with Zach soon. The idea of seeing him again spawned a ridiculous flutter of butterflies in her stomach.

Pushing to her feet, she dusted her jeans off then tugged at her ponytail to straighten it. Lord, she probably looked atrocious.

She opened the door, but instead of the man who'd been

occupying her thoughts more than he should have, a well-dressed, dark-haired, middle-aged woman stood there smiling and holding …a casserole dish?

Not far behind her, Brian stood propped against the hood of his car, watching. He nodded and gave a discreet two-fingered wave, which was the code they'd decided for "All clear."

"I hope you don't mind me intruding, but I wanted to come over and introduce myself." The woman held out her hand. "I'm Carolyn Carter, from down the street."

"Oh." Hannah accepted the gesture. "Hannah Dawson. Nice to meet you."

"Hannah." The woman repeated her name as if it were the lyric of a song. "What a beautiful name."

"Thank you."

Carolyn cast a backward glance at Brian before beaming a friendly smile in Hannah's direction again. "I know how hard it can be getting settled into a new neighborhood. I thought the least I could do was bring you over a casserole as a housewarming gift."

Oh, right. This was the part where she should invite the woman inside. Hannah rubbed her forehead and cringed at her social ineptness. "I'm sorry. Would you like to come in? I've been unpacking, and I'm afraid it's a bit of a mess right now." She used her foot to guide Costello back and out of the way. *Please, Lord, don't let him hump my new neighbor*. "Forgive my manners, but I'm not used to having company."

The woman stepped inside and immediately began looking around. "Don't worry about it, dear. I won't stay long. Like I said, I wanted to welcome you to the neighborhood. I've lived here for six years, and believe me, if I didn't come over to greet you, no one would." She held up the dish. "Do you like chicken and broccoli?"

"I love it." Hannah awkwardly took the offering and moved to the kitchen. "Thank you." After storing the casserole out of paws' way, she turned and found the woman bent over and scratching behind Costello's ear. The dog's tail wagged in ecstasy. "That's Costello. My cat is around here somewhere. He's Abbott."

"Abbott and Costello." The woman clapped once and laughed with delight. "That's precious. I used to love to watch their films when I was a little girl."

"So did their former owner. She named all of her pets after her favorite movie stars."

Carolyn Carter stayed for at least ten more minutes, doing her best to learn as much about Hannah as possible. Was she married? Did she have children? Had she always lived in Atlanta?

"I don't mean to pry, dear, but I can't help but wonder—" She leaned closer to Hannah and said, "Are you a famous actress or something?"

Hannah's eyebrows shot up. "Me?" She laughed. "No, I'm a nurse."

Carolyn glanced at the window. "Oh, I just assumed with the police cars patrolling the neighborhood and that man outside —" She waved her hand dripping with rings dismissively. "Never mind me. I'm an aging housewife whose only excitement is what I see on television. My imagination runs wild sometimes."

Hannah bit her lip, wondering how wise it would be to reveal the truth to her new neighbor. She wasn't stupid. Chances were the woman would leave and be on the phone within minutes, sharing all that she had learned with a network of their more curious neighbors. Hannah had been living here for almost three weeks, and this was the first time any of them had attempted contact. She'd feared becoming a source of gossip after calling the police during the first break-in, and now she had police cars and strange men coming and going at all hours. Yeah, she'd have been curious too, but she didn't want to scare the other residents unnecessarily by hinting they were in danger of burglary or anything.

"Well, I—"

She was saved from further explanation by the sound of the doorbell.

Hannah hurried to answer it, eager for any reason to usher this woman out.

Zach stood there, looking gorgeous and casual in jeans paired with a well-worn leather jacket. He tugged the sunglasses from his eyes as his lips spread into a killer smile—aimed right at her. He opened his mouth to speak, but his gaze drifted toward her guest. She saw confusion flitter across his face, but he recovered fast.

His grin kicked it up a notch when he leaned down toward her. Hannah wasn't sure what shocked her more. The fast, firm press of his warm lips against hers, or the feel of his hand sliding to the small of her back. She slid into the curve of his body without an ounce of protest.

Before she could react, he reached his free hand toward Carolyn. "Hi, I'm Zach. You must be one of Hannah's new neighbors."

Carolyn's face turned a shade redder than it had been as she accepted Zach's gentle handshake. She quickly brought her hand back to her chest. "Nice to meet you."

Hannah swallowed. Should she wrap her arm around his waist too? He obviously wanted to give the woman the idea they were a couple. Her left hand fluttered awkwardly at her side. She really, really wanted to touch him though.

"Um, Zach, this is Carolyn, my neighbor."

"I appreciate you coming over," he said, squeezing Hannah even closer to his side. "I've been so worried about Hannah since the break-in. It's good to know she's finally meeting some of the other residents."

Hannah's eyes widened—but probably not as much as Carolyn's did.

"The break-in?" The woman's hand fiddled with the necklace

at her throat.

"Yes, I'm sure you saw the police cars and the ambulance." He shook his head and sighed loud. He waved his hand toward the bruise on his face. "I almost caught the guys, but they clobbered me pretty good. I'm out of the hospital now, and I'm not going anywhere until I'm sure she's safe." He pointed his thumb toward the door. "My best friend Brian and my other friend, E.J., have been helping me keep an eye out. You haven't seen anything, have you? Any strange behavior in the neighborhood?"

She shook her head, a worried frown highlighting the wrinkles on her aging face. "My goodness. No. No, I haven't. We did wonder…" Her voice trailed off as her gaze drifted toward the door. "Do you think it's safe now?"

Zach chuckled. "Oh yeah. I'm not letting her out of my sight for personal reasons, but my friend Brian is tight with the cops. The guys who broke in are probably long gone."

"It is a nice community," Carolyn said, somewhat distractedly. "We have a neighborhood watch."

"We figure the robbers probably saw the moving trucks one day and figured it would be an easy hit." He lowered his gaze to Hannah's, and winked. "Hell, the cops think they might have even worked for the moving company."

"Oh, you poor dear." Carolyn reached out and pressed a gentle squeeze against Hannah's hand. "What an awful way to start out in a new home. I assure you, I've lived here many years, and I have never known of such a thing to happen. If you need anything— anything at all—please call me. I'll leave you the Wilkinsons' number too. They're right next door."

When Zach closed the door behind Carolyn a few minutes later, Hannah put plenty of distance between them. This man was like kryptonite to her control. He turned her brain to mush.

"What was that about?"

He turned and offered her a boyish grin. "That was me, feeding your nosy neighbors enough information to satisfy their curiosity and keep them out of your hair for a while."

"Why didn't you tell her the truth?" She swallowed. "Why did you pretend that you—" She shook her head and looked at the floor. "Why did you let her think—?"

"That we were a couple?" He moved around her and headed down the hall. He glanced in every room. When he turned, his jacket exposed a leather holster and the handle of a gun at his waist. "Would you have rather I told them I was your bodyguard?"

"I don't know. Maybe."

"No way." He stepped forward until they were within touching distance. "She might get curious, go on the internet and try to figure out who you are and why you need protection. Next thing you know, some tabloid has paid her money to show some photographers around."

"That's ridiculous." She frowned up at him. "My name hasn't been reported. No one knows that I was Ellie's nurse."

He nodded to the dog sitting beside her. "Did she see him?"

"Yes." What did that have to do with anything?

He pointed at Costello. "That dog is unique. I have never seen another dog that looks like him. His picture was in the paper. She might not know who you are, but it wouldn't be hard for her to figure out if she tried."

Hannah crossed her arms and exchanged looks with the dog. Alright, so maybe he had a point. She was paying him to be careful, right?

"What did you say?" Zach asked.

He was staring at her when she looked at him again. "What?"

"Did you say something?"

She shook her head.

"You didn't just say, 'Maybe I'm unique, but I sure am a pretty thing?'"

Spontaneous laughter burst from her lips. "No, of course not." Costello's tiny, brown eyes looked back at her with merriment, as if he also found it funny. "Are you trying to tell me Costello said that?" She knelt and scratched the dog behind his ears. In the baby voice she used only for the pets, she said, "You are a silly boy, but yes, you are a pretty thing, aren't you?" Glancing up, she wondered how Zach could have known that's what Ellie used to tell Costello often. *You sure are a pretty thing.*

Judging by the way he was leaning against the wall, his face much whiter than it had been, she figured it was best not to ask.

Maybe he *was* going crazy. Full-on, stick-me-in-a-straight-jacket insane.

Zach carried his duffle bag over to the sofa and sat it on the cushion. That'd explain the voices, and feeling strange emotions. He glanced over his shoulder and saw Hannah examining some figurines she'd removed from another box. She caught him staring, and her entire body language changed. Her shoulders tensed. Her back straightened. Her fingers tucked a loose strand of hair behind one ear.

The cat came sauntering into the room, sat down and gave Zach a staredown he was pretty sure that creepy kid from *The Omen* couldn't match.

*Oh, it's only you. I smelled you from a mile away. Shower much?*

Wait. Had the cat just insulted him, or was his imagination running away with him again? Zach lifted his arm a fraction and discreetly took a sniff. Deodorant. He'd showered this morning. What the—?

"Mreow."

The cat jumped onto the other end of the sofa, curled into a ball, and lowered its head.

Nothing. No more weird thoughts.

Wiping a hand over his face, Zach took a deep breath and tried to refocus.

His game plan before coming here had been to convince Hannah to move to a safe house, but she'd still been adamantly opposed to the idea. He needed to find out why. Convince her she was wrong. There was a rental house in an upscale, gated community they'd used before that was ideal. It had a guard at the entrance and private security patrolling the neighborhood twenty-four-seven. Since they were short-staffed, it sure as hell would help to have that extra peace of mind. To know he wasn't the only thing standing between Hannah and whoever the hell was after her animals.

He rubbed at a tense muscle in his shoulder. "Is it okay if I set my stuff over here?" He gestured to the sofa.

Her gaze strayed down the hallway, where the dog was preoccupied with some kind of toy. "I'm still not exactly sure how this is supposed to work, but I have four bedrooms in this house if you're more comfortable in a bed."

"Living room is better. I can keep an eye on the main entrances and exits from here. It's also close to your room, so I can hear if you need me."

He glanced around and liked the changes she'd made since he'd last been here. The walls still looked sort of bare. That reminded him.

He snapped his fingers. "Be right back."

She was watching him curiously when he returned, a small-framed poster in his hands. He walked over to the wall beside the television and held it up. "I was thinking you might like to have this. Maybe put it here on the wall?"

She gasped and rushed over to inspect it more closely. "A *City Lights* poster? Where did you get that?" Her face was happy as she examined it.

"I've had it for years." He tapped Charlie Chaplin's face on the print. "I crashed on a couch for a while with a guy who dressed up like Charlie. He made his living earning tips on Hollywood Boulevard, posing with tourists. I watched a lot of Chaplin movies with him. I bought this movie poster at a flea market a few years back. I figured you might appreciate it, so if you want it, it's yours."

"I love it." She looked at him hopefully. "You sure I can have it?"

"You want to hang it here, or is that too ugly?" He held it over the spot he'd envisioned. Maybe she'd rather hang it in an office, or not at all.

"It's perfect. Thank you."

He grabbed some of her tools and set about hanging it for her. "You don't meet too many people our age who are fans of Chaplin."

"Ellie loved movies—classic film. She introduced me to Charlie, and I fell in love with the way he made me laugh." She stood back and watched, her hands on her hips. "He was a genius."

Yeah, he had been. The actor-writer-producer-director had always been a favorite of Zach's, too. He'd never met a woman to share that opinion before. It was a novelty.

Hannah went back to the table and box she'd been sorting through. Her beautiful face looked relaxed with a smile now. Good.

"Hannah, I have some questions."

The paper stopped crinkling as her hands stilled. She glanced up and sat the trinkets aside. "Alright."

"You don't have to stop. We can both unpack while we talk." He tilted his head toward a box marked DECORATIONS sitting beside her. "Want me to go through that one?"

After a slight hesitation, she nodded. "If you don't mind, I'd appreciate the help."

Placing the box on the table opposite from her, he opened it and found picture frames and photo albums. "Tell me about yourself."

"What do you mean?"

"Tell me about your family or your friends."

She shoved something into the box she was messing with so hard it clinked against something else. "My parents are dead. I don't have any siblings. No other family. I don't have a lot of friends either. Never had much time for socializing."

He focused on the container in front of him again. "What about boyfriends?"

"That's kind of personal, don't you think?"

Probably. "I'm trying to get an idea who might have a grudge against you, Hannah. Usually, exes are a great place to start."

He flipped through the photo album, saw nothing but images of a man, woman and young girl who looked suspiciously like Hannah. Setting it aside, he picked up one of the photo frames. Two teenage girls goofed for the camera. One white. One black. Hannah and another girl.

She had at least one close friend. She'd spent a lot of time with the other woman—tall, black, pretty—when he'd been surveilling her years ago. Hard to believe they weren't still friends. He moved to set the frame on a sparsely decorated bookshelf while Hannah said, "I can't think of anyone I know who would be responsible for any of this. Not even any of my exes."

"Everyone always says that. More often than not, however, the perpetrator is someone they know."

Zach fingered another framed photo in the box. A handsome, blond guy stood with his arms wrapped around Hannah. It was a more recent photo, maybe a few years old. Her expression was so bright and optimistic, it warmed something inside of him.

Zach felt a hot rush of hostility seeing the man he remembered all too well.

Holding up the framed picture, he asked, "What about this guy?"

All of the color drained from Hannah's face. She ate up the distance between them and snatched it from his grip. "No, not even him." Her fingers trembled around the wood-edged frame. "I didn't know anyone had packed this." She walked into the kitchen, opened the trashcan and tossed the frame inside.

He guessed that meant she hadn't gotten back together with the guy. Good.

"Okay. Different questions." He took a deep breath. "Who helped you move?"

"Friends."

His lips twitched. "I thought you said you didn't have friends."

"My best friend, Sarah. She has four brothers. They helped me move."

"You didn't hire anyone?"

Hannah shrugged. "I rented a truck."

Anger radiated from her. Why? Because he was questioning her, or because she didn't like to be reminded of her ex, Eric Meester?

Zach couldn't remember the last time he'd met a woman so reluctant to talk about herself. Didn't she know that only intrigued him more?

She grabbed the box he'd been sorting through and carried it to where she'd been working. He got the message loud and clear. *Stay out of my stuff.* "Would you mind helping me move those boxes into the garage?" She nodded toward at least a dozen piled up in the corner. "I want to have them donated somewhere."

He shrugged and bent to lift one of them. The lid burst open and the damn cat poked its head out with a loud "Mreoow." Zach's heart nearly pounded out of his chest.

"Dammit, cat." He sighed, staggering back.

The cat jumped onto another box and stared at him. Its tail swished back and forth.

*I don't like you. Get out.*

Zach froze, meeting the feline's almond-shaped gaze.

*Get out.*

Zach knew the thoughts were not his own. Was the cat actually—?

*Hey idiot, I said, get out of my house. Go. Now. Scat.*

"Uh," Zach whispered. He glanced over his shoulder, saw that Hannah had her back turned and was reaching into a cabinet. He leaned closer to the cat and lowered his voice. "Did you say something to me?"

The cat lifted its paw and began licking.

Nothing else.

A cold sweat broke out on Zach's forehead.

Of course the cat hadn't been talking. Cats couldn't talk!

"Do you need some help?" Hannah asked.

*Yeah. I think I do. Professional help.*

"Nah, I got it." Zach moved warily around the cat as he lifted a couple of the boxes and carried them to the garage.

He didn't know what the hell was going on, but he knew one thing.

He was keeping an eye on that cat and dog.

# Chapter Seven

Hannah perched on the arm of the sofa beside Zachary and stared at the laptop in front of him. Was that her name in the internet search bar? Why?

*Well, duh. Because he probably thinks you're a total psycho after the way you reacted earlier.* He was probably checking to see what looney bin she'd escaped from.

She took a deep breath when he looked up at her. "I'm sorry. I was rude earlier, wasn't I?" She laid a hand on his shoulder and squeezed. "I'm not usually this awful. I swear. What do you want to know? Ask me and I'll tell you."

His mouth lifted into that grin she was becoming fond of—whoa, mama, he was hot—and she grew instantly aware of the intimate way she'd touched him. She drew her hand away, stood, then moved across the room to the chair and waited for him to repeat the questions he'd asked earlier.

She'd spent the better part of the afternoon kicking herself for her reaction to his questions. It wasn't that she was ashamed of her background. Far from it. She knew enough about psychology to know she'd been a little depressed and overly sensitive since Ellie had died. That was her only excuse.

That, and Eric, the jerkface, still held too much power over her emotions.

Zach closed the lid of the computer and leaned back.

"I understand. This can't be easy on you." He gestured to the computer. "I've been doing online searches to verify none of the media have identified you. So far, so good. You're only referred to as 'the nurse.'" He made quote gestures with his fingers.

She relaxed a little more. "Sounds like a bad title for a TV movie of the week."

"I bet you a hundred bucks you get an offer from a producer before this is over. Trust me. I know these people. They're probably doing everything they can to track you down for the story. They're like vultures." His mouth twisted with disdain.

Is that why he'd given up television? Because he didn't like the people he worked for? She was curious now. "How did you get your own TV show?"

Judging by the way his impressive arm muscles bunched when he clenched his right fist, she didn't think he was going to answer. Seconds passed. "I was working at a private investigations firm in Los Angeles. A TV producer suspected his assistant was selling spoilers to a magazine, and my boss gave me a shot at the case since it was low key."

"And you impressed that producer so much, he offered you your own show? How did you convince him you were psychic?"

His cobalt blue gaze turned dark. Cold. "It didn't take much." He leaned forward again and tapped the laptop, bringing her attention back to his earlier words. "The other good news is that the most recent article is from last week, which means the media interest is waning." He scratched the stubble at his chin. She got the message. Subject closed. "Who's been handling PR for you?"

Abbott jumped onto the chair and curled up on her lap, so she buried her fingers in the cat's soft fur and stroked. "Ellie's attorney is handling everything. He's been great through this entire process."

Zach stared at Abbott, whose purr got louder each time she

rubbed him. Brows furrowed, her bodyguard moved some papers aside and pulled out a folder. He pushed it toward her across the table.

His tone was curt. "Hannah, I had to consult my own attorney before talking to you about this, which is why I didn't say anything when you first came into my office. We adhere to strict client confidentiality, but this is a unique situation."

Pushing Abbott aside, she reached for the folder. It had Ellie's name typed on it. "What is this?"

"Ellie Parham hired me three years ago to do a background check on you."

What the hell? She sat up straighter, causing the cat beside her to grumble. Three years ago? "I started working for her four years ago. Part-time at first, but then she had her stroke." She shook her head as she skimmed the file. Nothing but a few reports. Reference checks. Credit report. Criminal history. Thank God that one was blank. "I don't understand why she would have hired you to do this. The agency I worked for already did background checks on us. She knew that."

"She never said why, but do you want my opinion?"

"Yes, of course." Her mind was gobsmacked.

"I think a woman of her wealth wanted to make sure anyone she hired could be trusted. I also think she was looking at you as a potential heir. Making sure you were everything you claimed to be. Making sure you were worthy of ten million dollars." He leaned back. "By law, she couldn't leave the money directly to her pets, Hannah. She could only leave it to someone with instructions the money be used to take care of them. Even then, there is no way to guarantee the person does, so I'm guessing she saw something in you that put her mind at ease on that front."

She supposed that made sense. If only Ellie had told her. If only the older woman had asked. *But Zach told you. He didn't*

74

*have to, you know.*

She examined his profile. So handsome. So serious. "I think I'm starting to understand."

"Understand what?"

"Let me show you something." When she returned with the envelope that contained Ellie's notes, he seemed hesitant to look inside. He gave nothing away as he glanced over the words the older woman had written. This man was good at hiding things. What else was he hiding? Hannah crossed her arms as she watched him carefully. "I suppose Ellie wanted me to hire you because she liked the work you did for her. That's why she left these notes."

Zach frowned when he looked up. "Yes, but why would she think you'd have a need?" He handed the envelope back to her. "Hannah, I don't want you to overreact to what else I have to tell you."

Tension seeped back into her muscles. "I won't." Abbott groused when she sat down and pulled him back into her lap, but then purred as she gently stroked her fingers through his silky fur. Having the cat close comforted her. "Tell me."

"I ran a background check on Ellie."

Her forehead tightened as she frowned. "Why?" Abbott pushed his furry body against her fingers, demanding more petting. She scratched him in that spot he loved behind his ear. *Purr. Purr. Purr.*

"I'm trying to narrow our list of suspects." Zach sank back against the sofa cushions and gave a loud, contented sigh. He let his head fall back on the cushion and his voice was languid when he spoke. "I wanted to make certain there were no long-lost relatives looking to cause trouble for you."

Okay. That made sense. "Did you find anything?" And why was he acting so weird all of a sudden?

He lifted his head and shifted his weight on the sofa. "That's what has me puzzled. Ellie Parham didn't exist until 30 years ago."

"But that's impossible." She stopped stroking Abbot's fur and met Zach's gaze. He lifted a hand and rubbed the back of his neck and explained what E.J. had found. Hannah shook her head. "No. There has to be some explanation."

"There always is." He was quiet for a while. "Do you know how Ellie got her fortune?"

That had been one of Hannah's first questions upon hearing the terms of Ellie's will. She nodded. "Mr. Russell, the attorney I mentioned earlier, said she came from a wealthy family, and she had an incredible financial advisor who secured her trust fund when the stock market collapsed a few years back. She barely lost a dime of what she'd made over the years."

She remembered how conservative Ellie had been with money, insisting Hannah use coupons from the Sunday paper and buy things only on sale. It wasn't hard to believe she'd never touched her trust fund.

Zach looked thoughtful. "I'd like to speak with your attorney. My gut tells me he's the person who could clear a lot of questions up for me."

Abbott made himself more comfortable in her lap. His four legs stretched until he was sprawled across her thighs. His purr vibrated against her leg as she slid her fingers through his silky hair. "We can go see him tomorrow." She looked forward to the opportunity to get out of the house.

Zach slid lower in his seat, spreading his legs wide and appearing so relaxed he looked almost…drugged? He'd been acting fidgety during most of this conversation. Should she be concerned?

"Are you okay?"

He reached up and tugged at the collar of his shirt. "Yeah." He moved to his feet and paced to the window. Wrenching the curtain aside, he peeked out. "Good. Yeah, we'll go in the morning."

What the hell was happening to him? Zach was getting excited, in more ways than one.

He tried to focus on the task at hand—finding out more about Hannah—but it was hard.

Kind of like he was getting hard.

Damn.

It had started when the cat had jumped in her lap. She'd started petting the animal, and a happy, relaxed feeling had washed over Zach. It had felt as if someone was running her hands through *his* hair. Pure ecstasy.

The more he'd watched her stroke the cat, the more his thoughts had shifted in a different direction. The woman was gorgeous. Even dressed in jeans and a t-shirt that featured a popular cartoon character, her hair pulled back and hardly any makeup on.

Not good.

He ran a hand through his hair to try and distract himself from the odd feeling of someone else's fingers there. No matter how attracted to Hannah he was, he couldn't let it happen. She was his client. Right now, the agency's most valuable client.

"I know it's a touchy subject, but I really do need to know if there's anyone in your life who might be responsible for this." He turned to face her. "Who knows where you live?"

A half smile tugged at her mouth. "That's easy. My best friend, Sarah, and her family. No one else."

"No one?"

"I wasn't joking when I said I don't have many friends, Zach." She shrugged. "Truth is, I hate people. I try to avoid them as much as possible."

Wait. She hated people? "You're a nurse."

"*Was* a nurse. I haven't decided if I'm going back to work or not." She motioned toward the TV in the corner. "I can't even watch the news anymore. People are horrible. I prefer my animals. Animals are much more innocent. Isn't that right, sweetie?" She cooed to the cat, who lifted its face to accept her kiss on its nose.

Lucky cat.

Something clicked. "You hired us to protect the cat and dog."

A weary smile pulled at the corners of her mouth. "Pretty sure I mentioned that."

He hadn't taken her seriously. No one was that selfless. "So if someone had a gun to your head and another person had a gun to that cat's head, who would you want me to save first?"

"The cat. Of course." She had a *duh* expression on her beautiful face.

He moved closer. "So if someone had a gun to my head, and another gunman had your dog, you would save…?"

Her eyelids drooped as she stared at him.

He arched a brow. "Not gonna answer?"

"I was thinking." She pursed her lips. "No offense, but I barely know you. You're a tough guy. You can protect yourself. I'm gonna have to go with the dog. We have history. You and I don't. Sorry."

If only she knew.

He glanced toward the framed photo of her and her friend, now placed on a shelf prominently in the room. The house was beginning to show clues of Hannah's personality, but he would have never guessed at the bitterness hidden deep inside her. She'd choose a cat or dog's life over a human's? That was nuts.

"Tell me about Sarah and her family."

Her expression relaxed. "I've known Sarah since middle school. We grew up together." She watched the cat as her fingers continued to caress its fur, and Zach couldn't prevent the slight moan from slipping past his lips. "My mother died when I was twelve. It was sudden. Brain aneurism." There was no emotion in her words. He tried to focus on that, and it worked. His libido cooled. "She and my stepfather had only been married a few months. When she died…" Her voice trailed off. She glanced up. "I had no other family. He turned me over to DSS, and I ended up in foster care. Sarah was in foster care too. That's how we met."

"What about your birth father?"

His voice became more taut. "He's not in the picture."

"What's his name?"

"Why?"

"I'd like to do a background check. Make sure he's not trying to cash in on a suddenly rich daughter."

Her lips thinned. "My mother left Ireland to get away from him. When she told him she was pregnant, he wanted her to have an abortion. I don't think he even knows I exist."

Damn. "Your mother *told* you that?"

Amusement lifted the edges of her mouth. "My mother told me he died in a car accident before I was born." She shook her head. "I overhead my stepfather telling the social worker. Otherwise, I'd have never known the truth."

Zach couldn't help but wonder if he'd found his first credible suspect. "Do you know his name?"

She rolled her eyes. "Liam Kelly. I'd appreciate it if you didn't contact him. Even if he's still alive, I'm not keen to meet him." Abbott finally grew tired of the petting and leapt to the floor. Thank God. Hannah's gaze followed the cat. "Besides, I've been lucky. I was never abused. Teenagers rarely get adopted, but I did. An older couple—a preacher and his wife. Donald Patrick was more of a father to me in five years than any man I've known."

"Are you still close to him?"

She shook her head. "Mr. Patrick died from a heart attack six years ago. Mrs. Patrick had a stroke and died a year later."

He stood behind the smaller sofa opposite her, his hands braced against the back of it. "That's tough. Sorry."

She blew out a breath and gestured awkwardly toward the kitchen—or more precisely, he realized when she spoke, toward the trashcan. "Since we're discussing my soap opera of a life, there was also Eric Meester, my ex-fiancé. It didn't end well, but I haven't seen or spoken to him in about three years. Last I heard, he'd moved out of state anyway."

Zach held still, waiting for her to elaborate. When she didn't, he asked, "How did it end?"

"I told you—badly. I'd rather not go into those personal details if you don't mind." She pushed to her feet and moved into the kitchen. A hint of bare skin beneath the hem of her shirt showed when she reached up to retrieve a glass from the cabinet. He swallowed, forced himself to look away.

"What about other boyfriends?"

She turned and leaned back against the counter, taking a sip of the water she'd poured. "I can give you a list of names. It won't be long." Her fingers toyed with the glass. "Nurses work odd hours. I'm not a nun, but I haven't had much time to date."

They spent the next hour going over possible suspects in Hannah's life over a frozen pizza Hannah heated up. She didn't give him much to go on. Eventually, she called the animals over to feed them.

"It's getting late." She poured their food into their bowls and his stomach began churning. Begging with short growls and barks, Costello scrambled to his bowl and dove in with gutso.

*Yum. Yum. Yum. So good. So good. I'm so hungry. Gotta eat.*

Oh, no. Not again. Zach leaned back in his chair and tried to make sense of the ridiculous sensations and thoughts running through his mind. He stared as the cat darted out of hiding and began eating, much more slowly, hunched over his food bowl.

*Delicious. Tuna is my favorite. I love her so much.*

"I'll get you a pillow and blanket." Hannah disappeared down the hall.

Zach made sure she was out of hearing range before he leaned down and whispered, "Hey kitty. If you're talking to me, here's your chance. Say something."

Licking his lips, the cat sat up and began rubbing his ear with his paw, over and over again.

Nothing.

"This still seems so surreal to me." Hannah's voice demanded his attention. He turned and saw her stacking some items on the corner of the sofa. "I mean, will you get any sleep, or are you supposed to sit here all night and…what? Guard over us?"

"I'll get some rest, off and on." He stood to help her. "Don't worry, Hannah. I'll keep you safe."

She slid her hands into the back pocket of her jeans. "I'm going to turn in. It's been a long day. If you need anything, feel free." She waved to the kitchen.

She started to move away, but he caught her arm. Big mistake. As soon as he touched her, heat sparked from his fingers and rushed to his groin. Judging by the way her eyes widened, then darkened, she felt it too. "Don't forget to get me that list."

A brief laugh shook her body. "I was kidding."

"I wasn't." He loosened his hold. "Ex-boyfriends. Friends. Stepfathers. Anyone you can think of. I only want to run a basic background check."

She stepped away, putting some distance between them. "You can't be serious." She leaned over and picked up the cat. "How would you feel if I asked you for a list of women you'd dated?"

Uncomfortable. Awkward. He'd want to tell her it was none of her damn business.

"I'm not asking because I want to know. I'm asking because I'm trying to protect you."

*Liar.*

At the strong, foreign thought, Zach's gaze met the cat's. Abbott was in Hannah's arms, staring right back at Zach with an intent look.

A look that called him a liar.

"Fine." Hannah whistled for Costello to follow. "I'll see you in the morning."

Zach waited until her bedroom door was closed before grabbing his mobile and dialing Brian's phone number. His finger quickly hit END before the call could be sent.

What would he say? That he thought he could actually hear what these animals were thinking? His friend would insist on him seeing a doctor, or get pissed because he'd think Zach was back to his old tricks.

*Try calling Alexandra King.*

His head snapped back on a *whoa* sensation of where the hell did that thought come from? Alexandra King. That was a name he hadn't thought of in a while.

He scrolled through the names in his phone's contact list. He stopped on the woman's number, surprised it was still in his phone. He could just imagine that conversation.

Hell no.

Shaking his head, he decided to check the perimeters. Hannah's bedroom door was closed, and he assumed the animals were in there with her.

A laugh bubbled up from his chest. Wasn't this his luck? Of all the cool psychic powers he could suddenly possess, he was some kind of lame pet psychic. He sobered. Wait. Was he actually believing this now?

He needed to wrap his head around whatever the hell was happening.

Stepping outside, he drew in a breath of fresh air. A woman's life depended on him keeping her safe. He needed to get his shit together. Needed to figure out what was wrong with his head, and soon.

He didn't want to be responsible for any more deaths.

The light coming through the curtains stung Zach's eyes hours later. There was also an unfamiliar weight on his chest. He blinked his vision into focus, and a pair of almond-shaped eyes stared back at him.

*Get out.*

Zach started, but the action didn't jostle the cat. It was lying on his chest as if it had been there a while. Watching him sleep.

*Are you an idiot? We don't want you here. Leave.*

The cat's left paw stretched toward Zach's neck. Its claws flexed and pierced his skin. A slight purr followed the action.

"Aw, look." Hannah's voice came from somewhere behind him. "Abbott likes you."

Zach wiggled his way into a sitting position, and the cat finally jumped away. He glanced at the clock. It was past seven.

He rubbed his throat. The jingle of the dog's collar and tags drew his attention. He wasn't used to getting up so early, not especially after only catching a few hours of sleep. Hannah was dressed in a pair of jeans and a different t-shirt. Her hands toyed with a leash.

"Sorry to wake you, but I always take Costello on an early morning walk." She leaned over to ready the dog, who was wiggling his butt in obvious excitement.

"Can't you let him out in the backyard?"

She straightened and frowned at him. "I could, but I'm not going to." She reached for the lanyard that held her key. "I usually take him for a walk in the morning and at night for exercise. Poor guy has only been getting walked in the mornings since this all happened." She nodded toward the cat, who was lounging on the floor near him. "Are you gonna stay here with Abbott, or should I grab his kennel?"

Zach sighed and rose to his feet. "You're not going anywhere alone. I'll grab the bag. Where is it?"

A few minutes later, Zach wished he'd remembered his sunglasses before venturing on their walk. He squinted against the early morning sun, even as he glanced around, taking in their surroundings. The mesh bag containing Abbott bumped against his side as he kept pace beside the woman and dog.

*I want out of this bag. Oooooh, look at that bird.*

*I want that bird.*

*I want it.*

Zach looked down and followed the cat's intense stare toward one of the neighbor's yards. A red bird was perched on a birdfeeder. A low growling sound came from the animal he was carrying.

But that wasn't all.

*I love the outdoors. I love going on walks. I love to pee.*

Hannah stopped walking, and Zach's gaze fell to the dog who had hiked his leg and was peeing on a bush. The dog's thoughts were much simpler and way less menacing.

He reached up a hand and rubbed at his eyes.

This couldn't be happening to him.

"Did you get much sleep?" Hannah's voice was a nice distraction from the strange thoughts scrambling through his brain.

"A few hours."

"Same here."

She didn't look like it. No bags under her eyes. Her green gaze seemed clear, focused, and beautiful.

An image of Hannah, her hair down and dressed in a tank top and shorts, lying in bed reading a book flashed through his mind. Blinking, Zach felt disoriented for several seconds. He glanced down and saw the cat staring up at him through the mesh front of the bag.

"Meow."

He realized Hannah and the dog had moved ahead of him. His

feet felt heavy as he followed.

"Hannah." She glanced over her shoulder. "Did you read a book last night?"

"Yes. Why?"

"Do you have pajamas—a tank top that has a funny-looking rabbit on it? I think it says—"

She gaped. "It says 'A makeover. You need to be run over.'"

He nodded.

Hell. This was real, wasn't it?

"How did you know that?" Hannah demanded.

He took a deep breath and attempted to smile. "Psychic, remember?" His fingers trembled slightly when he reached to adjust the shoulder strap of the cat's bag.

"Right." She looked almost as weirded out as he felt. "Is something about that important?"

"I don't think so. I get random, uh, flashes sometimes."

"Okay."

"Yeah. Okay." He swallowed. Hard.

The dog in front of them kept passing gas and then whipping his head around. *What was that? Who did that?* Zach felt a chuckle bubble from his chest.

"He does that a lot—gives little toots and then acts like he doesn't know who did it." She shrugged and added, in a baby voice, "Silly, Costello. Silly, silly boy."

"Oh, he's not acting." Zach shook his head. "He really doesn't know he's doing it. He's not too bright, your dog."

Hannah gasped. "Zach! Hush your mouth." But she was grinning. "Costello is smart when he wants to be. You'd be surprised."

He didn't want to ruin her perceptions of the dog, who he evaluated was as dumb as a brick, so he kept quiet.

They'd nearly finished their walk in silence when Hannah spoke again. "How long have you known you were psychic? Have you always been that way?"

Of all the questions to ask.

"No, not always." He gripped the strap of the cat's kennel. "I've always had –" He searched his mind for the best word. "Good instincts. It took me a while to realize I was psychic."

There, that was at least the truth. He didn't want to lie to this woman anymore than he already had.

Had he always been psychic and not known it? He'd trained himself how to read people's tells. Living on the streets that had been how he'd survived. And he'd always followed his instincts. They'd never let him down.

But psychic?

Maybe he had been. Hell. He had no idea.

"There was a case on the show once." He spoke aloud, but more to organize his thoughts than for conversation. "A little girl was missing. I helped lead the police right to her."

"I remember. That's one of the episodes I saw."

He nodded. It had been one of the last episodes of his time on the show, period. He'd quit soon after. Zach remembered how spooked he'd felt when the police raid had produced the girl and her kidnapper. He'd studied the police files, picked up on a few details while talking to some of the witnesses to her abduction, listened to his gut, and prayed his logic would pan out.

Seeing that little girl being carried out of the building in a police officer's arms had hit him hard. What if he'd been wrong? Lives were at stake. A real psychic, if they actually existed—maybe even Alexandra King—might have found that girl sooner.

So he'd quit and founded the agency with Brian, putting his "psychic" past behind him. They'd used his name to lure clients in, but he'd never accepted a case from a client expecting a psychic resolution.

"I can't imagine being able to do what you do," Hannah said, drawing him back to the present. "I have to admit. I'm a little skeptical about psychics."

"Then why did you ask me to communicate with your animals?"

"Ellie's note. And I was testing you," she admitted. "I don't know. I'd love to know what they're thinking. Am I doing this right? Do they love me or only tolerate me?" She shrugged.

"They love you very much."

"You sure about that?"

"Positive, but it doesn't take a psychic to see that."

The hopeful smile she turned toward him stole his breath. She had a beautiful smile. Pretty lips. Lush and kissable. "I think maybe I misjudged you." Her eyes narrowed as they moved over his face. "You don't like to be reminded that you're psychic, do you? You always try to change the subject when I mention it. Why?"

The lady was too damn perceptive.

This was his chance to tell her the truth. Explain it had all been a sham before, but suddenly it was real. His lips drew tight. He shook his head. "It's too hard to explain." He cleared his throat. "Hannah, did Ellie ever talk to you about her past? Can you think of any reason besides the money that she would have thought you'd need to hire me?"

That had been puzzling him since she'd shown him the old woman's notes last night. What had Ellie meant when she said the animals knew the secrets of her past?

*Are you an idiot or what? She knew Hannah would be in danger. She knew he'd come for her.*

Zach stumbled along the path. Another thought, clear, but not his own. He looked down at the cat. Its creepy eyes were staring up at him intensely from the bag.

"I have no idea," Hannah said. "Sorry."

"Yeah, it's okay."

The cat looked away, but Zach didn't relax.

The cat had said—or at least he was pretty sure it had been the cat—*he* would come for her.

Who the hell was *he*?

# Chapter Eight

Hannah went to step out of the shower and hesitated.

She peeked around the curtain to make certain neither Abbott or Costello were lying on the floor, watching her like one or both often did. Her gaze shifted around the room.

No animals in sight.

Her shoulders relaxed, and after she'd wrapped a towel around her body, she glanced at her reflection in the steamed-up mirror. What if Zach could see things through her eyes? What if—?

No. She was being silly.

Shaking her head, she wiped away the steam to clear her reflection. He'd freaked her out a little this morning when he'd mentioned her pajamas. Last night, she'd stayed up late reading with her bedroom door shut. When she was ready for sleep, sometime around three in the morning she'd cracked it open so the boys could go get water during the night.

Maybe Zach had looked in on her while she'd been sleeping. She shook her head again. No, she always slept under her covers, and she was a light sleeper. The only eyes that knew what she wore to bed these days belonged to a cat and a dog.

"You knew he was psychic, or at least possibly psychic, when you hired him. What's the big deal?"

Her reflection didn't respond to the hushed question.

She took a deep breath and reminded herself she still wasn't one-hundred percent certain Zach was psychic at all. If she took the time, she might be able to find a reasonable explanation for his insights, right?

Stepping into the bedroom to get her clothes, she immediately froze when she saw that Abbott was lounging lazily on the bed, staring at her. Costello was breathing heavier than normal where he was sprawled on the rug beside her bed, also watching her. His mouth was open in what seemed like a maniacal grin for a dog and his chest rose and fell with quick breaths.

But what if there isn't a reasonable explanation?

What if Zach could see what her animals saw?

Her fingers gripped the towel bunched above her breasts. It only fell to mid-thigh, leaving her more exposed than she would have liked.

*Uh-uh. No way in hell.*

She cleared her throat. "Um, boys."

Costello's ears perked up.

Her gaze darted to the closed bedroom door. One of Costello's toys was propped up next to it. Walking carefully to the entryway, she squatted down, felt around until her fingertips grazed the stuffed animal and then opened the door a tad. She flung the toy out of the room. The dog jumped to his feet and happily gave chase. She quickly shut the door behind him.

That left the cat.

His tail lifted and beat the comforter as he stared back at her. Abbott's head lowered defensively, obviously expecting no good.

"Abbott, get out of the room." Hannah pointed at the door. She kept her voice quiet as she spoke. "I'll give you tuna if you go in the other room until I'm dressed."

The cat didn't move.

Hannah sighed. "Please?"

The cat jumped from the bed and dashed to the door as if she'd threatened his life. She opened it, only to feel the weight of Costello's heavy body pressing against it from the other side, demanding re-entry.

Oh, for the love of—

Hannah shoved against the door, wincing at the loud slap of wood on wood as it connected with the doorjamb and groaning when the latch didn't connect. Costello shoved the door open again, so she pressed against it with her body.

She felt a big push from the other side, seconds before Zach's voice asked, "Hannah, everything okay?"

Squealing, she grasped her towel, stepped back and tripped over something furry that sent her sprawling in an unladylike heap to the carpet. "Don't come in here!"

But it was too late.

Gun drawn and pointed in front of him, Zach was already in the room, glancing around for an intruder or something.

Bloody hell.

His gaze dropped to where she scrambled to cover herself with the too-small towel. He froze but didn't try to avert his gaze.

Oh yeah. This was going to be one of those days.

"Um, sorry." He holstered his gun and reached a hand down to help her up. "I thought maybe someone had..." He sighed and looked away when she made no move to take his hand.

How could she? As soon as she stood, the towel would expose far too many parts of her for her liking. Somebody kill her already.

"I'm okay. Would you mind turning around please?"

He turned, slowly, and she awkwardly found her feet, tugging the towel off and wrapping it around her middle as securely as she could manage. A few steps and she could make it back into the bathroom.

Her eyes lifted and met his in the mirror across the room.

Oh, sweet heaven. He'd gotten an eyeful, hadn't he?

"I didn't see anything." But his eyes were dark and dancing with mischief.

Biting her lip, she tried to take a step back and nearly tripped over the same object that had gotten her before. She flailed before a strong grasp captured her upper arm and set her right.

"I think my pets are trying to kill me by leaving their toys scattered around." She lifted her gaze and met his. He was so close, she could feel the warmth of his body. His fingers were still holding her arm.

And she was practically naked.

Sweet heaven.

His gaze dropped to her mouth, and she could have sworn she felt a slight tug on her arm as his head lowered a fraction toward hers. His throat moved beneath a swallow.

"I should let you get dressed."

She managed a nod, even though that's not what she wanted. She wanted his lips on hers. Right now. "Please."

He hesitated. Swallowing again, he stepped back, glanced around the room, and disappeared.

Zach closed the door to Hannah's bedroom and wondered if he had enough time to take a cold shower before she was ready to leave.

Have mercy. All it would have taken was a simple little tug to feast his eyes on that hot body of hers. He'd seen enough to set his blood rushing to his groin, making him damned uncomfortable now.

Walking into the living room, he dropped to the floor and started doing twenty. His arm needed the exercise anyway. *Four. Five. Six.* He tried to think about anything but how she'd looked in that towel. *Nine. Ten. Eleven.* The creamy curve of her breast against the white fabric. *Thirteen. Fourteen.* Crap. This wasn't working. He hit twenty and shoved to his feet.

He forced his mind away from the naughty ideas still swimming in his brain and retrieved his phone. Work. Focus on work.

When one of the team transported a client who was at high risk, a backup always followed to make certain no one tampered with the vehicle while the client and her guard were away from it. He needed a second set of eyes this afternoon, and E.J. had drawn the short straw.

"No problem," the younger man said after Zach explained the situation. "How are things going?"

Zach leaned forward, fixated on the closed bedroom door at the end of the hall. He knew how he wanted things to be going. "Quiet." He rubbed at his tired eyes and took a deep breath to help cool his libido. "I don't know. I have a feeling it's too quiet." His gut was uneasy, and it had nothing to do with the woman in the other room.

"While I've got you on the phone, I got the information you asked for on Hannah Dawson's finances."

That got Zach's attention. "Anything worth mentioning?"

"Yeah. She was in a lot of debt when the old lady passed away."

"Really? What kind of debt?"

"Credit cards, mostly. A couple of personal loans. About $40,000 worth. Funny thing is, she had most of her student loans paid off before she got in deep."

"Noted." E.J. was proving to be really good at this. Maybe he could use the kid to cover a shift here while Zach took care of some business. "Be at the lawyer's office in an hour, and don't be late."

A flash of white and black caught his attention as he ended the call. The cat slowed its pace and stalked toward Zach as if it had purpose. Oh, crap. He was alone with the pets again.

"Hey, kitty." He took a step back and forced a smile he wasn't feeling. "How's it going?"

The cat sat down. It was damned creepy the way that thing stared at him sometimes. As if it could see straight through him.

"I bet you'd like a treat, huh?" Zach snapped his fingers and moved to the kitchen. He opened the cabinet doors above the stove, but he didn't see any treats.

*Not there, idiot. She keeps them here.* A clear image of the pantry-style closet flashed through his mind. Zach felt so disoriented by the unexpected vision he grabbed hold of the fridge handle to anchor himself.

Whoa. Zach dared a glance at the cat as he maneuvered his way to the closet, making sure his hands held onto something along the way.

"You know, cat, we could be friends if you stopped calling me names." He reached into the closet and grabbed a bag of cat treats. "See?" He shook the bag, and Abbott meowed and came toward him, rubbing against Zach's pants leg in a gesture he'd always assumed was a sign of affection.

*Okay, I own you now. You have permission to feed me.* The cat circled back and swiped his leg again. *Give me a treat…or a bunch of them.*

He poured some treats onto the floor, and the cat slowly snuck up to devour them. Zach reached down and petted the animal, hoping to make peace. Maybe if he did, the damn cat would get out of his head.

"Abbott, what did you mean that he was coming after Hannah? Who's he?" Was it Eric Meester? Had Ellie been afraid he'd come back once she was gone?

*Nom. Nom. Nom. These are so good. I like the tuna ones best.*

"Fine, but I'm gonna keep asking until you give me an answer."

He'd bribe it out of the little jerk with some treats. Yeah, he knew the cat's weakness now. Tuna.

Straightening, he rubbed his eyes and glanced down the hall, where the sound of a blow dryer was muffled behind the closed door. Maybe he had a few minutes. Stepping into the guest room and closing the door, he pulled out his phone and selected Alexandra King's number before he could talk himself out of it. Predictably, it rang twice before she sent him to voice mail.

He rambled an awkward greeting before snapping to the point.

"I know I'm not your favorite person, but I could really use some help with something. It's personal and … I wouldn't call if I didn't have anyone else to ask, so … give me a call back please. It's kind of urgent."

Hannah double-checked her makeup as she ran the brush through her hair one last time. She glanced at her reflection and figured she looked decent enough, with a turquoise sweater over a pair of white pants.

She was moving down the hall, sliding her arms into a jacket, when she spotted Zach sitting on her sofa, bent forward, scratching Costello's ears and staring eye to eye with the dog. Her footsteps slowed, and she couldn't help but wonder if she was interrupting something.

"Do you know who he is? What is the cat talking about? Huh, boy?" Zach's voice was above a whisper.

Spotting her, he glanced up and released the dog quickly.

"Ready?"

She nodded and reached for her purse, wondering if she should bring up what had happened—or almost happened—in her bedroom earlier. His expression was stoic and almost militant now. Had he already forgotten it? Was the attraction only one-sided?

Ugh. Story of her life.

The ringtone for a popular dance song snapped Hannah's attention away from the human-canine duo. She took a deep breath and stretched to grab her cell phone from the corner table.

A few minutes later, she couldn't keep the grin off her face as she pressed END. Turning to see Zach sitting again on the sofa, watching her, she felt her face drop a little.

"Oh. Shoot."

Zach's eyebrows lifted. "Whoa, lady. Watch the language. There are impressionable ears around here." With one last ferocious head rub for the dog, he stood and winked at her. "Anything I should know?"

Okay. Had he just winked at her? Talk about mixed signals.

"I guess I should've checked with you first." Her fingers rubbed a circle around the edge of her phone. "I have an appointment for Agatha Roundtree's class tomorrow. They just called to remind me of it." She bit her lip. "I can call her back and reschedule if I need to, but there's a long waiting list. It's taken me months to get in."

Zach's expression was oblivious. He held out his hand in a *whoa* gesture. "What kind of class is it, when and where? Are we talking spinning class? Crocheting? What?"

Hannah nodded toward Costello. "A dog obedience class. Tomorrow afternoon at Centennial Park." She shrugged. "Agatha Roundtree is supposed to be the best in the region."

"Never heard of her." He crossed his arms and looked down at the dog. Costello looked back, tilting his head and eyes upward. What a funny picture they made—Zach was tall. The dog was so short. They were like some sort of odd couple. "Dog obedience, huh?"

Her lips twitched. "You might have noticed—he has a bit of a humping problem."

"Yeah, I think I noticed that."

"And he can be kind of aggressive with his favorite toys." She flicked her wrist awkwardly. The action drew Costello's attention, and the dog's head tilted as if he was trying hard to understand what she was saying. "He's been that way since we got him. He's fixed—Ellie got him from the pound—but, well, I guess he's just kind of crazy."

The smile in Zach's eyes about knocked her off her feet. "I guess we'd better take him to obedience class then." He winked at her again and turned to grab the dog's leash.

That smile. That wink.

Oh, my. She was in trouble, or would be if he actually started flirting with her in earnest.

One minute he was all business. The next, as charming as a used car salesman. He confused her.

Blowing out a frustrated breath, she moved to find Abbott and secure him in his bag. If she was lucky, Zach would switch out with Brian soon, and she could take a step back to reassess her situation with a clear head.

Problem was, her luck these days kind of sucked.

Ellie Parham's attorney reminded Zach of the handful of entertainment lawyers who had worked on his TV show. The young guys had always been shoving something at him. Sign this. Sign that. Their ties had usually seemed askew and not quite made of the same high-grade silk as their senior partners. But the older ones—like this guy—had moved slower, dressed richer and taken time to look you in the eye.

His grip when he reached across the desk to shake Zach's hand was firm. His expression was much softer when he nodded at Hannah in greeting.

"Thank you for taking the time to speak with us." She glanced over her shoulder at the dog as she took her seat, the bag with the cat planted firmly beside her feet. "I hope it wasn't too much trouble fitting us in today."

"No, of course not." Franklin L. Russell waited for Zach to sit before he lowered himself into the comfy-looking chair behind his desk. "Anything for you." His smile when he looked at Hannah took on a flirtatious quality that Zach did not appreciate. The man was old enough to be her father. "How are the animals, Hannah?"

"They're fine." She met Zach's gaze when she spoke. He could feel her mentally needling him to speak.

He turned his focus to the older man. He had to tread carefully here. "I have some questions about Miss Parham that might aid in the security of Miss Dawson and her animals."

"I'll answer anything I can, but I believe I already told your associate everything he wanted to know."

Zach leaned forward. "That's the interesting thing. My associates and I have been completely unable to find any evidence that Miss Parham existed prior to 1983." Zach tapped his fingertips against Russell's desk. "Can you help me understand that?"

Russell sighed and glanced toward Hannah in clear aggravation. His gaze had lost its welcome. "Are you trying to suggest my late client, who was a dear woman and a close friend, was not who she claimed to be?"

"You tell me."

"Zach," Hannah's voice interrupted his stare-down with the attorney. She said nothing, just pursed her lips and shook her head. He got the message loud and clear. *Take it easy.*

An image of the older man and Ellie Parham appeared in his mind like a flash going off. The two were flipping through a book and laughing.

*He knows more than he's telling you. They were close. Really close.*

The idea was not his own, although he'd been headed in that direction fast. Zach looked down at the mesh bag and saw the cat staring back at him.

*He knows who she really was.*

Abbott lifted a paw and began licking it.

Zach swallowed.

"Mr. Collins, are you alright? You look a little pale all of a sudden."

Hannah's warm fingers touched his hand. "Zach?"

Damn. He was still getting used to that, those flashes.

"Mr. Russell, I'm curious." Hannah squeezed his fingers and then removed her hand. She focused on the lawyer. "Why would Ellie leave documents instructing me to hire Mr. Collins after her death? Did she ever confide that information in you?"

Every cell in his body froze as Zach waited for, dreaded, the answer he knew was coming.

Franklin L. Russell's name had been on the two checks Zach had handled years ago. One, delivered to his office as payment for services rendered to Ellie Parham, and the other made out to Eric Meester.

This asshole had been involved in what they'd done to Hannah three years ago. He knew everything.

He could *ruin* everything.

The older man leaned forward, bracing himself with his elbows on the desk. He looked at Zach for several long, intimidating seconds before turning his gaze back to Hannah. "No, I'm afraid she didn't. As her legal advisor, I would have warned her against it. Our firm has worked with other private investigators I would have recommended first."

Zach sighed, tipping a mental hat to the man who was as good an actor as any he'd ever known.

Hannah looked disappointed. This was another sin compound on his list of many he'd have to atone for someday.

He would have to find a way to visit the man without Hannah. Find out whatever the attorney knew, because he definitely knew something.

# Chapter Nine

"I think we should make our move soon. This afternoon."

Fox's grip on the phone tightened, even as he reached with his other to pick up the makeup kit sitting on the hotel dresser. Although he'd already come to the same conclusion, he asked, "What makes you say that?"

His partner's voice was hushed. "Collins left last night. His assistant is standing guard, and the kid is green. Real green. From the sounds of it, he's spent more time playing games on his phone than keeping an eye out. She's also taking the dog to Centennial Park this afternoon."

Glancing at his clean-shaven reflection in the mirror, he had to give his prodigy credit. Planting the bug in the home had given them plenty of useful information while they waited for a prime opportunity like this. He would have preferred not to make a move in public, but nothing about this job had gone as planned.

Fox slid his hand beneath the mattress to retrieve the small gun he'd hidden there.

"Good work." He made sure the safety was on and slid it into his bag. Now all he needed was the perfect disguise. "I'll meet you at the park in an hour."

Hannah considered E.J. as she prepped Costello's bag for the training class. The young man had positioned himself on her couch where he'd occupied himself with his Smartphone for most of the morning.

"Do you want something to eat? I can fix something before we leave."

"I probably shouldn't take advantage." E.J. lifted his head, mischief dancing in his eyes. "But if you twist my arm, yeah, man, I'd love to eat."

Hannah raised her eyebrows. It was hard not to like this guy. "You might regret those words, but I'll see what I can scrounge up for us."

"Mmmm." Tucking his phone into his jacket pocket, E.J. slid onto one of the seats at the breakfast bar. He rubbed his hands together. "You sure you don't mind?"

"I actually enjoy cooking." She found some eggs and readied a pan. She made a mean omelet and wouldn't mind one for herself. "I'm running low on supplies. I haven't been to the store much since I moved in here."

"I'll talk to Zach. Maybe make a run for you after he gets back."

"Thanks. When did Zach say he'd be back?" She hoped she didn't sound as hopeful as she felt. She didn't want to offend E.J. Her reasons for wanting to see Zach simply had more to do with liking him around than anything wrong E.J. had done.

"Shouldn't be too long. He's taking care of some personal business."

Personal? "Oh. Is he married?"

"Zach? Hell, no." E.J. snorted out laughter.

"What? Is he gay or something?" She peppered her voice with amusement to make a joke out of it.

"Yeah, that's even funnier." E.J. shook his head. "Nah, he likes the ladies. Trust me."

At least she could reassure Sarah of that now. "So how long

have you been doing this, E.J.? You seem awfully young."

His fingers tapped out a rhythm against the tabletop. "Nah, I just turned 21." He reached into his jacket and retrieved a Slim Jim. "Zach and Brian took me on about—what was it?—two months ago."

Not for the first time Hannah noticed the tattoo peeking out from the neckline of his shirt. She recognized the skull with initials from her rounds in the emergency room as a student nurse. *Should I mention I know what it means?* She couldn't remember which gang it signified, but that detail didn't matter to her.

She only cared if E.J. was a danger to others.

E.J. must have caught her staring because his hand reached up and tugged at his collar. "My granddad works in their building. He put in a good word for me. Brian thinks I could go for my P.I. license someday. Zach's been helping me study about laws and regulations."

"Your grandfather must be proud."

Costello whined, and E.J. bent down to scruff his head. "I'm sorry, boy. Here ya go." He handed the dog a chunk of the beef jerky. Perhaps the only danger E.J. presented was giving her dog high cholesterol.

"Yeah, my grandpa's a good man. So are Zach and Brian. They gave me a chance when not a lot of people would have. I—"

His words hung between them for several seconds. When Hannah flipped the finished omelets onto plates, she turned to measure his reaction. "You what?"

He shrugged, and she recognized the vulnerability in his expression. And maybe even a hint of guilt? "Sometimes I think I don't know what I'm doing." He scratched the back of his head and chuckled.

Zach obviously trusted this young man, so she would, too. She slid a plate in front of him. "Everyone has a special set of skills.

All you have to do is figure out how yours will benefit the agency."

He wolfed down his food almost as quickly as she'd seen Costello snatch a treat. "I'm pretty good with a computer. Zach wants to bring in people who can work in cyber security. I'm hoping maybe—" He shrugged. "I dunno."

Funny. Sarah loved computers, too, so much so she had gone back to school for it. Hmm. How much persuasion would her friend need to give E.J. some lessons? Oh, probably a lot. Hannah smiled at the thought.

"Know what else I'm good at?" Oblivious to her amusement, E.J. glanced over his shoulder, both ways, then leaned closer. "I'm a helluva pickpocket. I can boost a car in under thirty seconds." He snapped his fingers. "Like that. Snap. It's done."

Her eyes widened as she slid a piece of her omelet into her mouth. Sometimes E.J. reminded her of a little kid with all of his enthusiasm and mannerisms—but then words like that came tumbling out of his mouth. "Um, that's…impressive."

He shook his fork at her. "Nah, I'm gettin' away from all that. I promised my grandpa."

She hoped he kept his promise. It was no easy feat, leaving a gang as she assumed he'd done. She wanted to ask him how he'd done it, but she wouldn't pry.

"Okay, I have a confession of my own." She smiled conspiratorially. "I used to want to be a pickpocket like Dodger in *Oliver Twist*."

"That a movie or somethun'?"

*Oh. My. God. Please tell me he's kidding.* Hannah blinked away her bemusement. "A book by Charles Dickens."

"Huh." He shrugged. "Pickpocketin's easy."

"Well, show me."

"Nah. Zach wouldn't like it."

She was about to remind him Zach wasn't there when the phone in his pocket went *beep beep beep* and he fumbled to silence it, muttering, "Stupid game."

"If you get stuck with guard duty again, remind me. Ellie had a Wii somewhere that we used to help keep her active. I think it's in a box in the garage."

He pointed his fork at her. "Now you're talkin'." He laughed and shook his head. "You all right, Hannah." He gestured to the dog that was staring up at him in anticipation of more scraps—not that there were any. "What time we gotta have 'em at the park?"

She checked her watch. "A couple of hours." Hannah nudged the remainder of her omelet toward him and leaned against the counter, propping her head in her hand. He grabbed the plate and devoured her leftovers. "Wanna do me a favor?"

"Sure thing."

E.J.'s boss knew more than she wanted about her. It was only fair to get some intel on Zachary Collins, too. "Tell me what you know about Zach. What's his story?"

"He's one of the best guys I know." He hopped to his feet and grabbed both their empty plates. "Dishwasher?" She opened it for him and together they began loading the dishes into the machine. "Thing about Zach I've noticed is he don't give himself enough credit. He knows everything about laws and junk when we go over them, but he always acts like Brian's in charge. I heard somethun' bad went down on a case he was workin' six months ago, and he's been workin' behind a desk ever since. I ain't seen him put as much work on a case as yours. Usually he stays in the office, handles paperwork, bills, research, whatever."

"Really?" It pleased it her to think she was a special case for Zachary Collins. Because of her money? Probably, but still. She felt irrationally flattered. "What happened six months ago?"

E.J. shrugged and bumped into her. "Oh, sorry." He closed the dishwasher door and stepped back. His mouth was pulled from ear to ear. "By the way—" He held up the watch she'd been wearing a few seconds ago. "I lifted this off you."

"What?" Her mouth dropped open and she grabbed the watch out of his hand. "You sneak! Show me how you did that."

"Alright. Alright." And, laughing, he did.

Hannah was so engrossed in his lessons, she forgot all about her questions.

Zach's grip tightened on the phone as he listened to his contact at the DMV confirm what E.J.'s research had found.

Eric Meester lived in New York. He had a wife and a kid. Steady job and no reason to return to Georgia anytime soon.

Zach ended his call and swore. He'd come to the office and pulled the dossier on Meester from three years ago. The man's criminal history had been enough to send up a red flag then. Mainly he'd been cited for writing bad checks and incurring a shitload of traffic tickets.

Zach's mind went back to one of his last meetings with Ellie Parham.

*"Thank you for meeting me here." The old woman had patted the seat on the park bench beside her. "I read the report you mailed to me, Mr. Collins. I appreciate that you gave me a discount on your fees. That was very kind of you."*

*He'd cut her a break because the old lady had looked like she barely owned a suitable sweater, let alone could afford his fees. She'd been holding some kind of yappy little dog that had wanted nothing more than to crawl into his lap.*

*"It didn't take much to run a background check on your nurse, Miss Parham. No need to thank me for billing you accordingly." A small lie, but it didn't bother him.*

*"Call me Ellie. I like to think I'm good at reading people, and when I look at you, I see a kindred spirit." She had reached over and patted his knee. "I can trust you, can't I, Mr. Collins?"*

"I like to think so." He'd been working hard to make himself the kind of person people could trust. "And you can call me Zach."

Her smile had grown bigger. "I care about Hannah Dawson, and I'm worried about that man she's mixed up with. I'm sure you can understand why."

He'd shrugged. It had seemed as if the guy had cleaned up his act a lot since meeting his fiancé. Zach was in no position to judge anyone. "It's hard to tell a person's true character by reading a piece of paper, Miss Parham, er, Ellie."

"That's why I'd like to hire you to do a more extensive investigation on Eric Meester. Follow him around. Make sure he really is worthy of my Hannah."

He'd started to stand. "Look, I—"

"I'll pay double what I gave you before. Just as a retainer." She'd reached into her purse and pulled out an envelope. It had been thick with money. All cash. "I need to be sure he's a good man. I need to know he loves her and not just her money."

"Her money? Does she have a lot?"

"Why, she's a nurse!" The old woman's voice had sounded astonished he'd even questioned it.

Zach had thought about taking the envelope. Thought about it and decided against. The old woman had probably cleared out her entire savings to offer the payment. No way could he accept it. Pushing her hand away, he'd said, "If I can ease your mind that this guy really loves her, then what?"

"Then I'll die a very happy woman. My mind will be at peace."

"This means a lot to you?"

"It means everything, Zach."

"Then keep your money. I'll do it as a favor." He'd winked at her. "I'm a sucker for a pretty lady."

"Oh, Hannah is beautiful, isn't she?"

"I wasn't talking about Hannah." He'd stood, taken her hand,

*and kissed the back of it before departing.*

Zach had followed Meester around for only a week before he'd come to the conclusion Ellie had been right. He'd been playing around on Hannah with a woman from his office—make-out sessions in his car, not a full-fledged affair, but it had seemed headed in that direction—and Zach had overheard him bragging to another colleague that he'd only proposed to Hannah because she was financially responsible and had a good career.

"She's beautiful. She'll make a great mother. I care about her, sure, but five years down the road, I'll be traveling a lot if I get promoted. What would it hurt if I took up with a few women on the road? It's the perfect setup. Right?"

Zach had put it all in his report to Ellie, and hadn't been surprised when she'd contacted him a few days later, wanting one more favor.

Ellie hadn't asked Zach to rough Meester up or anything. Simply deliver an envelope and wait for an answer. It'd shocked the hell out of Zach when he'd peeked inside the envelope she'd given him and seen a check for fifty thousand dollars made out to Meester, from Franklin L. Russell. The fist he'd delivered to the asshole's gut when Meester had read the enclosed letter and accepted the check without hesitation had felt good. He hadn't been able to resist.

He'd added a few words, whispered into Meester's ear while he'd been still been winded and hunched over. "If you don't hold up your end of the deal, I'll be back."

Zach had spent several months worrying the creep had recognized him, that he'd press charges, or that the whole mess would somehow come back to bite him on the ass. Why had he gotten so involved? He should have known better.

If Hannah ever found out about this—

His phone vibrated against the table before chiming, and his heart did a somersault when he saw the caller's name. He took a deep breath and answered, "Alexandra, you called me back."

"What do you want, Collins?"

Damn. She wasn't going to make this easy on him. He glanced at the time. "I need—" He blew out his breath. "I need someone to talk to about psychic stuff."

"Psychic *stuff*?" The disdain in her voice warned him not to push his luck. "You mean, like a case you're working? You need a consult? How much does it pay?"

"I'm not going to jerk you around, Alexandra, because you deserve better. I'm sorry for the way things went down with the show." She'd guested on two episodes as a competitor to his character. He'd made it clear to the producers he preferred doing the show alone. Too risky having a real psychic on set to expose him for a fraud. "I know what I'm gonna tell you is gonna sound as crazy as hell, but…" The words caught in his throat. He swallowed. "I just realized that I really am psychic, and I don't know what the hell to do about it. I feel like I'm going crazy."

Silence.

"Alexandra, are you there?"

Even though he'd half been expecting it, her soft, feminine laughter took him by surprise.

"I'm not joking." He should have known this was a mistake. "Dammit. Forget it. Forget I ever called."

"Wait." Her entreaty stopped him. "Collins, are you for real? You're admitting to me that you faked it all those years on TV?"

He clenched his teeth. "Yes."

"I could go to someone with this. It could be in the news by tomorrow."

"I know." But something told him she wouldn't.

She said nothing for several seconds. A long sigh blew into the phone. "Why do you suddenly think you're psychic?"

He explained it as briefly as he could manage.

"Hmmmm," she said.

"That's all you have to say?"

"What do you want me to say? I'm trying to figure out if you're yanking my chain or if this is real."

"You're psychic. Can't you tell if I'm lying?"

She snorted. "I'm a medium, Collins, not a telepath." Her sigh blew into the phone. "Look, I've got to run to work. If you're serious—really serious—about this, maybe we can meet up sometime and talk."

"You're in Atlanta?" He thought she'd been based out of Denver or somewhere similar.

"No, but I will be later this week. I'm attending a con at the Marriott Marquis."

"DragonCon?"

"Never heard of it. Do you want to meet or not?"

He glanced at the files on the table. How could he plan anything in the middle of a case? Then again, whatever was happening in his head was friggin' crazy. He needed answers. Zach nodded. "Alright. Let's meet."

*Someone just kill me already. Please.*

Hannah's face grew warm as the woman in the skinny jeans clapped her hands and said, "Attention please. Try and get your dogs to settle down if they're misbehaving. We can't start the lesson until everyone is here."

The trainer's assistant was talking about Costello, who'd tried to hump every other dog in the class since arriving at the park.

"Costello, no." Hannah tried to rein him in with the leash, but the dog was strong. He barely spared her a glance before lunging at a fluffy poodle who was having none of it. Hannah tried to dig in her heels, but he dragged her along as if she were a paper doll. "Costello, sit!"

A hand from behind reached to grasp the leash, startling her so much she almost lost her grasp on the nylon.

"Whoa, buddy. Calm down for a second." Zach's voice and warm breath teased her ear as he managed to draw the dog into her. The press of his body against her backside was warm and solid. She pulled away, let him take Costello's leash, and drank him in. First thing she noticed was the clear spiral tube behind his ear. She'd noticed E.J. wearing a similar one in the car. Zach was dressed in jeans, a gray sports coat and a black t-shirt that hugged his chest tight, highlighting plenty of muscle definition. Clearly he was a man who worked out, and often.

Mercy.

"Thanks," she said, tucking her hair behind her ear. "I wasn't expecting you."

"Are you kidding? I wouldn't miss this for the world."

Brilliant. He wanted to watch her and Costello act like fools. Seriously, someone needed to put her out of her misery already.

"Yo, Zach." Not far away, E.J. was sprawled in the grass with Abbott's mesh carrier sitting beside him. None of the dogs had noticed him yet, but the cat's stare was totally focused on the activity in front of him. "Not that me and the cat don't like hangin' back and chillin', but does this mean I can go now?"

"Sure. Go home and get some rest." Zach picked Abbott up and slid the carrier's strap over his shoulder. Even as he was bumped around a bit, the cat's wary gaze did not waiver from the other animals. Zach waited until E.J. was on his feet to lean in and whisper something to the other man that Hannah couldn't make out.

"Yeah, no problem, man." E.J. brushed off his pants and reached for Hannah's hand. Cradling her fingers between his, he leaned closer and lowered his voice. "Good luck with that dog, you hear?" He cocked a finger gun at Costello, who was trying to pull at the leash in Zach's strong grip.

Hannah squinted against the afternoon sun and slid the sunglasses on top of her head down over her eyes.

Zach was wearing a pair of his own, but the yellowing bruise beneath them wasn't completely hidden from view, giving him a dangerous-looking edge. One of the other women's voices carried the short distance. "Maybe that's her husband. Maybe the boy was her ride?"

So did the response. "I don't know, but if he stays, I might not be able to handle the distraction."

Murmured giggling followed, and Hannah quickly moved forward to take back Costello's leash. "Thanks, but I think I've got it."

He held his arms out and stepped back. "Then I'll be right over here keeping an eye out."

Before he could get far, Costello suddenly charged to the left, barking like a crazed maniac, then darted in a circle around both of them, chasing away any dog that came remotely close to them. The long leash clotheslined the back of Hannah's calves as it tightened with the dog's movement. She stumbled forward—landing right in Zach's waiting arms.

"Oh!" She gripped his forearms and felt solid muscle beneath her fingers. Her chest was pressed against his, and she felt nothing but heat radiating between their bodies. Sweet heaven.

Laughing, Zach shuffled his feet a little. She felt his left hand press against her lower back and saw that his other was securing Abbott's carrier to his side. "Damn dog has us tangled together." He whistled. "Costello, stop!"

Amazingly, the dog stopped running, looked at Zach and sat down.

"Here." Once again Zach took the leash from her grip and began unwrapping it from around them. "You know, Hannah, I think your dog might need training."

She feigned a gasp. "No, *not* Costello."

"Maybe a little bit." The heat of his teasing look seared her clear down to her toes. "Why don't we try this again?" He returned the leash. She was free to move away, but she kind of didn't want to. "Me and the cat will keep watch from over there."

She nodded and started to turn away until she heard him call her name. "Yeah?"

Hannah couldn't see it behind his glasses, but she imagined he winked at her. "Good luck."

# Chapter Ten

Zach's mind and body were feeling an overload of sensations.

His arms still tingled where Hannah had touched him, and his jeans were a hell of a lot tighter than they had been a few seconds before. If she'd pressed any closer she would've felt something she wouldn't appreciate.

Or maybe she would.

He'd caught the glimpse of awareness in her face when he'd been untangling them. She was every bit as attracted to him as he was to her.

Good—but not good.

A surplus of thoughts were racing through his head. Some of them were his own. Some weren't.

*The grass smells good. Smell the grass.*

*Gotta pee. I'm peeing.*

The one that rang out the loudest was an agitated gripe that translated to *That damn dog is gonna get me killed.*

Zach tightened his grip on the carrier at his side and made a soothing sound to the cat. "Don't worry, Abbott. I got your back. Those dogs will have to go through me to get to you."

The cat's face actually turned up. Poor animal looked scared to death.

*You? Is that supposed to make me feel better?*

What the—?

"Really, cat? I promise to keep you safe, and you insult me?"

A loud throat-clearing sound brought his attention to the fact he'd been talking—loudly—to the animal in his care. Hannah's eyes were wide and watching him, but it was a redheaded woman he hadn't noticed before who was closest to him, still making strange sounds with her throat.

"Obedience class is about to start. If you don't have a dog, please give us some space. Thank you." She gestured them away with her hand.

The newcomer was the trainer, judging by the way she addressed the small group of seven women and one man with dogs. She paced in front of the group, examining the line of canines with the attention of a drillmaster.

"This is the beginner's class, but I fully expect you to do these tasks at home. The more you work with your dog, the more obedient they will become."

*Oh great. I'm gonna have to put up with this at home too? He'd better not expect me to participate.* The cat made a growling sound to accompany this thought.

Zach crossed his arms and tried to focus on staying alert and watching the activity around Hannah, but the animals' thoughts and feelings were as much of a distraction as the lady herself. His eyes kept trailing back to her. Beside her, a collie of some sort nearly tackled its owner when she introduced treats as a reward, but Costello immediately sat when Hannah stood in front of him and waved a treat bag.

*He's an idiot. They're all idiots. Look at them, pandering to their people. Disgusting.*

Zach snickered at the cat's opinion.

Hannah and Costello had moved closer to them as she tried in vain to get Costello to stay on command. She took a step and so did the dog, right behind her, chasing the treats.

*I'm a good boy. Gimme a treat? Pleeeease gimme a treat.*

"Costello, stay."

The dog would sit for about two seconds then follow her.

*I'm a good boy. See? If you gimme a treat, I'll stay. Promise.* The dog whined.

Zach shrugged. "Give him a treat, then tell him to stay."

"But I thought I was only supposed to give him a treat when he actually followed a command—as a reward?" She glanced around. "Try it."

*Yes. Pleeeeeease. Pleeeeease gimme a treat first.*

Hannah gave Costello a treat, firmly told him to stay and stepped back.

*Okay, I'll stay. Can I get another treat though?* Costello sat in the spot, not following. His stare was fixed on Hannah.

She frowned when she looked at Zach. "How did you know—? The psychic thing?"

For the first time in his life, he could agree to that without feeling guilty. "Maybe a little bit of common sense too."

After an hour, the trainer clapped her hands and told everyone the class was dismissed. "Before you leave, please check with one of my assistants. They'll sign you up for the next class and let you know where it will be held. Remember—practice is key."

After exchanging a few words with the head trainer, Hannah led Costello over to where Zach still stood. "She thinks Costello has a dominance problem we need to work on in private. I've got to schedule an appointment for her to come to the house. Wait here?"

"Sure."

She led Costello to the younger woman in a dark polo shirt holding a clipboard, but a line of women and dogs preceded her. Zach sighed. They might be here a while.

*I could go for some tuna right about now. How about you? Or maybe some bird if you have one?*

Zach's stomach growled and he chuckled. He squeezed the bag close to his side. "Alright, buddy. Let's get you home first."

An average-looking man in glasses and a dark polo stepped up to Hannah and said something that made her nod, step away from the line, and hand over Costello's leash. The guy knelt down and rubbed Costello's ears, still speaking to Hannah.

The pungent scent of cigarette smoke assaulted Zach's senses. He glanced around. There wasn't a soul near him.

Costello's growl as the man fiddled with his collar reached Zach's ears, luring him forward. Something wasn't right. His gut was suddenly tight with apprehension and fear.

*Bad man. Get away. Don't make me hurt you. Get away from us.*

Costello's loud snarling bark ripped the air. His long snout showed bared teeth in warning as the man leaned back, holding his hands in the air. Zach saw the man's right hand lower to slowly reach for the satchel at his side.

That smell.

Costello's reaction to it.

This guy wasn't one of the trainers. It was the same one who'd broken into Hannah's house!

Zach reached up to activate the microphone in his headset as he began advancing on the scene, not wanting to alert the man that someone was onto him. "E.J., there's trouble. Call the cops and get down here."

"I'm on it," E.J.'s voice responded.

Zach had told E.J. to find a discreet lookout spot and not to leave until they had Hannah back safe at home.

As he watched, the man on his knees in front of Hannah and the dog leaned as far back as he could comfortably go. His eyes had a surprised and slightly frightened gleam to them.

Good. Maybe he'd abandon whatever plan he'd had here. Once

the man put distance between himself and Hannah, Zach would tackle the sonofabitch.

"Costello, no." Hannah commanded, but the dog released another series of barks and growls that would have made great sound effects for a werewolf film. A wave of panic washed over Zach. What if the dog bit someone? What if he did worse?

No. He knew what the dog was thinking. *Bad man. Get away from her or I'll kill you.* Costello was only focused on one person. Protecting Hannah from the bad man.

Zach's attention fell to the gun suddenly visible in the other man's hand.

He reached for his own gun, holstered beneath his jacket, but what good would it do? Hannah was too close. Too damn close to getting in the crossfire. "Hannah, step away. Now." His voice was loud and firm.

Everything happened so fast, Zach barely had time to process any of it. The barrel of the gun pointed at Hannah. Costello, teeth snapping, tearing himself free from Hannah's grip. The dog ran sideways in an arc away from her, circling the stranger, barking at him ferociously.

"No, Costello. No!" Hannah yelled.

The stranger redirected the gun's aim toward her pet.

A woman behind Zach screamed, "That man has a gun!" but he didn't have time to question whether she was pointing at him or the other guy. People began running, all around them, away from them, getting in Zach's way, disrupting his line of fire. Feet pounded the ground mixed with soft squeals of panic.

The man's finger squeezed the trigger as Zach finally reached Hannah's side.

There was no time to think, only react.

Shoving Abbott's carrier against Hannah's middle, Zach dove toward the dog, covering him with his massive body.

Stinging pain spread through his lower back as his body stiffened on impact with the dog. Beneath him, Costello wiggled and whined as if Zach had done something awful to him.

*What are you doing? Get off me. Please don't hurt me. I'll be a good boy.*

"Shhh, Costello. It's okay. I'm not gonna hurt you."

"Zach." E.J.'s deep voice helped focus his attention on the fact the stinging in his back had passed. "Bro, you okay? You've been shot."

He reached a hand around and felt a long object buried in his skin above his belt. Animal tranquilizer. Damn.

Making sure he kept the dog close to him, Zach pushed to his feet as a pair of hands grasped his arm and helped him find his balance. He blinked at E.J., swinging his head around to look for Hannah.

She was right behind E.J., holding Abbott's bag in a death grip against her middle. A couple of young guys were flanking her protectively. One of the men asked if Zach needed help and said the cops were on their way. Sirens in the distance confirmed it.

"I'm fine. Where is he? Where'd he go?" The creep who'd shot him was nowhere in sight.

"He took off. You alright? You want me to go after him?" E.J.'s fingers tightened around Zach's arm as he spoke.

"Let him go." Zach stuffed the dart in his pocket in case the contents needed analysis. Who knew what the hell was in it, or how strong it was? "We've got to get Hannah and the animals out of here."

It wouldn't be long before the tranquilizer kicked in, and he'd be no good to her then. Dammit. He made sure E.J. had Costello's leash before reaching for Hannah and pressing her forward through the throng of people that had suddenly gathered around them.

E.J. walked backward, his eyes scanning the area. "Sorry, man, I should've jumped in sooner. We could've had that mother—"

"Let's get out of here," Zach interrupted, glancing around. For all he knew, the shooter was still hanging around, or had accomplices. People gawked and stared as they rushed past, but no one seemed suspect.

They reached the parking lot, and Zach dug into his jeans for his keys. He was still alert and feeling normal, but he knew better than to chance driving. He went to hand the keys to Hannah and—

Whoa!

The parking lot swam around him, and he fell forward, landing against some poor schmuck's car.

"Zach." Hannah rushed to steady him. "Oh my word, are you okay?"

Somehow he managed to shove his keys into her hand. "E.J., follow us. Make sure no one else is." Blinking, he focused on Hannah. She looked so worried. He reached out to touch her face and ended up swatting at air. "I need you…to drive. Can you do that?"

She nodded and reached an arm around his waist. He used her as a crutch getting to his truck, and God only knows how he managed to get himself into the seat.

Helping her bodyguards stay vertical was getting to be a habit.

E.J. had situated himself under Zach's right arm while she took the left. Zach had been dozing off and on through the car ride home, only seeming alert a few times—most memorably when he realized she was driving him home from the hospital.

"I told you no hospital." He'd clasped her arm. "Dammit, woman, you've got to start listening to me."

A few seconds later, his soft snore had been her only entertainment on the drive home. He might have ordered her not to take him for medical attention, but Hannah wasn't crazy. Animal tranquilizers could be deadly for an average-sized man, but Zach was tall and muscular. Most likely, the dart had held tranquilizer intended for a medium-sized animal. That would've taken a few minutes to kick in, plus Zach had the benefit of adrenaline to keep him steady during those first few minutes.

Once the ER doctor had declared Zach was safe to leave—he simply needed to sleep it off and as long as he had someone to keep an eye on his breathing for the next 24 hours, he could do that at home—Detective Ryan had turned up, demanding answers about what had happened in the park. If only she could've given him any.

The detective had reluctantly assigned a patrol car to follow her home and said it would be on watch outside her house for the next 24 hours, barring any catastrophic emergencies. "Hopefully I can get to the bottom of this mess before then," he'd said before taking his leave.

Now, she had to figure out what to do with Zach in the meantime.

"Let's put him in my bedroom," she told E.J., and they awkwardly maneuvered down the hall with Zach's much taller body between them. "Once he's settled, I have to call Brian to check on Costello."

"Brian?" Zach snapped to attention. He suddenly laughed and began singing, "Brian, the babe they called Brian. He grew, he grew, and grew, grew up to be, grew up to be, a boy called Briaaaaaaaaaaaaaaaaaaan."

Plopping Zach on the bed, E.J.'s eyebrows drew together. "What the hell was in that gun? Heroin?"

"Heroine? Ha." Zach poked a finger at E.J. "Who's your favorite heroine? I always liked Wonder Woman. She could kick ass." He fell back, flat on the bed, out cold.

The tension began to leave Hannah's shoulders. "The doctor said it was ketamine."

She knew the drug was given as injections to people to ease

their pain. She'd taken more than one patient to have it done.

"I've seen it put people straight to sleep and others sing, talk nonsense and have hallucinations." She checked Zach's breathing and pulse and nodded. "I think he's going to be okay. There wouldn't have been enough in that dart to do much." She hoped.

A quick call to Brian assured her that her dog had suffered no injuries in the park. Zach's partner had agreed to take the dog to the vet to put her mind at ease while she and E.J. dealt with Zach at the hospital.

Handing the phone off to E.J., she wandered into the bedroom where Zach lay sprawled on her comforter. Abbott jumped onto the bed, sniffed around Zach's face and then curled up by his side.

Hannah perched on the side of the bed and reached out to pet the cat. "What are we gonna do, Abbott? Why won't these people stop coming after us?"

Her soft words roused Zach, who lifted up suddenly and glanced around the room. His arm brushed against Abbott's fur. "Heeeey, cat. Buddy. What's hanging?"

Abbott narrowed his eyes but didn't turn away from her. Could cats roll their eyes? Cause she was pretty sure hers did just that.

Zach's hearty chuckle filled the room. "He called me an idiot again. Said 'You almost got us all killed, idiot.'" His laugh deepened with amusement. "He said not to worry. He'll keep an eye out until I'm not acting sooooo stupid."

The bed shook with Zach's hilarity. The movement agitated Abbott, who stood, arched his back and moved down near Zach's feet. After a few minutes, Zach became more serious, piercing Hannah with blue eyes that had an unguarded, dreamy quality in their depths. Her shoulders tightened a little.

"What?"

"You are so beautiful. Do you know that?" He shook his finger at her. "You have a good heart, too. It would never work between us."

Her eyebrows lifted and she tried to fight a laugh—but it was no use. "You're delirious. You don't know what you're saying."

"I know you want me to kiss you." He turned on his side and reached toward her. His fingers couldn't find their target because she was too far away. Hannah leaned forward a little, disarmed by his words. Had it been so obvious to him—how attracted she was to him? Gah, she was mortified to think of it. His hand fell and dangled off the bed. He groaned. "I want to kiss you. I really, really do, but I'm no good for you, Hannah. I'm not a good guy."

She entwined their fingers, fighting the urge to brush the hair back from his forehead. "You were willing to take a bullet for my dog, Zach. I think that makes you one of the good guys." She bit her lip. "Did you know it wasn't a real gun?"

"Hell no." His grasp tightened. "I sort of reacted. If I'd thought about it first, I probably wouldn't have—hey is that a butterfly on the wall?"

She turned, saw nothing and sighed. He was really out of it.

He rolled onto his back and reached toward the ceiling. "Wow, this room is really tall. I can't touch your ceiling at *all*." His hand fell to his stomach. "Oh, Hannah. You're really gonna hate me soon."

"I don't think—"

"You will!" His loud exclamation startled Abbott, who made a grousing sound and jumped off the bed. Zach gestured toward the cat. "See, he knows it. I'm a phony, Hannah. I'm not psychic. I'm not—hey, cat, that's not very nice thing to say. I'm trying to be honest here. Okay?"

Hannah glanced down. Abbott had collapsed on the floor near her feet. His tail swished around like crazy. She could imagine him cursing Zach in his little mind for disrupting their routine.

Not psychic? Right.

She wasn't sure when she'd become so convinced of that, but she was.

Needing a short break from, well, everything, she used the excuse of getting Zach a glass of water. She leaned against the sink and took a deep breath. How much more of this could she take?

Zach was still awake when she returned, babbling nonsense as if he were still having a conversation with the cat. He held something in his hands—a photo?

"I really miss him, cat. I screwed up. I shouldn't have left him behind."

Rather than sit on the bed, Hannah sat in the chair in the corner. "Who?"

"Dylan. My little brother." He sighed, long and hard.

She hadn't asked him many personal questions because she'd sensed they weren't welcome. Maybe this was her chance to get to know him better. "Are you close to your brother?"

He shook his head. "I left home when I was a few months shy of graduation. Haven't seen him since."

Left home? As in, ran away from? Wow. She hadn't expected that. "What about your parents?"

A sneer lifted one edge of his mouth. "My dad was a cop. Died when I was a kid. He stopped a robbery, got shot. Died." He tossed the photo onto the bed. "My mom married a real asshole a few years later. Never liked me. Hated my guts, so I left."

"You left?" His comment from earlier made more sense. *I shouldn't have left him behind.* "Your mom didn't look for you?"

"I dunno. She's dead now. Cancer. That's what I heard."

She moved closer and reached for his hand. "I'm so sorry, Zach."

"I shouldn't have let the asshole make me leave." Zach struggled to sit up, only to fall back when he couldn't hold himself up. "I don't even want to talk about what happened in Kirkland. What's the use? Won't change anything."

Maybe she shouldn't pry too deep, too soon. It seemed kind of…invasive. She leaned forward. "Zach, you're not a bad person."

She picked up the photo, not wanting it to get lost or damaged. The picture was old and faded. A teenager she recognized as Zach stood with his arm wrapped around a younger version of himself.

He didn't respond, and she wondered if he'd dozed off again. Then he said, so low she barely heard him, "You only say that because you don't know me."

Well, duh. Her point from earlier still held. Besides, her animals seemed to like him, and they were impeccable judges of character. She remembered the one time Eric had come to the house, looking for her after she'd first started living with Ellie. Costello had nearly maimed her ex five seconds after meeting him. A tiny smile played at her lips. Eric hadn't come around again after that.

She cleared her throat, told herself not to, under any circumstances, say what she was thinking, but the words tumbled out anyway. "I'd like to know you better." She swallowed. There was a good chance he wouldn't remember any of this tomorrow anyway. "But I guess you know that."

He pushed himself up onto his elbows and fixed his gaze on her, brows drawing together. "It's no good, Hannah. This is karma trying to put me in my place." He shook his head, seeming almost like himself again. "I can't cross that line. I want to, but I can't. You're my client."

True. Sarah's similar warning came to mind, but while she was being open and honest, Hannah had to admit she didn't care whether it was appropriate or not. She had feelings for this man. Strong feelings. Maybe it was time she wandered out of her comfort zone to find out if those feelings were real.

"Well, I won't always be your client." Tentatively, she slid her hand over his. "Right?"

He didn't answer. His forehead was creased in thought.

"Besides, I'm not your client." She turned her thumb toward the cat lying on the floor beside them. "They are, remember?"

He blinked slowly and seemed to be considering her words. "You know what?" He shifted and sank backward a little. "You make some good points."

Zach suddenly pushed himself forward again, toward her, and curved a hand around her face, whispering her name. Hannah leaned toward him, waiting for his next move. He was going to kiss her. There was probably something wrong with her for taking advantage of his current state, but who knew if the chance would come again?

He whispered her name a second time, then a third, his warm breath so close it tickled her lips.

"Yes?" She tilted her head a little, giving him easy access.

His soft snore teased her ears.

Hannah pulled back a little and cocked her head at him. "Seriously? *Now?*" She felt like a fool for expecting—and craving—his kiss. She should have known better. He wasn't exactly in his right mind at the moment. Sighing, she pressed her hand over his heart—oh yeah, it was still beating steady—and let it rest there for longer than was probably wise. He was so warm and solid and *alive*. She liked touching him.

She started to stand, but his hand jerked her against him, causing her to tumble onto the bed. Right on top of his warm, hard body.

"Where ya going?" He slurred. "Thought we were gonna get sum'sleep?"

A few more minutes, and he would be out for a while. She laughed and tried to untangle herself from him as gently as possible. His grip was tenacious.

Hannah finally gave up and relaxed against him. A few minutes like this wouldn't hurt anything. He shifted and she slid beside him, fitting into the crook of his arm as if it were the most natural thing in the world.

"M'better." He tilted his head until it rested against hers. "This is nice."

She slid her arm across his chest, hugging him, and settled more comfortably against him. She hadn't been this close to a man since Eric, and it was a strange feeling to be so comfortable with a man she barely knew.

Did she actually trust him?

Yes. She did.

She felt so safe with Zach. All of the tension she'd been holding inside seemed to melt away beneath his touch. The sad truth was she'd never felt so safe with anyone—not even Eric.

"He was an idiot." Zach's mumbled words hinted that sleep wasn't far off.

"Who?"

"Eric Meester." His arm tightened around her, pressing her even closer against his side. "No man with half a brain would have left you at the altar."

How had he known she was thinking about—?

Wide-eyed, she lifted her head and realized his eyes were closed. A soft snore escaped his lips.

Hannah sank back into the curve of his arm. Maybe it wouldn't hurt anything if she stayed here a while longer—and did some serious thinking while she was at it.

Zach realized two things when he opened his eyes.

He was in Hannah's bed, and he was alone.

No dog. No cat. No beautiful woman nearby to distract him.

Letting his head fall back onto the pillow, he rubbed the early morning crud from his eyes. Damn. He hadn't slept that good in a while. He felt totally refreshed and relaxed. Had he taken something? He couldn't remember.

The bedroom door opened slightly, spilling a crack of light into the room. The sound of music and laughter from outside grew louder, too. Blinking, Zach saw a black and white tail slowly circling the end of the bed like a shark's fin. It stopped, sank out of view, and Zach waited for the attack.

Abbott pounced onto the bed and walked up Zach's chest. The cat rammed its head against Zach's nose, and purred.

"Hey, buddy." Tentatively, Zach's fingertips grazed the animal's fur. When he wasn't swatted or hissed at, he dug in for a more vigorous petting. "You sure are in a good mood today."

The cat sat on his chest and began kneading Zach's muscles. Zach ruffled the fur on the cat's head.

The cat immediately stopped kneading and looked straight into his eyes.

*Whoa. Don't get too friendly. Just because I've decided to trust you doesn't mean you can take liberties like that.*

Zach dragged both hands back. "Okay."

The cat did a slow blink and started kneading again.

*We can trust you, right? The woman who feeds me needs to be protected at all cost. You're gonna help her?*

Zach nodded. "Of course."

He was rewarded with another head ram. The cat's fur swiped his nose, tickling it.

Abbott stopped kneading and sank down.

*This thing on my neck. Take it off.*

Zach glanced at the cat's neck, seeing nothing but his collar.

*Take it off, idiot.*

"Okay, dammit. Give me a second." His fingers fumbled to undo the clasp. The leather strap tinkled when it fell against him.

The cat jumped up and ran away.

"Hey!" Zach frowned at the cat's backside as it shot out of the room.

Dumb animal had tricked him.

Slinging his legs over the edge of the bed, Zach couldn't help but chuckle at the wily animal's deviousness. No, Abbott wasn't a dumb animal. He was too damned smart for his own good. Now he supposed he would have to chase the cat down to get this back on him.

"Geez." Rubbing his face again, he fingered the collar in his other hand. Glancing down at it, Zach's smile faded.

There were three tags hanging from the collar instead of the two he expected to see. He flipped each one over. A tag showing Abbott's name and Hannah's phone number. A rabies tag. On the third tag was an unfamiliar address.

"I'll be damned."

Was this a clue the cat had been trying to give him?

"You're getting extra tuna tonight for that, buddy." Clasping the collar firmly in his hand, he hurried in search of a computer. Where was his smart phone? Where was—?

He stopped in the hallway, suddenly remembering what had happened to him yesterday.

Tranquilizer.

Had he and Hannah—?

He glanced down to verify he was still dressed in his clothes from the day before. His belt was still clasped at his waist. The pants probably hadn't come off.

Shit. He remembered some things, but there were holes.

He remembered tugging her down against him and feeling content with her resting in his arms. He remembered almost kissing her.

Oh no, had he actually sung?

He groaned.

The sound of paws hitting the floor heavy brought his attention back to the present. Costello charged down the hall and leapt up against him, nearly knocking him over.

*It's our man. Are you okay, man? Are you okay? I'm so happy to see you! Will you feed me?*

As soon as Zach petted the dog, Costello bounded back toward the living room.

*He's okay! Man is okay!*

E.J.'s voice said something he couldn't make out, and Hannah laughed. Music started playing again.

Rounding the corner, his assistant and the woman he was supposed to be protecting were hopping around like children. Suddenly, Hannah threw up her arms.

"Awwww, girl, you won again? Damn, that ain't right." E.J. spun around, punching the air. He spun back around. "One more time. One more."

Zach's eyes were drawn to the TV where a grungy-looking cartoon man stood with a guitar.

Guitar Hero.

A lunatic was out to get them, and they were playing Guitar Hero?

"E.J." Zach barked the kid's name. "What the hell are you doing?" He glanced around. "Why the hell are we here? I told you to take her somewhere safe."

Hannah spun around with a red guitar strapped around her neck. E.J. turned too, and his expression looked like a child who'd been caught with his hand under the Christmas tree a week early.

"Calm down, Zach. It wasn't E.J.'s fault," a deep voice said.

Zach hadn't noticed the man sitting in the corner until he stood. Kellan crossed his arms and nodded. "You okay?"

"What the hell are you doing here?"

His tall, blond employee didn't even flinch. Kellan was like that. He didn't react. He thought things through. It's one of the things that had made him a great bodyguard—before he'd started sleeping with their client. "Brian called me. I've been here since last night. You've been in a coma for about nine hours. We were starting to get worried."

Zach looked down at his watch. Damn. "What happened?"

E.J. filled him in on the details of what had happened in the park, and after. "Man, you was actin' punk." His laughter was punctuated with a fist pump.

Zach didn't really know what the hell that meant, but he figured it wasn't good.

Hannah lifted the guitar strap over her head and handed it to E.J. "I'll let Costello out, then I'll fix us something to eat." She gave him a shy, wary look as she brushed past him. She whistled, and her dog bounced after her.

*Feed me. Feed me. Feed me. Oh, gotta pee first. Gotta pee.*

She opened the patio door and stepped outside. She slid the glass door shut behind her and then leaned against it to watch her dog.

She was giving them some privacy.

He focused on Kellan. "What about Katie? Shouldn't you be on set with her today or something?"

Kellan uncrossed his arms and stepped over to the window. "She's on vacation, visiting her grandma up in Canada. She didn't want a shadow for that." Letting the curtain fall back, he looked at Zach and nodded to the ground. "Looks like you've made a friend."

Zach glanced down. Abbott was standing right beside him, observing the action. His furry face looked up, then his tail started swishing.

*What?*

Zach almost spoke to the animal, but then reminded himself others were present. He shook his head and gripped the collar tight.

"I need to figure out an address. Where's my phone?"

E.J. scrambled around the room, trying to remember where he'd put it. Kellan pulled out his mobile and moved closer. "What is it?" He typed in the address Zach read, and while they waited for the result, Kellan sighed and said, "I know you're pissed at me right now, but there's no reason I can't help out on this case for a few days."

"Don't feel obligated."

Kellan cursed. "Look, I didn't plan for it to happen. It just did." He rubbed the back of his neck. "If you only knew how much I've been beating myself up over it, but I can't change how I feel about her."

Zach felt his temper wane. Hadn't he crossed the line himself, with Hannah, a little? He'd never had a problem keeping his mind on business when a woman was involved in it, until her. He shook his head. "Just tell me what the address is."

Kellan glanced at his phone and shrugged. "It's a bank." He named one not far from where Zach lived.

The patio door slid open and Costello bounced back into the room and over to Zach.

*Heeeey. It's so good to see you. Will you feed me now?*

Zach knelt and grabbed hold of the dog's collar. Costello sure did wiggle a lot for such a chunky mutt. It took Zach twice as long to unclasp Costello's collar as it had taken him to undo Abbott's.

"There's something here too. What is that?" Zach couldn't make sense of the series of numbers on Costello's third tag.

Kellan reached for it. "I bet it's a security code."

"For what?"

"Safety deposit box. Katie has one at that same bank. I've taken her there to put something in it." He handed the collar back to Zach. "A code like that, I bet it's used for a box with extremely valuable contents."

Hannah had wandered over and was biting her fingernails. "What's going on?"

Zach turned toward her. "I think we could have a lead on this case." He explained about the collars and asked if she was familiar with the bank.

She shook her head. "That's not the bank where she had an account. I can check with Mr. Russell and see if he's familiar with it."

"Go give him a call."

He found a pen and wrote down the address and code then had Kellan take pictures of both with his phone.

"You know what this means, don't you?" Kellan asked.

Zach nodded. "These people aren't after the animals. They want whatever's in that bank."

# Chapter Eleven

"Ellie told me those extra tags had something to do with their microchips. I've never really looked at them. Why would she lie, Zach?"

And more, what else had she lied about?

Hannah meant to break the uncomfortable silence between them, but her question seemed to only add to it. Zach's fingers tightened around the steering wheel, causing a tiny squeak against the vinyl. She hated it when he morphed into Mr. Macho Bodyguard instead of Mr. Grin and Winky Face. It made her… tense.

Her lawyer had had no record of a bank account at the facility found on Abbot's collar. When she'd told him that news, Zach had instructed his men to follow a detailed plan.

Kellan was to stay at the house with the animals, and E.J. was supposed to follow her and Zach to the bank, keeping an eye out for anyone trailing them. Zach hadn't said much more to her than "I'm sorry, Hannah. I need you to accompany me. Bring a copy of any official papers you have showing you're the benefactor of Ellie's will."

So she had, secretly thrilled at the idea of having some alone time with the man after what had happened between them yesterday. Did he remember any of it? If he didn't, should she remind him, or play it cool and see how things played out? Besides that, there was a tickle of excitement in her gut over solving the mystery of what Ellie had kept hidden at the bank. It didn't seem logical her elderly patient had left behind more money, but then again, Hannah would've never expected Ellie to have had ten million in assets either. So many questions and possibilities swam in her mind, it was an effort to keep them from spilling out.

Zach, on the other hand, was focused, quietly keeping his attention on the road and the vehicles around them. Not one word had come out of his mouth since they'd entered the car.

"Zach?" He still hadn't acknowledged her question.

He shifted in his seat. "She obviously had some secrets." He took his eyes off the road to glance at her, briefly. "I wouldn't take it personally, Hannah."

He returned his attention to the cars in front of them, so she sighed and did the same.

They should have been to the bank already, but they'd gotten trapped in lunchtime traffic. Hannah lifted her phone for about the tenth time, saw no missed calls or urgent text messages from Kellan, and tried to relax. Was this how parents felt the first time they left their children alone with a babysitter? It was all she could do not to call Kellan and ask how things were going.

"I don't have a good feeling about this." Zach swore beneath his breath. "Maybe we should've waited longer."

The bank came into view up ahead and Hannah began scanning for available parking. She recognized the building from a news story she'd seen on television. Supposedly the secret formula for Coca-Cola had long been housed here in a vault.

Zach parked in a garage across the street and Hannah reached for her door handle. "Hold it," he barked. "Wait on me."

He moved out of the car and rounded the front, his gaze intently sizing up the people walking nearby. He opened her door and reached to help her out. "Let's be quick about this, okay?"

She nodded and let him guide her through the bank entrance. He kept her close with a hand on her lower back as they maneuvered their way through the doors.

"Do you know what to do?" His warm breath tickled her ear. Having him so close was a bit distracting.

"I think so."

"Good." He pressed her forward toward a glass office designating the bank's manager.

There was nothing quick about gaining access to Ellie's safety deposit box. The bank manager refused to accept Ellie's death certificate or the estate affidavit naming Hannah as the benefactor of her will. The older man also kept looking at Zach as if he expected Zach to produce a gun and yell, "This is a robbery." The fact that Zach still sported the hint of a bruise near his eye and kept shifting anxiously probably wasn't helping their case.

Hannah finally caught the man's gaze and explained, "Mr. Collins is my private security."

The man did not look convinced. "I will have to check our records. If we don't have a signature card on file for you, I'd advise you to retain a probate attorney to help you gain access to the box."

The manager focused on doing a search on his computer. After several minutes, he asked for Hannah's driver's license. He glanced at it carefully before returning it to her.

"We've got your signature on file, Miss Dawson. I'll need the access code now."

He had her signature on file? Seriously?

She jerked her head toward Zach and began to tell him that it was impossible since she'd never entered this bank before today. If his expression hadn't signaled her to keep her mouth shut, his fingers squeezing hard on her arm would have done it.

She reached into her purse for the numbers taken from

Costello's collar. If her voice shook while she read them aloud, no one commented about it.

A genuinely friendly smile lit up the manager's face for the first time since he'd introduced himself. "Excellent. Follow me."

They followed him to a private room and waited while he retrieved the safety deposit box. When he returned, it was much larger than Hannah had been expecting.

He sat the eleven-by-fourteen box on the table in front of her. "Would you like some privacy?"

She exchanged looks with Zach. "Yes, please."

"I'll be outside if you need me."

The sound of the door clicking shut seemed somehow ominous. Hannah swallowed. What if she found something awful in the box?

"Tell me, Mr. Psychic Detective. Do you know what's in there?"

He shook his head. "Go ahead. Open it."

Her fingers trembled a little as she raised the lid. The box did not contain nearly as much as she'd expected. Two black velvet bags tied with string sat in one corner while a leather-bound journal sat on top of a thick large manila envelope.

Hannah reached for the journal and realized it was a photo album, filled with old pictures. As she flipped quickly through, three people were featured the most—a much younger Ellie, slim with long blond hair, a handsome man often touching or holding her hand, and a second man with short-cropped hair and glasses. Hannah stopped when she glimpsed a wedding photo. Ellie and the handsome man, dressed in wedding attire, posed in front of a church.

"Ellie was married?" She handed the book to Zach. Ellie had never said one word about a husband, ex or otherwise.

"It appears so." He nodded to the box. "What's in that envelope?"

She quickly tore it open. "Looks like official documents for Eleanor Nichols." She flipped through the papers. A birth certificate. Social security card. A passport with numerous stamps. And a wedding certificate. "Eleanor Constance Nichols and Caleb James Lightner. August 10, 1953."

Lifting all of the papers from the envelope, she heard a rip and carefully tugged out the papers at the back. Paperclipped together were a clump of old newspaper and magazine clippings from the sixties and seventies.

*London jewel theft remains unsolved.*

*The Fox steals legendary diamonds—again!*

*Sophisticated jewelry heist stumps New York cops.*

There were at least a dozen more with similar headlines, from various cities around the world.

"Why would Ellie have these?" Hannah whispered more to herself than Zach, but he answered anyway.

"I think I might have a good idea."

Hannah returned her attention to him and saw that he was holding one of the black velvet bags in one hand. A gasp escaped her lips as a large white diamond poured into his other palm.

Zach's gut was knotted. They needed to hurry up and get the hell outta there.

Hannah must have felt the same, because her steps quickened as they rushed to the car. No sooner had Zach started the vehicle than a voice spoke in his ear.

"Silver Buick with tinted windows parked at the curb. It hasn't moved, and no one has gotten out of the car. I dunno, man. Seems fishy." E.J.'s voice was heightened with excitement.

Zach spotted the vehicle as he directed his car onto the street. The hairs on the back of his neck rose as he lifted a hand to push to talk on his microphone. "I see it."

"What do you want me to do?" E.J. asked.

"Hang back and keep an eye on it. Did you get the license plate?"

"Yeah. Kellan's working on it now."

"Good work. We'll meet you back at Hannah's."

He ended the conversation and directed his truck toward the intersection. The Buick pulled out and followed. "Damn."

"What's wrong?" Hannah asked, turning to look behind them.

He grabbed her shoulder to keep her from turning fully. "I think we have a tail."

"What?" Her voice rose higher, and she clutched the shoulder strap of her seatbelt with one hand. "What do we do?"

He shook his head. "Nothing. They already know where you live. No use in trying to shake them."

"But—"

"Stay calm," he urged, taking a different route. The car followed their turns, speeding to keep pace.

Hannah jerked out her phone and started typing.

"Who are you texting?"

"Sarah. I want her to know I'm okay. I haven't talked to her today."

Her tone was calm, but he felt the fear she radiated like a punch in the gut.

"What should I do about those jewels, Zach?" Hannah's face was painted with panic as her hands gestured wildly. "Should I call the police? The FBI? Who handles jewelry thefts anyway?" She swallowed hard. "I wonder how much of the money in her will was stolen. I bet I'll have to give that back too."

"Whoa, lady. You're jumping to conclusions." He cocked a half smile at her. "Let us get home safely before we determine where those jewels came from. For all you know, Ellie bought them and they're perfectly legit."

"Do you believe that?"

No. Not at all. He shrugged. "Why not? It could be something that simple." He nodded to the phone in her hand. "Do me a favor and call Kellan. Put him on speakerphone." She managed to have him connected in a matter of seconds. "How are the animals?" he asked his associate.

"Curled up asleep. Everything is clear here." Kellan grew more serious. "The plates on that Buick are stolen. The cops should be catching up with you guys any second now."

Zach had expected as much. Blue lights appeared in the rearview behind the Buick. The other car jerked to the left and disappeared down a side road with a police car in hot pursuit. Zach kept his SUV steadily driving ahead.

He gave Kellan their estimated time of arrival and told Hannah to end the call.

If Hannah hadn't been in the car with him, Zach would've been bumper to bumper with the police cars. He'd have liked nothing better than to be there when the cops caught up to the guy who had been terrorizing her for weeks.

He turned his attention to the woman beside him. She was still clutching her phone so tight her knuckles were white. Anxiety radiated from her like heat—or maybe it was because he was so good at reading people that he felt it. He jerked his head sideways, scanning the left side of the road, trying to ignore the insane urge he felt to reach out and cover her hand with his.

His awareness of her as a woman was becoming a problem. He knew that. He didn't know what the hell to do about it.

"Do you think the police will catch them?" She was calm and almost normal again. *Thatta girl.*

"Eventually." That knotted feeling had loosened in his gut, but it was still there. "Don't worry, Hannah. You'll be safe soon."

"Promise?" Her voice was tinged with laughter, as if she were aiming to lighten the mood. When he glanced in her direction, he caught the shine of the tears she was trying hard to hold back.

Dammit. There was only so much a man could take. His fingers

reached across the seat and covered hers. "Damn straight I do."
He'd see to it, one way or another.

Hannah managed to hold it together until she excused herself
to her bathroom at home. She hated crying. She hadn't cried at
Ellie's funeral—she'd waited until she was alone at night to weep
for her lost friend. She hadn't cried the night someone had broken
into her house and scared the hell out of her. She hadn't shed a
tear when Eric had told her he'd made a mistake and couldn't
marry her. She'd saved all those emotions for when no one was
around to see her fall apart.

All it took this time was for her cat to jump on the counter
beside the sink, where she stood trembling and trying to pull it
together. Abbott, bless his furry little soul, actually jumped up
and put his paws on her shoulders as if he were asking *Hey, are
you okay?*

Hugging the cat, she collapsed to the floor sobbing. Abbot
gave a screech and shot away from her as if his tune had quickly
changed to *Hey, are you crazy or what?* And who could blame him?

Why had Ellie chosen her? She wasn't cut out for this. Oh,
Lord, Ellie. What if the older woman had somehow stolen those
diamonds? What if her entire fortune was a fraud? She felt a sting
of betrayal, wondering if she'd even known the sweet elderly lady
she'd come to view as a surrogate grandmother. She'd thought
they had a special friendship. She'd thought—

Hannah tried to wipe away the tears, but it was no use. More
flooded after them. If she had to give back all of the money, what
would that mean for Sarah and her mom, not to mention all of
the debt Hannah had managed to escape?

Costello drove his head against her arm.

"Don't worry, Costello." She sniffed. "No matter what happens,
I'll take care of you. You and Abbott are the only family I have."

She buried her face in his fur and sobbed some more. He was such a good dog when he wanted to be.

And then he ruined the moment by wiggling out of her hold, jumping up, and humping her shoulder.

"Hannah?"

Oh, no, no, no. The sound of Zach's voice was like another stab in the heart. She didn't want him, of all people, to see her like this. Crying. Hopeless. And being humped by her ridiculous dog.

"M'okay," she murmured and pushed her hands against Costello's fur to jostle him loose. "I need a few minutes please."

She heard Zach move but didn't realize he'd actually stepped into the bathroom until she felt the brush of his body against her side. Strong hands gripped and turned her into him, and she realized he'd actually lowered to the floor beside her. His arm curved around her and pressed her close. She sank her face into his chest and curled her fingers into his shirt with a force that should have torn it from him but didn't.

"Go ahead and let it out." He was so gentle and kind. "You've been through a lot, Hannah. You shouldn't keep it all bottled up inside."

"But—"

"No back talk. You're scaring the animals. Abbott was a nervous wreck when he came and told me you were—" His sentence was interrupted by an awkward chuckle. "Well, never mind. They love you, you know that, right?"

She sniffed and glanced to where Abbott paced anxiously, his back arched as he brushed against the cabinet door, his tail stuck straight in the air. "I love them too."

"And we're all gonna get through this."

She nodded against him, but the tears refused to stop. She lost track of time as she clung to him and cried, neither of them saying another word. This was so humiliating. Hannah hated herself for falling apart. Pulling away, she sniffed and tried to force a smile. "I'm okay now."

The gentle touch of Zach's thumb wiping away a tear was so tender, it made her heart ache. What would her life be like if she had someone like him in it? Someone to make her laugh, caress away her tears, kiss her?

Her eyes met his, and she saw unmistakable desire glittering in their cobalt-blue depths. She wanted him closer, needed to feel wanted in return, for a few minutes. She reached up and touched his dark hair, pleased by the silky texture, and wondered if she dared let her fingers trail lower.

"Hannah." Her name was a whisper as he leaned closer. She held her breath until his lips met hers. So warm. So soft. With skilled ease, he coaxed her to open for him, exploring her mouth, hot and greedy. Gah, she needed this. It had been so long. Too long.

Arousal sparked a fire in her veins. She moaned and pressed into him, hungry for some kind of human contact that didn't involve danger. But in the back of her mind, she knew he was dangerous. This man could destroy her in a way no one else had. She sensed it, but was powerless to resist the urge to lower her defenses and let him inside.

His grip on her forearms suddenly pushed her away. "I need to go."

Zach moved to stand, sliding away from her. Hannah's cheeks grew warm. He'd rejected her. Why? Because she was his client. That thought only made her more confused. How could she possibly pay him enough after this? Consoling an emotionally unstable woman wasn't part of their contract. Sweet heavens, she was mortified.

Instead of leaving her, Zach reached down and scooped her into his arms.

"You should get some rest," he told her. "You've had a rough day."

"But—"

"No buts. I've got an errand to run. Kellan and E.J. will be right outside if you need them. When I get back tonight, we'll figure out some things, alright?"

She nodded and tried not to cling to him when he gently lowered her onto her bed. Their eyes met and they both stilled, their warm breaths mingling as he hovered above her.

She wished he would kiss her again. She wished he'd do *more* than kiss her.

When he turned to move away, she reached out and grabbed his hand. "Thank you, Zach."

His fingers squeezed hers before letting go. "Relax for a little while. I'll be back soon."

When he shut the door behind him, Hannah wiped away the last of her tears and tried to will herself to sleep. If she was lucky, she could escape reality for a few hours. If she was really lucky, Zach would be waiting for her in her dreams.

# Chapter Twelve

"So they found the jewel?"

"Oh, they found it alright." Glancing at his watch, Fox slid into the passenger seat of his partner's car.

It had been touch and go for a few minutes, but he'd managed to lose the police after weaving through some one-way streets and ducking into a back alley, where he'd ditched the car and fled on foot. He'd wandered into a touristy part of the city, blended into the crowds, and phoned his accomplice. Years of evading the police had come in handy.

"Did they leave it at the bank or move it?"

"That's a damn good question." He peeled away part of the disguise that altered the shape of his nose. Stupid latex was starting to itch. "Collins is smarter than I gave him credit for. How in hell did he figure out the collars?" He swore and slammed his fist against the dashboard.

"What does it matter? All we needed to know was where the old lady had stashed the diamond. Now we can move forward with our plan. We don't need the Dawson woman or her pets anymore. This is good, right?"

He hated working with a moron. His fingers drew into a painful fist, but he resisted the urge to strike out again. "I want this Collins guy out of the way. He's too good at figuring things out. That makes him dangerous. Besides, we don't know for a fact the jewels are still at the bank. Collins could have moved them."

The sound of his partner swallowing hard betrayed the younger one's sudden unease. That grated on his nerves almost as much as his partner's naivety. "It shouldn't be too hard to find out. They haven't discovered the bug I planted yet. We can listen to—"

"*You* can listen," he interrupted harshly. He brushed the side of the gun holstered at his side. "I've got more important things to do tonight."

Zach walked past the law firm's secretary and straight into Franklin L. Russell's office, the older man's assistant dogging Zach's heels like a yappy pup. Not that he paid her much attention.

"We need to talk," he informed Russell, who glanced up from studying paperwork with no hint of surprise in his expression.

Russell looked past Zach to his secretary and said, "It's alright, Margaret. Please give us some privacy."

Once the door was shut, Zach planted his hands on the edge of Russell's desk and leaned forward. He tried to keep the bite out of his tone, but it spilled onto every syllable. "Let's agree to be honest with one another from here on out. I've got a short list of suspects of who's behind this shit, and you'd better believe you're at the top of the list."

"Careful, Mr. Collins. That sounded dangerously close to an accusation."

"Good." Zach pushed himself away from the desk and braced his hands on his hips. "I'm glad I made myself clear."

Russell's gaze never wavered from his. The attorney leaned back in his chair and crossed his legs. "Perhaps you'd better explain yourself."

Zach did, recapping the events of the day for the man who never betrayed an ounce of surprise—until the mention of the jewels they'd found. Russell's eyebrows shot up for a brief second before he cleared his face of emotion.

"So I have to ask myself, who would Ellie have confided in about the collars?" He paced calmly now as he spoke. "It wasn't Hannah. From what I understand, that only leaves one person. You." Zach leaned forward and grabbed the edge of the desk again. "From where I'm standing, that gives you the biggest motive to be behind all of this."

The attorney's mouth curved up. "It's a plausible theory, but there are far too many holes in your scenario for it to hold much weight, Mr. Collins." He gestured toward the closed door. "For example, if I knew about the collars, why not simply take them? Why go to such elaborate means when I could have simply paid a visit one afternoon and taken a peek when Hannah wasn't looking?"

Damn. He'd called Zach's bluff.

"Besides," Russell added, leaning forward again. "What good does knowing about the collars do if I'm not able to access the box? From what you indicated, Hannah is the only person with the authorization to get in and out of the vault."

And that made her a target, every bit as much as Abbott and Costello had been before. Shit. Zach straightened and ran a hand through his hair.

"When Ellie insisted on hiring you, I tried to convince her to use someone else," Russell said. "But I'm beginning to understand what she saw in you." Sighing, he stood, shrugged out of his jacket and laid it across the back of his chair. "She always had an amazing ability to judge people."

The attorney moved to a mini bar and poured himself a glass of Scotch. He lifted the glass of amber liquid to his lips, swallowed, and focused on Zach again. "Care for a drink, Mr. Collins?"

"I'd prefer some answers."

Shrugging, Russell gestured to the two chairs facing the desk. He angled one to face the other before taking a seat. "I'll deny telling you any of this if you try to make it public. Understand?"

Zach lowered into the second chair and nodded.

Russell tilted the glass and emptied it in one gulp. His eyes glassed over as he stared at the wall above Zach's head. "Ellie would be horrified if she knew the trouble Hannah was having. She was afraid of it, though. She went through a lot to ensure Hannah never became a target, but I suppose no plan is fool-proof, is it?"

"Come on, Russell, tell me what you know." Zach didn't want to be away from Hannah for too long. Especially now that he'd realized how much danger she was in.

Russell leaned back in his chair. "Ellie and my father were childhood sweethearts. Their families were well connected in Atlanta society. I have no doubt they would've ended up married if Ellie hadn't gotten a taste for independence and decided to travel Europe with her cousin one summer—back in 1960, I believe it was. My father told me that it didn't take her long to stop writing, and after a few months, she finally called to tell him she'd met someone else."

"Caleb Lightner?"

Russell's eyes widened. "Very good, Mr. Collins." He nodded. "Yes, she married him shortly after that. My father was heartbroken, but he had his career in law to fall back on, and eventually, he met and married my mother."

"Go on."

"I remember meeting Ellie and her husband one June when I was, oh, maybe eight years old. They showed up at our beach house in Savannah one day. They were staying in her family's summerhouse down the road. After that summer, I considered them to be Aunt Ellie and Uncle Caleb. My mother and Ellie got along very well. We spent holidays together. Ellie would often send me postcards from the exotic places she and Caleb traveled during the year."

"They never had children of their own?"

"No, I assume they were unable. I think that's why Ellie always had a dog or cat—or both—to nurture. Abbott and Costello aren't the first animals she rescued from a shelter."

Zach reached into his pocket and retrieved the photo of Ellie and two men he'd taken from the photo album they'd found.

"Is this your father?"

Russell leaned forward to look. His shoulders lifted with tension. "Where did you get that?"

"Is it your father?" Zach repeated, tapping the image of the second man.

"No. That's Roglitz." His chest heaved beneath a deep sigh. He lifted a hand and rubbed his eyes. "He's the man who murdered Ellie's husband."

"Murdered?" What the hell?

Russell nodded. "These are not good memories."

Zach tried to ease off. It was obvious this man had cared a lot about Ellie and her husband, but he could only afford so much empathy now that the stakes were so much higher. "Please, Mr. Russell. If you know anything that could help save Hannah's life, I would love to hear it."

Setting his empty glass aside, the older man leaned forward and fingered the picture. "I had just started making a name for myself in my father's law firm when he called me to his house one day and said he had an urgent matter to discuss with me. He'd retired early. Cancer. It was sometime in the 80s. I can't remember." He shook his head and stood up. Zach watched as he refilled his glass and took another drink. "That's when I learned more than I cared to know."

"What did you learn?"

"Caleb had been killed, and Ellie was back in Atlanta. She needed our help to escape some of the things she'd done." He took another swallow of the amber liquid. "My father was a stand-up attorney, but he would've done anything for her, as he knew I would." He turned and waved his glass toward Zach. "Are you sure I can't interest you in a drink?"

Zach shook his head.

Russell loosened his tie and returned to his seat. "My father told me that Caleb and his best friend, Peter Roglitz, had been performing jewelry heists for years, and Ellie had gotten involved once she'd married him. Together they'd performed some of the biggest heists in Europe. Have you ever heard of the Fox, Mr. Collins?"

Zach reeled back, feeling a little confused and overwhelmed.

"Neither had I, but Interpol had been chasing after him for years." A harsh laugh escaped his throat. "Funny thing was, the Fox wasn't just one person. The Fox was Ellie, Caleb and Peter combined. They were a team."

Zach leaned back in his seat, trying to take it all in. The elderly woman Hannah had adored had, in fact, been a world-class jewelry thief? He blew out his breath on a ripple of disbelief.

Russell continued his story. "As these things usually go, Roglitz decided he wanted Ellie for himself, enough to get his best friend out of the way permanently. He killed Caleb and tried to make it look like an accident, but Ellie knew better. She'd loved her husband and never even realized Roglitz harbored secret feelings for her. She helped the police put Roglitz away, and since the murder had happened in Chicago, he was sent to a prison in Illinois. He was only sentenced to forty years."

Zach was beginning to connect the dots on his own. "Ellie came to your father because she wanted to change her identity."

"She wanted a new life," Russell agreed. "She had lost her husband and felt nothing but remorse for the things she'd done.

I suspect she was worried Interpol would soon be on her doorstep too, but Roglitz wasn't stupid. Admitting that he or Ellie was the Fox would've gotten him even more time in prison and hurt his chances of ever getting out. She was also worried Roglitz would escape, as he'd threatened, and seek her out for revenge. We helped her change her name and secured the trust fundher parents had left her so it couldn't be touched. She spent the rest of her years living here in Atlanta modestly, with only her animals to keep her company, until Hannah came along."

As the older man spoke with such a sincere tone to his voice, it became obvious to Zach that Russell had known nothing about the jewels Ellie had hidden. He'd honestly believed the old broad had been on the straight and narrow.

Zach felt a pang of sympathy for the attorney.

"What happened to Roglitz? Is he still in prison?" Either way, the man would have to at least be in his eighties by now—and what kind of threat could he pose?

The attorney wiped a hand across his face. "He's been denied parole every time. He should've gotten out last month, but since Ellie had passed, I didn't think—" His eyes widened. "You don't think he's behind this, do you? The man would be too old to be a threat."

Moving to his feet, Zach itched to get to his car so he could call and initiate a background check on Roglitz. Old or not, the man was his best lead so far in this case.

Thrusting a hand through his hair, he turned to the attorney. "If you were so protective over Ellie's identity, how did her inheritance to Abbott and Costello get leaked to the press with that photo?"

A sarcastic rumble of laughter shook Russell's chest. "Damn reporter came across it in the probate records." He shrugged. "Some good came from it. It helped us get Hannah her inheritance sooner." He shook his head. "But without that reporter coming across the probate records—" He swore.

Without a word, Zach turned and headed for the door. This was good information. Things were starting to make sense. He'd feel better piecing the rest of the puzzle together with Hannah and her pets in sight.

"Mr. Collins?" Russell's voice caught him on the way out the door. He turned and acknowledged the entreaty. "Did you really find jewels in that vault?"

Zach nodded. "Yes."

He sighed, long and hard. "I suppose she had to have a few secrets left, didn't she?"

Zach turned again to leave but hesitated. The old guy looked defeated. "I'm sure she was protecting you by keeping some of the details to herself."

Russell lifted his glass and pointed at Zach. "She did that, didn't she, protected people? Or some might even say manipulated. Like she did with Hannah. Tell me. Does Hannah know what we did then?"

Zach shook his head. "With Eric Meester? No. She knows Ellie hired me to do a background check on her."

The older man settled the empty glass on the desk beside him and stood, sliding his hands into the front pockets of his tailored slacks. "I hope she doesn't hate us for our involvement, but God help us, I'm sure she will."

A heavy feeling weighed down Zach's tongue, but he spoke anyway. "I don't think she will if we tell her the truth before she finds out on her own."

Was it really so bad—what they'd done to her and Meester? The man hadn't deserved her. She'd been headed for heartbreak.

Sure, but she'd deserved to make the choice herself. Not be manipulated. His conscience nagged him.

Russell nodded, looking again much more like the calm and

collected attorney with whom Zach was familiar. He met Zach's eyes. "Get them out of Atlanta before it's too late, Collins."

Zach turned and hurried to his car. He'd been thinking the same thing. But first, he had an appointment to keep.

He spotted Alexandra as soon as he walked into the artsy lounge at the Marriott Marquis. The Pulse lived up to its name, with attractive young people spread among the red seats, sipping drinks and mingling while music vibrated through speakers he couldn't see.

Alexandra kept flicking glances at the watch on her wrist. He'd passed signage promoting the Healthy Mind, Body and Spirit Wellness Conference with times listed for various activities. She must be scheduled for one.

He slid onto the empty seat next to her. She flung her long, blonde hair over her shoulder and crossed her shapely legs so she was angled toward him. Dressed in a black pantsuit with high-heeled boots, she looked pristine and professional.

"I was about to give up on you, Collins."

"Sorry. I got held up with business. Thanks for waiting."

She pursed her lips and narrowed her eyes as she met his. "I almost didn't. Call me crazy, but I'm intrigued by what you said on the phone."

He noticed some women at the bar watching him with a familiar look that implied they recognized him from TV. Damn. The people at this conference might know him, and that made him uncomfortable.

"Maybe we could go somewhere more private," he suggested, shifting awkwardly.

"No way, Collins. I'm on a panel in thirty minutes. A girl has to make a living. Do you wanna talk or not?"

He recapped what he'd told her on the phone and asked the question that had been at the heart of his thoughts ever since.

"Can a person develop abilities after experiencing a head trauma? How does it happen?"

She shrugged. "It's different for everyone. Most psychics I know have had their abilities since childhood. Are you certain you didn't have these abilities before?"

"I don't know. I was always good at reading people. Had good instincts. But psychic?" He shook his head. "I don't know."

"The thing with the animals—that's new?"

"Never happened until now."

She looked thoughtful. "You could be a telepath, but they're extremely rare. Probably always been a clairsentient. Maybe an empath. Do you feel the animals' thoughts or hear them?"

He held up a hand in a half shrug. "Hear them, mostly. Sometimes it comes across as feelings."

"Maybe a clairaudient then."

He leaned closer. "Woman, I don't know what the hell any of those words mean."

Her eyes softened for the first time since their meeting began. "I know it's scary and confusing when it first happens." Her hand covered his. "You're not crazy, Zach. That's the most important thing for you to understand."

Her words were like a salve to his worried mind. "I hope to God you're right. How do you turn it off?"

"Yeah, right. Good luck with that." She rolled her eyes and reached into her purse. Pulling out a pen and piece of paper, she scribbled something. "I'll give you some websites to check out and my email in case you have questions. I have a friend who's a clairaudient—someone who senses thoughts and feelings in the form of sounds. I'll see if we can't put you two in touch. I can't tell you how helpful it is to know there is someone else out there who can understand what you're going through."

Relief relaxed his muscles. "Geez, thank you."

She arched an eyebrow at him and handed him the paper. "For what it's worth, I didn't know you were faking it on the show. I think you probably weren't."

"I don't know anymore."

Her eyes widened, and he'd be damned if her pupils didn't suddenly dilate right along with them. Her mouth fell open in a slight gasp. "There's a woman here with you."

Hannah? He glanced over his shoulder. The crowd around them had scattered. He saw no one. "Where?"

She nodded toward the wall at his back. "Curly, dark hair. Sad eyes. Older. I think her name is—" She closed her eyes and shook her head. She mumbled something he couldn't understand. "Has your mother passed?"

Zach's shoulders tightened painfully. "What?"

"She keeps saying, 'Tell him I don't blame him. Tell him I understand why he left.' Does that mean anything to you?"

He couldn't speak. What the hell was going on?

Alexandra's eyes opened and she looked at him, but she seemed to be looking straight through him. "She keeps asking, 'Why haven't you talked to Dylan?' Do you know someone named Dylan?"

"My brother," he whispered as a chill ran down his spine.

Alexandra's face scrunched as if in pain. "She wants you to know that your leaving was a good thing. It snapped her out of it. She keeps saying that—'snapped me out of it.' She says thank you for what you did to help them. Something about money. You gave them money? Does that make any sense to you?"

When he'd heard that his mother had succumbed to cancer, he'd been told she hadn't been with the asshole anymore. He'd wondered when and how that had happened. Maybe she'd left him. He *hoped* she had left that jerk. As for the money—

He nodded.

"She forgives you for not coming home." Alexandra's hand

circled in a repetitive motion. "She wishes you would find Dylan. She says you both need each other, and she's sorry for driving you away. She wants you to know she protected Dylan, after you left." Alexandra squeezed her eyes shut again. "So much sadness. So much pain."

Zach felt the burn of tears and rubbed at his eyes. Dammit. He hadn't expected this. Was this happening?

Alexandra reached out and clasped his hand. Her eyes opened, and he saw the sheen of tears. She shook her head and her eyes focused, returned to normal.

"I've got to go," she whispered. Her eyes drilled into him as if she were seeing him clearly for the first time. "Will you be okay?"

He swallowed the lump in his throat and nodded. They both stood and she released his hand.

"Good luck, Zach. If you need anything…" She let the offer linger between them. With a nod, she walked away. It took effort for Zach to do the same.

"Hannah, we have some serious talking to do." Sarah threw a thumb over her shoulder towards the back yard, where Kellan, E.J. and Brian had retreated to give Hannah and her best friend some privacy.

Sarah placed her purse on the counter and gave Abbott a wide berth when the cat came stalking in to say hello. It was as if Abbott knew about Sarah's phobia and always delighted in tormenting her with his presence. But this time, Sarah barely gave the cat a second glance. "Why the hell are there two gorgeous studs in your house and you didn't invite me over sooner?" She craned her neck for a look outside. "Damn, girl. That's some serious man candy."

Hannah bent to pick up Abbott and confine him to the bedroom. Before she could get more than a few steps, a knock on the door preceded its opening. Zach stepped inside and hesitated when he spotted Sarah.

A tiny squeak from Sarah's O-shaped mouth was the only sound in the room as the other woman openly gawked at the latest addition to Hannah's Man Candy Club.

"Sorry. Am I interrupting something?" Zach moved forward to scratch Abbott's ears in greeting.

Behind him, Sarah dropped down low, flung out her arms and feigned an open-mouth "That man is *hot*" expression that ended with a little hand fanning. She followed this by holding up three fingers and shaking her head. Clearly, she was ignoring the fact that *puny little* E.J. was here, too.

Zach turned around as Sarah straightened and assumed one of her saccharine sweet smiles. Hannah fought a giggle when her best friend topped it off with a few flirtatious bats of her carefully made-up eyelashes.

"Sarah stopped by to check on me." Hannah cleared her throat, tying to chase away the amusement stuck there. "Zachary Collins, this is my best friend, Sarah Taylor."

Zach accepted Sarah's hand in his. There was that tiny squeak from Sarah's throat again, and Hannah was surprised her best friend didn't just swoon and get it over with.

"I've heard great things about you." Zach pulled away. "Sounds like Hannah is lucky to have you."

Sarah shifted from one foot to the other while the fingers on her right hand fiddled with the necklace at her throat. "Thank you. Likewise."

Hannah expected Sarah to launch into a round of twenty questions as part of her usual protective interrogation, but her friend seemed to have been rendered speechless. Zach nodded toward the back yard. "Full house. Sorry. I asked them all here to strategize. If you ladies will excuse me..." His expression looked intense when he caught and held Hannah's gaze. "We'll talk when I'm done outside, alright?"

Her body slowly relaxed. She'd been so worried when he'd left earlier. Something about his presence calmed her in a way no one else's did.

Sarah brushed against her side as they both stared through the glass doorswhere all of the men stood in a loose huddle in the yard talking. "Mmm-mmm. You saved the best for last, didn't you?" Sarah glanced over and realized Hannah was still holding Abbott at the same time the cat leaned over and brushed his head against Sarah's shoulder. Her friend squealed and shot across the room, wiggling her body as if she were trying to shake off the cooties in the process. "Creeeeepy cat."

Rolling her eyes, Hannah deposited Abbott on her bed and shut the door before returning to find Sarah once again propped up against the kitchen island and staring at the men outside. Hannah leaned onto the counter beside her and sighed. The men seemed to be having an intense discussion, judging by their facial expressions. Zach looked up, caught her staring.

Both women immediately turned away.

"So are you and Mr. Fine Ass doing it yet?"

"What? No."

"Mmm-hmm. I notice you didn't ask which one I meant." Sarah moved away from the counter but kept casting glances out the door at the men. "I saw the way he was looking at you, and more important, I saw the way you were looking at him."

"We barely acknowledged each other." She snorted. "Besides, weren't you warning me not to fall for my bodyguard?"

"That was before I saw the man in person." She angled for a better view of the yard. "Girl, please tell me all those men are not your bodyguards. I'd probably sleep with them all at some point."

"Even E.J.?" she teased.

Sarah waved a dismissive hand. "Except him."

Heat crept up Hannah's neck. "You're awful. One is married and the other is taken." And Zach was…what? She hoped Sarah didn't ask, because Hannah didn't know.

Sarah winked at her. "Doesn't mean you can't look." Joining Hannah across the room, Sarah sank onto the couch beside her and slapped her knee. "You know I'm teasing. Let's get real. How are you holding up?"

Hannah explained all that had happened and watched her friend's eyes grow wide. "Did you tell the police about the jewels?"

"Not yet. I think that's why Zach asked everyone to meet. I'm not even sure the police would be interested if I can't even give them a clue where the jewels came from."

"This is starting to sound like one of those Lifetime movies of the week." Sarah glanced toward the back yard again. "Hannah, are you sure they're keeping you safe?"

All things considered, she thought so. "I'll be fine."

Sarah clasped her hand in her own and squeezed. "What about—you know? I was only half teasing before about getting involved with one of them. Are you really ready for that, if it happens?"

Oh, it was already happening, but she had no idea if it was all one-sided or not.

And she wasn't sure what to do about that.

# Chapter Thirteen

"We're relocating you and the boys for a while. No arguments."

Hannah wasn't surprised by Zach's declaration, but a part of her still wanted to cross her arms, poke out her bottom lip and say, "Uh-uh. I'm not budging." The part of her that was still in denial that she was in danger—that any of this was happening to *her*— also wanted to dart onto the front doorstep and yell "Screw you!" to the unknown persons upending her life.

But she wasn't stupid. "Okay. Where are we going?"

Zach sighed and his shoulders sank as he fell into the chair across from her. "Kellan has—" He exchanged a look with his associate that seemed to carry a message "— a *friend* who is going to let us use her place for a few days."

"Where exactly is it?" Sarah asked, perching on the arm of the sofa beside where Hannah sat. She reached down a hand and squeezed Hannah's shoulder.

"A safe place. Don't worry." When Sarah opened her mouth to demand more details, Zach held up his hand. "I promise we'll let you know when we get there."

"And who is we?" Sarah crossed her arms. "You expect me to let my best friend go off with four guys I don't know from Adam without knowing where you're taking her? You must be outta your freakin' mind, Jack."

159

Hannah reached out a hand to calm her friend's temper from growing. "Sarah, I trust them. It'll be okay."

"Well I don't." Sarah whirled a ferocious glare around the room. "I'll only agree to this if someone lets the police know what the hell is going on first."

Brian stepped forward. "We've already spoken to Interpol, and they're working with the local police. But the APD can't offer the type of protection Hannah needs right now."

Zach moved to his feet. "I'll be staying with Hannah and the animals twenty-four-seven while the other guys chase down information. We'll have Internet and phone, and I'll be doing my fair share of the work from the safe house, too."

Sarah's slim body tensed, and she turned to look at Hannah. Hannah didn't need to be psychic to know what her friend was thinking. *Twenty-four seven. Alone with Zach.*

Oh boy.

"I don't know about—" Sarah's words were interrupted by Hannah's fingers squeezing her knee. Sighing loudly, she rolled her eyes and finished, "Fine. But I expect a phone call as soon as you get there and at least a dozen times a day."

Zach reached for his jacket. "I've got to run home and pack a few things. Hannah, be sure to pack whatever you'll need for a week for you and the boys."

She loved that he'd started referring to her pets that way, same as she did. She reached down to pet the dog whose body was pressed against her feet. Were the animals getting as attached to Zach as she was? She didn't know if that was a good or a bad thing.

Zach glanced around the room. "Is there anything you have of Ellie's that might help us? A diary? Old photos? Any documents you might have put in storage?"

Not really. Most of what Ellie had owned had been material objects—trinkets and the such. "I'll look again. Maybe I missed something."

Zach shrugged into his jacket as he inched toward the door. His actions roused Costello from his resting spot, and the dog staggered over to Zach with a walk that resembled a tired old man's.

Zach gestured to her pet. "Do I need to pick up anything for them while I'm out?"

Hannah shook her head, but before she could answer, Zach frowned down at the dog and said, "Absolutely not. No eating pig ears in my car. That's *disgusting*."

When he glanced up and saw that almost everyone in the room was watching, Zach gave an awkward chuckle and cleared his throat. "Yeah, I'll be back in an hour."

The other men scattered after asking if Hannah needed help packing. Sarah shooed them each away territorially.

"Are you sure you can handle this?" She grabbed Hannah's shoulders and forced her friend to face her. "Be honest."

Hannah wasn't the shrinking violet Sarah sometimes painted her as, but she knew Sarah meant well. "Remember when we first met?"

Sarah's face twisted into a confused expression. "Yeah, of course."

Sarah had been admitted to the same boys and girls home as Hannah because a neighbor had complained to the Department of Social Services that Sarah and her brothers were being neglected while their single mom worked two jobs. A group of older, trouble-making teens had cornered Sarah in the yard, taunting her with insults because she wore her brothers' hand-me-down clothes. Hannah had gotten fed up with what she'd been overhearing and charged in to Sarah's defense, reminding the others that many of them sure as hell didn't look much better.

"I don't like bullies," Hannah explained. "But I'm smart enough to know when I need help."

"I won't be there to have your back. Maybe I should come with you." Sarah's voice was quiet and thoughtful.

"No way. Your mom's last chemo is when—Friday?" When Sarah nodded, Hannah took her by the arms and shook her. "She needs you, you idiot. I've got four hunks looking after me right now. I'll be *fine*." She let the word roll off her tongue suggestively, then winked and smiled in a way that suggested pure naughtiness.

Sarah laughed and rolled her eyes. "What are you talking about? You wouldn't know what to do with four hunks if you tried."

Maybe not, but she had a pretty good idea what she'd do with at least one of them.

Gesturing to the kitchen, she told Sarah, "Go and help me gather whatever canned food I have to pack. I've got to find Abbott's kennel and Costello's car seat."

"Don't forget to pack some condoms." Sarah howled with laughter.

Thank heavens the door was shut so none of the men outside could hear them. Hannah's face flamed at the teasing—but that didn't stop her from going to check and see if she had any condoms left to pack.

Just in case.

That weird feeling in Zach's gut didn't start acting up until he was halfway down the stairs after leaving his apartment. His feet slowed their pace and he scanned the parking lot below. A neighbor he barely recognized was removing groceries from the trunk of his car. Otherwise, the place was empty.

*Careful.*

The hairs stood on the back of his neck in that familiar sensation that he was being watched.

He swore and quickened his steps. He probably *was* being watched by the scum after Hannah. Tossing his bag into his SUV, Zach grabbed his mobile phone and called Kellan.

"I'm being followed." He slid into the driver's seat of his navy Chevy Yukon. It was a company car. They'd gotten three at the same time—same model, same color, tinted windows. "Are you driving your car or one of the Yukons?"

"Since I'm on the clock, Yukon. Why?" His tone was slightly defensive.

"Good. I've got a plan. Let me talk to E.J."

Twenty minutes later, Zach pulled into Hannah's driveway and into the garage beside where Kellan had already parked his vehicle. E.J. was waiting for him.

"Did you get some?" Zach asked.

"Yeah, man. Piece of cake." E.J. held up two license plates and smiled. Zach wasn't sure he wanted to know where E.J. had gotten them. They needed to swap the current plates on both Yukons in case the person following him had noted Zach or Kellan's plates. He hoped to God neither of them got pulled over by the cops for it.

"Can you go switch them out for us? Make sure you put the other ones in the back of the cars so we'll have them."

E.J. sounded downright giddy when he said, "Damn, being a P.I. sure is exciting. I'm on it, boss." With a salute, he set about the task.

Zach couldn't help the agreeing smile that tugged at his mouth. E.J. was right. It'd been a while since he'd felt this excitement on the job. It felt good. Normal.

Hannah appeared carrying Abbott. She'd changed into jeans. Tight t-shirt. She looked fresh. Appealing. Costello came romping into the room and lunged for Zach.

The feeling of the dog's excitement and energy was so strong it almost knocked him over with its potency. Zach reached down and gave Costello a proper greeting. The dog squirmed against his legs, curling his long body this way and that to make certain Zach's fingers made contact with his furry head.

"If only everyone were this happy to see me." He winked at

Hannah and loved the way her delicate skin turned red.

"Next time I'll run into the room and jump on you too, and we'll see if you still feel that way," she teased.

His imagination ran wild with that scenario—and liked where it led. He wanted to hold his arms wide in open invitation. *Remember your boundaries.* He stepped back. Tried to focus on keeping her safe.

Zach helped load the items Hannah had packed into his car. He made sure Hannah hadn't followed him and Kellan into the garage before asking, "Think this will work?"

Kellan closed the car door and slapped him on the back. "Best shot we've got."

Hannah appeared with a strange-looking strappy thing in one hand and Costello attached to a leash in the other. "Since I don't know how long we'll be in the car, I need to put him in his seatbelt." She shooed the two men aside, then looked at both SUVs and hesitated. "Um, which one?"

Zach opened the door for her and stepped back to watch. The dog hopped into the backseat and Hannah bent over to fasten him in using the strappy thing. Damn, she looked great in those jeans. He realized his eyes were honing in on her shapely backside when he should have been offering to help.

*Going for a ride. Yes. I love to ride! Where are we going? Can I eat while we go for a ride? Hey, what is that? Can I eat that?* Costello sniffed the cloth piece of the harness Hannah was struggling to get looped into position.

"We're going for a ride," Hannah told the dog in her baby voice. "Are you excited to go for a ride? Huh? Are you?"

*Yes! I'm so excited to go for a ride. Let's go.* The dog whined and wiggled as she tried her best to get him situated.

Zach snickered. "Do you, uh, need any help with that thing?"

"No, I got it," she called from inside the car, but she seemed to be struggling—mainly because Costello kept wiggling around and jarring the buckle loose.

Done, Hannah grabbed her remaining bag and Abbott, who seemed comfortably tucked inside his mesh kennel. She sat the cat on the backseat beside Costello, hooked the bag in with a seatbelt matching the other strappy thing and then settled herself into the front seat with an exhausted-sounding sigh.

"I hate to tell you this, but I need you to get down, out of sight."

She frowned. "Seriously?"

"Down," he ordered. She hesitated, sighed, and climbed into the back seat. She sank down to the floorboard in front of the animals and gave him a defiant look.

Brian and E.J. had left minutes earlier to get into position, so Zach gave Kellan a thumb's up sign over the hood before sliding into the driver's seat.

Turning the engine on, Zach took a deep breath and waited for Kellan to leave first. "I hope these windows are tinted dark enough."

He gave Kellan a sizeable lead. They'd pulled onto I-85 when E.J.'s voice in Zach's ear said, "If anyone is following you, boss, I can't tell. I think they took the bait and followed Kellan like we'd hoped."

A second later, Brian's voice said, "Got 'em. A silver Honda has been on Kellan's tail since we got on 17th Street."

Zach's gaze shifted from the traffic in front of him to the rear-view mirror. He activated his microphone. "We don't know how many people are involved. I wouldn't be surprised if we were both being followed."

"My friend is running these plates, but my guess is that it's another stolen car," Brian said.

"Be careful, Brian. Leave it to the cops to give chase if it's stolen." Zach thought about Brian's new daughter. Panic tightened his chest. If Brian got hurt— "Don't play the hero. You hear me?"

Amusement flavored his best friend's tone when he replied, "Don't worry. I'm not about to take any careless risks."

For the next ten minutes, Zach kept his eyes on the cars around him. Hannah remained quiet, even as Costello whined and struggled relentlessly to free himself of his restraint. He couldn't spot any cars following them besides E.J.'s, a ways back. Maybe the plan had worked, but Zach wouldn't feel safe until they'd made it to Lake Lanier and established a safe base.

*I want in the front seat. Why can't I get in the front seat like I always do?* Costello whined. *Are we there yet? I want in the front seat.* More whining.

Zach's fingers tightened around the wheel as he silently told the dog to shut the hell up. Situation was bad enough without the animal's whiny chatter running nonstop through his head.

Hannah cooed, "Settle down. Sit."

*Am I in trouble? I want in the front seeeaaaat.*

Geez. This was worse than traveling with kids. Making sure it was safe to do so, he shifted and sent the dog an uncompromising look. "Costello, sit!"

The dog's ears lifted and his head tilted in surprise, but he stopped struggling to get free and sat still. Even the whining stopped.

Zach felt pretty damn pleased with himself as he returned his attention to the road.

"Thank you," Hannah said. "I've never taken them on a long road trip before."

"It's only an hour's drive."

"To where?"

He explained about the condo their client—now Kellan's damned girlfriend—owned outside of Lake Lanier. "It's secluded, but not too secluded, and in a gated community. We should be safe there."

He hoped like hell they'd be safe there. He would be the only thing standing between her and the psychopaths chasing her.

# Chapter Fourteen

Fox pounded his fist against the steering wheel when he realized he'd been made. Quickly, he directed the car to the left—away from where the tinted SUV was traveling—and kept an eye on the sedan that was following *him* now.

Collins and his team were good.

They'd used a decoy, and he'd fallen for it.

He should've taken Collins out at his condo, but when it had become obvious the private detective was planning something, he'd waited to find out what it was.

He should've known better. The pressure was starting to get to him. He was making careless mistakes.

Not good.

He reached into the hem of his jacket and touched the warm metal tucked carefully in his holster and checked the rearview mirror again, noting the sedan had fallen back. Now was his chance to get off its radar.

It was easy enough to lose his tail in the late afternoon congestion on I-85. Once he was certain he was no longer being followed, he called his partner.

"Tell me where they went."

Hesitation was the initial response. "They were careful not to discuss it inside the house. I didn't hear where they were going."

The man swore, loud and fierce.

They needed the woman to get inside the vault. Breaking into that facility without the proper help and equipment would be next to impossible with so little time to prepare.

"I think—" his partner said slowly, as if the words were hard to speak "—we might have another option."

"Tell me."

"The woman has a friend she cares a great deal about: Sarah."

"Keep going."

"Perhaps if we used her, we could draw Hannah out of hiding."

Maybe his partner wasn't as stupid as he'd begun to believe. "Figure out how we can get to this Sarah. We need to move, and fast."

"Wow."

Hannah blinked a few times so her eyes could absorb the awesome sight in front of her. A 15-foot floor-to-ceiling window overlooked a view of the lake, surrounded by trees and a dock that implied the stretch of water was their own private alcove. A giant flat-screen television was angled on the wall in the corner, in front of a set of navy leather sofas. She could feel Zach watching her, so she shrugged and stepped further into the open living room.

She cleared her throat. "This is some place."

"I think Katie had it remodeled when she bought it. Dammit. Kellan should have mentioned that open window." He frowned at the uncovered view. "We should go somewhere else."

"You don't think we're safe?" She glanced around, spotted a control panel on the wall—hadn't she seen something like that on HGTV?—and decided to toy with it and see if her hunch was right. Ah ha. Bingo. She messed with some controls, the room filled with a humming sound, and a set of blinds slowly slid across the window from an unseen alcove. "See? Problem solved."

His face was still scrunched in a glower. "Kellan said to be sure to check out the back deck." He dropped their bags to the floor and moved to the back patio doors. His eyes widened. "Oh, yeah. This is a bit extravagant."

The back deck had been transformed into a tiki bar complete with a roof made of rattan and palm leaves. Tiki masks and totem poles lined the wall behind the bar, and a couple of bamboo loungers faced the railing. A privacy wall divided it from the neighboring condo's deck.

"This place is like a—"

"A mini playboy mansion?" Zach suggested for her, bending to move their luggage. "Some people have too much money."

Yeah. She supposed some people did. Kind of like she did now.

His body froze in the middle of a lean. "I didn't mean—"

She held up a hand. "It's not like we both weren't thinking it." A sigh parted her lips. "I'm still getting used to it, that's all."

The sound of Costello's toenails clambering against hardwood caught her attention, and she turned to focus on the dog. His pudgy body bounced as he ran from room to room, inspecting all of the new spaces. Abbott still hadn't left his carrier, choosing instead to peek out, wary. When Zach dropped a bag beside him, the cat finally tiptoed carefully out of his comfort zone.

"Katie bought it as an investment. She rents it out when she's not using it. She also lets crew members on her show stay here sometimes with their families."

"That's nice of her." Two steps led up to the rest of the home. The bedrooms? Hannah decided to investigate, watching Costello dart up the steps. "She must really care about Kellan to loan him this place for us. Do you think I should pay her the rental fee to be fair, or—?"

Zach frowned. "Or what?"

Hannah suppressed a smile. This place was amazing. "She might be trying to score brownie points with him or something. I don't want to throw a monkey wrench in her plans."

Zach grumbled something she couldn't understand. He had lagged behind. He had one hand buried in his hair, and his eyes looked…furious?

"What's wrong?" she asked.

He shook his head and trudged up the steps slowly. "Nothing."

Really? It didn't look like it. Hannah let him pass as she thought about the things she'd seen and overheard that might have caused discontent between Zach and Kellan. "You *really* don't approve of his relationship with her, do you?"

He snorted. "I don't condone it, no."

"Why not?"

"Why not?" He turned and repeated with distaste. "It's unprofessional. It'll never last between them. It's—" He stopped himself short, and she couldn't help but wonder what else he was thinking. It was, what? Wrong? Asking for trouble?

Yeah, she'd considered the same arguments. Wondered if the adrenaline and excitement of having a bodyguard was the only reason she felt such a strong attraction to Zach, but she didn't feel the same toward any of the other guys on his team. Then again, she hadn't shared such intimate moments with them either.

She felt closer to Zach than she'd felt to anyone in a long time. Too close. She crossed her arms. "Are we ever going to talk about what happened between us?"

Zach's eyes widened slightly as he turned to face her. "Between *us*?"

She rolled her eyes. "Don't play dumb, Zach." She softened her voice. "You said some things, when you were drugged. Maybe you don't remember them, but—"

"Oh, I remember enough." Zach shook his head. "Hannah, I can't get involved with a client."

She felt her shoulders sag in disappointment. "What about after, when I'm no longer a client?"

He blew out his breath slow and looked away. "Woman, you're killing me."

So she'd been wrong. He didn't feel anything for her. Lust, maybe, but what man didn't respond to a woman throwing herself at him? A part of her wasn't surprised. Eric hadn't wanted her either, not when everything was said and done. She swallowed and nodded. "It's okay. I understand."

He swore, low and harsh, and crossed the distance between them. Grabbing her upper arms, he tugged her hard against him. Hannah inhaled sharply as his lips found hers, his kiss possessing a passionate desperation that matched her own. Sliding his hand up, his fingers curled around the back of her neck, pressing her closer—not that she needed persuasion. She wrapped her arms around his middle and opened her mouth, inviting him in.

He tasted as good as she remembered.

Zach groaned. Almost immediately, he pulled away. "Hannah, you're killing me." He kissed her again, as if he was every bit as reluctant to separate as she was. He took a deep breath and took a step back. "I don't think you understand at all."

Her head felt dizzy. Drugged. Hannah grasped his arms to keep her balance. "Then maybe you should explain it to me."

"I want you, badly. But I can't. Not yet. I'm having a hard enough time doing my job without this added to it. Please, Hannah."

"Not yet?" So he did want her? She sucked in enough air to clear her head as relief soothed her mind. "After this case is over—?"

"All bets are off," he assured her, his eyes dark and dangerous. Smoldering.

"Then we need to get busy solving this case, don't we?"

His throat moved beneath a swallow as he edged carefully away from her. "The sooner, the better."

She bit her lip, eyeing him from head to toe. "The sooner, the better."

He swallowed again and ran a hand through his hair. "Alright, then." Shaking his head, he turned away from her, ducked into both of the bedrooms and said, "Take the room in back. The view isn't as nice, but the brush provides privacy."

And just like that he was back to business. Mr. Macho Bodyguard. A part of her was disappointed, but the other part understood. He had to focus.

She glanced at the other room. Sweet mercy. There would only be a wall between them at night? That didn't seem like nearly enough to keep her hands off him.

"I'm taking the couch." He picked up the cat that had followed them. "That way I can keep an eye on the door."

"Makes sense." Her hands dug into the back pockets of her jeans. Why did she feel so disappointed he wouldn't be sleeping in the room next to her?

"You should be safe here, Hannah. If anyone had followed us, we'd know it by now. Relax, okay?"

She hadn't realized her muscles were bunched until he pointed it out. Relax? After what had happened? Yeah, right.

She reached for Abbott and then realized what a stupid move that was when her fingers brushed against the muscles of his arm. Tiny zingers of heat and electricity shot through her hand at the contact. The cat groused and she lifted him against her, letting his paws rest on her shoulder.

Zach jerked back as if she'd burned him. "I'll go get the rest of the stuff."

Hannah ventured into her new room and glanced around. Her lips still tingled with the sensation of Zach's kiss. And they were alone in this secluded place until the person after her was caught. How would she stand it?

Abbott meowed, and she sat him on the bed before sinking down beside him.

She'd start with a cold shower. Hopefully the rest would take care of itself.

Thirty minutes later she came out of her room and found Zach setting up a work station at the dining room table. His entire body froze as he watched her approach, so she glanced down to make sure there wasn't a hole in her shirt or something. She'd changed into a pair of shorts and a long-sleeved t-shirt but left her feet bare. She was more than decently covered. Why was he staring?

She brushed a hand down her front and cleared her throat. "I thought I'd try to go through some of the old documents I found in Ellie's stuff." Where had he put that box? Ah ha. There it was in the corner. "Maybe I can find something to help."

"Sounds good."

She picked up the box and moved it to the sofa. Call her a glutton for punishment, but she wanted to stay close to him. She stretched out on the cushions facing him and lifted some documents to read. She'd actually found some old letters amongst Ellie's belongings that she'd never felt comfortable looking at until now. It had seemed like such an invasion of privacy.

*Sorry, Ellie, dear, but you lost the right to privacy when you turned out to be a world-class jewel thief.*

She lifted a letter and found her gaze straying beyond it toward her bodyguard. What had he meant when he said he was having a hard time doing his job without this attraction between them?

Hannah grabbed her phone, peeked up to see if Zach was watching her, and bit her lip. "I forgot to text Sarah." Her face warmed at the lie, so she ducked down a little, used her knees to block her view of him.

She pulled up the Internet—fancy that, they had wireless—and typed Zach's name into the search field. Nothing but what she'd already seen. She pulled up the Atlanta newspaper's website and entered Zach's name again. *Bingo.*

An article from October, a little over six months ago, popped up. *Suspect in Ponzi scheme kills self, co-workers.* She clicked on the link and skimmed the details. She was wondering what it had to do with Zach when she stumbled across the words, "*Sources claim Johnson was being followed by a private investigator from the Collins Security Firm, founded by reality television star Zachary Collins. On the day of the shooting, Johnson realized he was being tailed and confronted the investigator before returning to his office in Kirkwood, retrieving a gun and killing two of his co-workers before turning the gun on himself. An official from the Atlanta Police Department said there are no plans to file charges against the private investigator involved.*"

Hannah's gaze lifted to the man now seated at the table, typing on his computer. Had Zach been the private investigator involved in the case? There were few details in the article, so she looked for follow-ups. Nothing.

She wanted to ask him about it, but couldn't bring herself to let him know she'd been snooping. Had Zach blamed himself for the shooting? Was that why he'd put himself behind a desk for the past six months like E.J. had said?

Oh, Zach. Surely he wasn't blaming himself?

A deep feeling of sadness for what he must've gone through rushed through her. She wanted to rush over and put her arms around him and—

Zach's mobile phone rang and snapped her out of her reverie.

"What did your contact at Interpol say?" He moved to his feet and started pacing beside the table. He looked so intimidating when he moved. Dangerous. Kind of like a caged panther.

Then again, Costello ambling slowly behind him like a tired, imitating, goofy child kind of ruined the effect.

Hannah cleared her phone and set it aside. She preferred watching him. A few minutes later, he disconnected his call and turned his attention to her.

"We're still waiting to hear back from the agent in charge of the Fox's case. Shouldn't be much longer. Hopefully, once the diamond is back in the right hands and the media gets wind it's been recovered, there will no longer be a need for anyone to come after you."

She hadn't thought of that. "Thank you."

He explained that the car that had followed Kellan had gotten away. Yes, it had stolen plates and the police had found the car abandoned. Kellan and E.J. were trying to track down and interview any old friends and acquaintances Ellie Parham might have known while Brian was following leads on the man who had murdered Ellie's husband.

"We should have some answers soon." He gestured to the papers she held. "Anything?"

"I've barely started reading, but not so far." A worried feeling settled in her chest as she thought about the effort his team was going through to protect her and the boys. "How's Brian's wife and baby? Is anyone helping them while he's at work?"

The suggestion of a smile pulled at his mouth. "They're good. Don't worry about them."

"I do. Brian should be home with them. It's my fault he's not." There had to be some way she could make amends. "Let Brian know I'm willing to pay someone to help his wife until she's adjusted. I know an agency. Some nurses. I can call them if it helps."

He moved to the other end of the plush sofa and sat down. "You know, for a woman who claims to hate people, you're not very convincing."

"Hate is a strong word." She crossed her arms and tucked her feet closer.

"Alright. Why do you dislike people so much? Tell me."

Eric. What he'd done to her—

She shook her head. She didn't like to talk about it. Instead, she nodded to the stack of papers. "Take Ellie. She lied to me for years. I trusted her as if she was family." Then there were the friends who'd stopped calling after her breakup. People she'd trusted to stick to her side, but who hadn't. Only Sarah had. "You can't trust anyone, Zach. You can't."

She expected him to say, "You can trust me." That's what people always said when she uttered that declaration. But Zach didn't. His eyes darkened, turned oddly cold, and he moved to his feet again.

"Hannah, you're a good person who cares." He hesitated, and then turned back toward her. "Brian is always telling me I shouldn't base my actions on other people's. That I should do what's right, no matter what."

She lifted her gaze to his. "Do you?"

"I've been trying." He sighed. "The point is, I don't think you should give up on people. When I think of what you did for Brian the day his wife went into labor, and what you did for me when I was shot." His cobalt eyes warmed. "Those aren't the actions of a woman who hates people. Those are the actions of a woman who cares too much to give up being a nurse."

Darn him for seeing so much and making her feel all noble and hopeful again. She shifted uncomfortably. She needed a change of subject, fast. "How long have you and Brian been friends?"

His glance dropped, and he turned his back again to move toward the table. She thought he wasn't going to answer, but his tone was casual when he said, "A while. Since we were seventeen."

"You told me you ran away from home. Is that true?"

He stilled. "I told you that?"

She nodded. He'd been doped up on ketamine, but he'd told her.

"Yeah, it's true." His smile was almost shy as he moved items around on the table. "I hopped a bus to California. He was the first person I met. He'd been running away from his family. We sort of clicked. Decided to team up and look out for each other."

"I'm glad you did." She'd heard horror stories about teenage runaways. She couldn't help but wonder what Brian and Zach had been forced to do to survive. A chill ran through her veins, and she rubbed her arms to chase it.

She watched him. His eyes were lit with amusement. "We never fell into prostitution or drugs or any of that shit you see on TV. We weren't on the streets long. As soon as we both turned eighteen, we enlisted in the Marines. We would have done almost anything for a good meal and a warm shower."

"How do you do that?"

"Do what?" His forehead creased.

"Know what I'm thinking. It's like sometimes you can read my mind or something."

His Adam's apple moved beneath a swallow.

"Wait. The Marines?" She didn't know Zach had been a Marine. She sat up higher. "What happened after you joined the Marines?"

His shoulders sank. "I was doing a training exercise with some other recruits. The vehicle we were in overturned in a ditch. Doctors said I was lucky. I only had nerve damage in my left arm. Earned me an early and honorable discharge."

"Oh my goodness, Zach." She moved to her feet and hurried to his side. "What kind of nerve damage? Ulnar nerve?" Her fingers gently massaged along his arm muscles.

"Yeah."

She glanced up at him through her lashes. "Why are you grinning?"

"I'm grinning?"

"You're grinning. Stop it. I'm not feeling you up. I'm checking you out."

"It's not as bad as it once was. I had surgery. Take meds. It only flares up every now and then."

He pulled his arm away, and Hannah realized touching him hadn't been the best idea. She didn't want to stop.

"When I touch you do you…see stuff?" His head tilted a tad and his expression looked puzzled at her words, so she added, "You know. Psychic visions or whatever you call it?"

His body tensed. "No. That's not how it works with me."

Good.

"I thought you did it that way on your show." At least, she was pretty sure she remembered him holding objects and giving his impressions to the camera. She could've been wrong.

His chest moved as he released a deep breath. "Some of that stuff was—" He paused. One of his hands moved to the muscles at the back of his neck. "It was staged, Hannah."

"Really?" Since she'd come to conclusion Zach had to be at least a little bit psychic, she couldn't help but wonder why. Then another realization hit her, distracting her from the question. "That's why you don't like to talk about the show. I'm right, aren't I? You're ashamed you staged some things."

His eyes widened enough that she noticed. "Yes."

She couldn't help the smile that tugged at her lips. Poor man. He really had more integrity than she'd first credited him. "It's okay, Zach. I kind of expected it. Most people do." She found herself stepping closer to him. Close enough to reach out and reassure him by laying a hand on his upper arm. His very muscled, smooth, hard upper arm.

"Hannah, I—"

"Don't worry about it." She shook her head, not wanting to make him feel uncomfortable by this detour in their conversation. She cleared her throat and jerked her hand away. *No touching, remember?* Her gaze turned hopefully toward the back door. "What are the chances I can go read those letters on the back deck? I'd love to get some sun." And put some space between them before she combusted.

His hands settled on his hips and his lips pulled tight as he moved to the back door, pushed aside the door-length blinds he'd closed earlier, and glanced out. Through the slabs, Hannah saw a boat not too far in the distance.

"I'm sorry, Hannah. It's too dangerous. Maybe later when there's not so many people out."

She sighed and crossed her arms. "I'm going crazy, trapped inside all the time. How can you bring me to a place like this and tell me I can't go outside?"

"It's not safe."

"Fine." She threw up her hands and settled back on the sofa beside where Abbott had curled up for his afternoon kitty nap. But it wasn't fine. Not really.

Frustration nibbled at her calm. Frustration that she was trapped inside again. Frustration not to have any answers yet about Ellie's past.

And frustration because she couldn't throw herself at her sinfully sexy bodyguard. She reminded herself of the vow they'd made to avoid anything remotely romantic or sexual until her case was resolved. Patience. That's all she needed.

Good things came to those who waited, and she had no doubt Zachary Collins would be good. Oh, so good.

She squirmed uncomfortably at the thought. *Focus on helping Zach solve this case. Keep your mind out of the gutter.*

Costello's paw nudged Hannah's foot playfully, and she glanced down at the dog now sprawled on the floor. His tail started thumping a strong beat against the hardwood floor as soon as her eyes met his.

"What are you doing, silly?" She moved the papers out of her lap, reached down and rubbed his stomach. "Are you a little bored too?"

The dog made a long mewling sound that was a cross between a growl and a whine and that sounded remarkably like "Uh huh."

From across the room where he'd reclaimed his seat at the table, Zach heaved a loud sigh and began typing on the laptop. He was back in Macho Bodyguard Zone, stone-faced, focused, and completely oblivious to her again.

Wasn't he as frustrated as she was?

Pacing on the back deck, Zach listened to his partner give him a rundown of what they'd all found so far.

Absolutely nothing.

Ellie Parham had been a mastermind at keeping her secrets secret, and whoever the hell was after that diamond wasn't giving them much to go on either.

"I'll check in with you again tomorrow," he told Brian. "Go home and spend some time with your family, man. Tell Jenny I'm sorry about this."

Ending the call, Zach stilled and rubbed at his eyes. He itched to be out there, actively investigating like the others, but who was he kidding? He was better suited to babysitting than footwork anyway. If the others couldn't find anything, he was an arrogant sonofabitch to think he could.

Not to mention he was now either psychic or crazy. Probably better to keep him on the sidelines.

Hannah had been right. He'd known—and he had no idea *how*—but he'd known exactly what she'd been thinking earlier. No voice whispering in his ear or a vision flashing in his mind, but more of a feeling. Kind of like intuition. That thing he'd always referred to as his gut.

He wished he could talk to someone, figure out what the hell was going on in his head. He hadn't had a chance to contact the person Alexandra had recommended.

What about Hannah?

Could he talk to her? She was the only one here. He'd almost told her everything earlier. Dammit, he wanted to unload everything on her, ask her for help, beg her not to leave him when she found out he was fraud and an asshole, but she was still his client.

But she was more than a client.

Zach hesitated before going back inside. Part of him wanted to rip up Hannah's contract and refuse her money so he could take her to bed. How could he? They needed the money. *Brian* needed the money. What would she think of him, if he revealed that he'd been nothing more than a con artist on TV? Opened up and let her know about Eric Meester? She wouldn't want anything to do with him. That gleam of hero worship he sometimes saw in her eyes would disappear.

Dammit.

He wanted to solve this case so he could—what?

He wouldn't tell her everything, but there were some things she deserved to know. He owed her that much.

Costello's ears perked up and the dog flipped from his side onto his feet to shamble over to Zach when he stepped back into the room. Hannah was still curled up on the sofa, the cat stretched out beside her. She was nibbling at her lower lip as she intently studied one of the letters in Ellie's collection.

She needed to go put on some more clothes. She was making him nuts. He couldn't handle the distraction of talking to her half naked again. It took all of his willpower to meet her gaze instead of leering at her sexy tanned legs. The V-neck shirt she wore dipped low and showed a lot of cleavage. Too much cleavage for sanity's sake.

She glanced up, caught him staring, and stretched her legs out. "What did Brian say?"

"Not much." His chest rose and fell on a deep breath. "Hannah, we need to talk." His body remained tense as he moved to the smaller sofa facing her. Lowering himself to the seat, he leaned forward, his elbows resting on his knees, and forced the words out. "I haven't been entirely truthful with you."

She lifted her gaze to his. His heart skipped a beat, but he refused to cower again. "About what?"

"When Ellie hired me a few years ago…" He almost choked on the words.

She shifted the papers aside and drew her legs up beneath her so she could hug her knees. "Yeah?"

He reached up to grip the back of his neck. "She asked me to do more than a background check on you."

Zach pushed to his feet and began pacing. If he paced, he'd have an excuse not to look at her. Looking at her made this too damn hard. *Don't be such a coward, Collins. Own up.* He stopped directly in front of her. Met her gaze.

"Ellie also used me to mediate a deal with your ex-fiancé."

"A deal?" Hannah sat up straighter. "What kind of deal?"

Zach's voice was hesitant as he said, "She—*I*—paid him $50,000 to stay away from you."

# Chapter Fifteen

It took several seconds for Zach's words to process, and even then, Hannah had a hard time grasping their meaning.

*She—I—paid him $50,000 to stay away from you.*

Why? Why would Ellie have even wanted to do such a thing? Hannah stood, hoping some movement would clear the confusion from her brain. Eric had been a huge part of her life until—

She hugged herself and paced away from the sofa. Turning, she frowned at Zach. "Maybe you should back up and explain what the hell that means."

He did, explaining all that Ellie had hired him to do.

"She asked me to deliver an envelope to him. I had no idea what was in it, until I got curious and peeked inside."

Looking away, Hannah nodded. Why did she have to relive this now? "You talked to him?"

"Not really. Ellie asked me to wait for an answer to whatever was in that envelope. He accepted and…I left." His expression suggested there was more to that story, but he didn't elaborate. "I can only assume that he left you."

"Yes," she hissed between clenched teeth, embarrassed by the memory. She closed her eyes. "On our wedding day."

Zach swore something incoherent. "Please tell me you're joking, Hannah."

If only.

She felt a little nauseated at the memory, remembering how she'd been squeezing into her wedding dress at the church when Eric's best man had knocked on the door to hand Sarah a note. Eric hadn't had the guts to tell her in person he had gotten cold feet and changed his mind.

Three scribbled lines of apology with no real explanation, that's all he'd given her.

That had been such a humiliating time in her life, although it hadn't taken long for anger to overtake embarrassment. For days she'd wallowed in heartbreak and despair, blaming herself, wondering why she hadn't been good enough to be Eric's wife.

One day she'd looked at herself in the mirror and hadn't recognized the desolate woman staring back at her. She'd hated it so much, hated feeling like she was throwing away everything she'd worked so hard to accomplish in her life, that she'd kicked herself in the rear.

The memory made Hannah feel better. It hadn't taken long for Hannah to feel nothing but blinding hot rage toward Eric too.

Oh, no, but she'd surpassed rage when the credit card bills showing her deposits for the caterer, florist, musicians and photographer had arrived. She hadn't necessarily wanted a large wedding, but Eric had persuaded her that his family would expect it.

She'd called and asked him to split the debt—which had disgusted Sarah, who'd felt he owed it all—but he'd been cold, blaming her for pressuring him into a marriage he'd never wanted. "You can afford it. I can't," he'd insisted. That had been so not true, it had made her laugh.

She'd pawned her engagement ring, using it to pay a small portion of what was owed.

She'd maxed out the rest of her savings to pay for the nearly forty-thousand dollars in wedding expenses Eric had made sure were in her name only. Credit cards. Why had she charged every-thing? Oh yeah. She'd had plenty of face-palming moments in those days. When Ellie had suggested Hannah work as her live-in caregiver to reduce her living expenses, it had been a godsend idea.

"Dear Lord," she whispered now. "Are you telling me that's why he stood me up at the altar? Because Ellie paid him to?"

"Hannah, I'm so sorry. When I offered him the deal, it was weeks before your wedding. The bastard had plenty of time to call it off before then. Shit."

"Tell me," she whispered, opening her eyes and looking at Zach. "What did you find on the background check for him? Why would she do that?"

She wanted, *needed*, to know.

Zach said nothing for several seconds, simply met her gaze with steely-eyed conviction. "Don't do this to yourself, Hannah."

She snorted. "He came to see me once, about eight months after the wedding. He apologized and wanted to know if I'd forgive him for what he'd done. I suppose he thought he could get more money out of the deal."

Zach's eyebrows furrowed. "I hope you told him to piss off."

"Of course I did." She crossed her arms. "Tell me the truth. What was inside the envelope? What did it say?"

"A letter from her attorney, stating that you had an admirer who wanted Meester out of your life. Ellie's name was never mentioned. Russell's name was on the check and the letterhead."

"That's all it took?" She shook her head, trying to focus on what he'd said earlier. "You still haven't told me why Ellie paid him to stay away from me."

His right hand curled into a fist, causing his arm muscles to flex. "I suspect she'd been planning to make you the benefactor of her will. She was a smart lady. Probably didn't take much to convince her he would have used you if he'd been in your life when you inherited her money."

So even then, Ellie had been protecting her assets. How could Hannah have not known how manipulative her elderly patient was? What else had Ellie done to meddle in Hannah's life?

"It might have been manipulative, but she did you a favor." Zach's voice was quiet. "Eric Meester was no prince. He was seeing a co-worker behind your back." He sighed. "I'm sorry, Hannah."

This was so humiliating. She tasted bile in her throat and prayed she wouldn't lose her breakfast in front of Zach. "I honestly thought he loved me." Tears welled in her eyes. She brushed them away as an epiphany overcame her. Her pride felt more wounded than her heart now. The blinding hot anger she'd suppressed for years bubbled in her gut like a poison, claiming a new target. "And Ellie. How could she do that me? What kind of person was she? I didn't know her at all."

Zach swore and moved closer, but she edged away from him. If he touched her, she might fall apart or lash out at him, and she didn't want him to see her that way. She was stronger than this.

He wasn't making it easy on her. He followed until she had no escape between his body and the wall. His arms were warm and strong as they curled around her and drew her close. She had no choice but to bury her face in his shoulder and lean into him.

"I'm sorry, Hannah. I'll understand if you hate me for not telling you the truth."

She sniffed. "Why would I hate *you*?"

"Because I played a part in what Ellie did. Because I didn't tell you sooner."

She snorted into his neck. "Don't be stupid, Zach. You were only doing your job. Besides, I didn't know you then."

"You don't know everything about me now. I don't want you to ever think I'm like him. That I value money more than you."

She didn't know everything about him? Geez. How much more

was there? Every muscle that had relaxed tensed again in anticipation of the worst. His arms tightened around her, refusing to let her pull away.

"I don't want there to be secrets between us." He pushed back and grasped her face with fingers that trembled. He took a deep breath. "I understand what Ellie saw in you, because I see it too. A woman who cares more for others than herself. A beautiful, beautiful woman, inside and out."

Tiny thrills of happiness began to battle the sadness that had hijacked her emotions. What was he saying?

His eyes were dark, concerned, his expression serious as he searched her face. "When you walked into my office last week, I didn't know how to react. I thought you'd come to sue me for my involvement in what had happened. A smarter man would have turned you away, but I couldn't."

"Why not?" She sniffed and wiped her tears with the back of her fingers.

"Honestly? The firm needs the money. We've barely been making the bills these last few months."

Money. Of course. She should have known. She tried to move away, but he held her still.

"That wasn't the only reason. I didn't refer you to someone else because I wanted to keep you safe. I felt like I owed it to you. You deserve a hell of a lot better than me, and you probably won't want anything to do with me after you know the truth about what kind of man I am. I want you to know everything, but—" He swallowed. "I'm falling for you. I wish I weren't because it's a complication I don't need right now, but there it is. That's the truth."

Hannah gasped and reached to clasp his hands. Falling? As in, he was falling in love with her? "Really?" Hope surged in her chest again, chasing away the hurt and anger that had threatened to consume her.

His eyes were intense, dark. "Really."

The sound of something vibrating against wood was followed by loud chimes. Zach blinked and released her, and she fell against the wall for support as she watched him retrieve his phone from the table.

He turned and met her eyes as he barked his name in greeting. The conversation was short and mostly one sided.

Zach said a few more words and disconnected the call. He never took his eyes from hers.

"That was Kellan. The man who murdered Ellie's husband—" He cut himself short.

Hannah moved closer. When he looked away, she grabbed his arm and demanded, "What about him?"

"He was released from prison three months ago."

"Seriously?"

He nodded. Excitement radiated from his eyes.

"You can't think he's responsible for this. Zach, he'd be in his eighties now. How could he—?"

"I don't know, dammit, but it's the best lead we have." He moved away and shuffled some folders on the table, their previous conversation shuffled away along with them. "Probably has an accomplice. I don't know, Hannah, but this feels right. Feels like we're finally putting the pieces together."

It made sense, in a way. Roglitz had been in love with Ellie, and the way he saw it, she'd betrayed him by helping the police put him away. Hannah's mind raced, trying to finish connecting the pieces of the puzzle.

Ellie.

Would Hannah ever be able to forgive her late friend for manipulating her so extensively? In many ways, Ellie's betrayal felt worse than Eric's. She'd loved the older woman like the grandmother she'd never had, only to discover now the woman had been a stranger to her. A jewel thief. A con artist. A master manipulator. Three things she was finding hard to forgive.

And Hannah was still paying a price for caring for the woman.

"That man. Roglitz." She sank onto the sofa, because her knees were suddenly jelly. "Do you think he'll try to rob the bank to get the diamond?"

"I think that's their plan." His eyes darkened and his shoulders tensed. "I think they want to use you to get inside the vault."

A chill crept up Hannah's arms, so she rubbed some warmth back into them. This man who was terrorizing her was an experienced killer and international jewel thief. He would have no qualms about killing her when he'd gotten what he wanted.

It was too much. All of this was too much.

"Hannah, you're safe. I'm not letting anything happen to you."

She nodded, but how could he make such a promise? Life was too unpredictable. *People* were too unpredictable.

"Zach, if something does happen, I want you to promise me something."

"Dammit, Hannah."

"Make sure Abbott and Costello find a good home. Together. I don't want them separated."

He swore again, harsher, and sat beside her. Twining the fingers of his right hand with hers, he squeezed. "Nothing. Is. Going. To. Happen. To. You." He bit out each word on a whisper. His other hand gripped the back of her neck and pulled her closer, until their foreheads touched. "I promise."

He'd said he didn't deserve her. Why did he think that? He made her feel safe. He made her feel calm. She should ask him what he meant, but right now, she didn't want to hear it. Maybe she never did. She didn't want to find out her ridiculously bad judge of character included him, too.

Hannah wasn't above seizing an opportunity when she saw one.

Her free fingers gathered his shirt tight and teased the bare skin it exposed above his belt. He was so warm and alive. His skin was so taut. So masculine. And he'd said he was falling in love with her.

"Hannah," he groaned and tried to pull away.

Her lips sought his and found their target with little effort. He kissed her back softly at first, then with a hunger that stole her breath. He slid his arms around her, crushing her to his chest as his tongue teased her lips apart and demanded entry.

Bloody hell, he was a good kisser.

She melted against him and offered no resistance when he scooped her up and carried her into the bedroom, teasing delicious kisses across her face as he walked. He hesitated before lowering her to her feet.

"Are you sure this is what you want?"

"This is definitely what I want. This is what I *need*, Zach. Right now. Please." She kissed the worried line at the edge of his mouth as her hands tugged at his belt. "We can talk later, or not. I don't care."

At that reminder, he hesitated, so she grabbed his face and hauled him down to her. "Zach, please."

He released her so that she slid down his body, but she never took her fingers off his belt. With a tug, she tossed it and traced the line of his zipper with her fingertips. His length was hard and bulging against the denim of his jeans. Poor baby. She'd have to see what she could do to help relieve him of that pressure.

Taking a deep breath, he grabbed the hem of her shirt and jerked it over her head, forcing her hands away from him. With a growl, he kissed her again, working quickly to free her of the rest of her clothes as he moved her backward until her legs met the bed. Naked, she tumbled against the mattress, laughing softly as she watched him toss his shirt aside and tug off his shoes and socks.

Oh my, but he was cut. She couldn't wait to trace the contours of his muscled chest with her fingers. He dropped onto the bed, settling himself between her legs. His hands curled around the back of her thighs, lifting them around his jeans-clad legs. "You're so hot," he whispered in her ear, nipping her lobe gently.

She trembled beneath him and slid her arms around his neck. "You have too many clothes on." She struggled to catch her breath. Sweet heavens, she was practically panting with anticipation.

"Patience." He murmured the word against her mouth as he ground his hips against her, wringing a moan from deep within her. She squirmed beneath him as he licked a trail down her neck to her breast, nipping her nipple and then lapping it with his tongue over and over again.

Her hands slid between them, desperate for more, wanting him inside her. Now. Fast and hard. They could do slow and sweet later. She didn't care. She tugged the button free, released his zipper and slid a hand inside, gasping when she felt his hot erection through his briefs. Oh, yes, he was a big boy, wasn't he? She licked her lips at that revelation as her fingers explored the shape of him.

"Hannah." He groaned before claiming her mouth again, desperate, hungry. He moved away long enough to rid himself of his clothes, and Hannah had a moment of clarity when he ripped open a packet with his teeth and crawled between her legs again, lifting one over his shoulder and trailing kisses along her inner thigh as he inched closer to where she wanted him to be. She was so wild for him, she'd forgotten about protection. She moaned and fell back, lifting her hips in desperation for more.

They both groaned when he entered her body, taking his time as he stroked her slowly, pulling all the way out before sliding in again, oh, so slowly.

"So tight." His eyes were shut as he maintained a steady pace.

Hannah whimpered, arching her back, trying to urge him to move faster, harder. His hands tightened their grip around her thighs, lifting her leg over his hip so he could thrust deeper. He kissed her, sliding his tongue between her lips and making her moan. His pace quickened, and her heart hammered as she teetered on the edge of orgasm. He slipped a hand between them, teasing her clit as he stroked into her, and she came loudly, delighting as her release tipped him over the edge too, loving the way he moaned into her neck as he bucked against her.

He rolled them onto their sides, keeping himself inside her, lifting her leg over his hip and kissing her so sweetly she felt tears of joy threaten to spill free.

"I feel good inside you." He nuzzled her neck. "I don't want to leave."

"Then don't."

"Mmmm." He shifted, and she could feel him growing hard again. "You okay?"

Smiling, she squeezed him with her muscles and felt him twitch inside her. "Oh yeah. I'll be even better when we do that again."

He groaned. "Woman, you're insatiable. Give me a few minutes. Damn, you're so hot."

"Hot as in temperature, or hot as in—?" She squeezed him again, felt him harden, and loved it when he groaned and ground against her.

"Every way imaginable." He licked the shell of her ear as he pressed her back against the mattress. "You're incredible."

Oh my, she was panting again and he wasn't even moving yet. She wound her arms around his neck and pulled him closer. Licking his bottom lip, she murmured, "By the way, I'm pretty sure I'm in love with you." Tangling her fingers in his hair, she pulled his mouth back to hers.

They could talk later.

# Chapter Sixteen

*Um, man. Hello?*

A loud whiney sound pierced Zach's contented dream-like state, and he slapped a hand toward the nightstand to mute the annoying alarm. Just a few more minutes. He could sleep for just a few more.

The whining grew louder.

*Man, I have to peeeee. Please take me to pee.*

More whining.

Zach sat straight up and felt the weight of another body shift away from him. A feminine grumble was the only sound Hannah made as she burrowed deeper into her pillow. She was barely covered by a sheet, and her naked back and thigh reminded him that he, too, wasn't wearing a stitch of clothing.

He'd done it. He'd slept with her.

Zach ran a hand over his face, blinking the sleep from his eyes. Glancing down, he saw Costello looking up with an eager gaze as the dog whined and pawed at the side of the bed. As soon as Zach made eye contact with him, the mutt's tail started slamming a beat against the hardwood floor.

*Pleeaaase!*

"Alright, buddy, hold on." Zach slid his legs over the side of the bed and looked around for his jeans. The dog was sitting on them and bounced away as soon as Zach stood.

*We're going to peeeeee! And then can we eat? Can we eat after we pee, man? Can we? Ohhhh, we were supposed to eat an hour ago. I'm sooooo hungry. And I have to peeeee. This is a nightmare!*

Zach snickered as he put his pants on and followed the excited dog to the back door. Slipping the leash on the mutt, he padded outside and saw that the sun was still bright in the sky. How long had they been asleep? A few hours?

*Okay, let's eat.* Costello turned and bounded back toward the house a minute or two later, practically dragging Zach behind him.

Zach was pretty sure he knew the animals' feeding schedule by now, so he dug around the boxes until he found their late lunch and poured them into bowls without disturbing Hannah. Abbott sprang out of somewhere unknown and darted toward the foul-smelling canned food Zach dished out. Geez, it reeked.

*Mmmmm, mmmm, you're not so bad,* the cat thought as he gobbled the treat. *I could learn to like this guy. This. Is. So. Good.*

When he returned to the bedroom, Hannah was sprawled out on her stomach on the bed. She looked sexy as hell tangled up in the sheets, with her dark long hair tousled across the pillow.

He loved this woman. How had that happened? What the hell was he gonna do about it?

He stretched out beside her and reached over to push her hair away from her eyes. Murmuring, she nuzzled into his hand. Her eyes blinked open, and her sigh warmed his fingers.

"Hi," she said sleepily.

"Hi." He couldn't keep the grin off his face. "Have a nice nap?"

"Mmmm-hmmm." Her fingers slid out from beneath the pillow and explored the muscles above his jeans. "Why are you dressed?"

"Your dog had to pee."

Her eyes widened and she sat up, clutching the sheet to her chest. "Oh no, what time is it? I should have already fed the boys."

He stilled her movement. "Relax. I took care of it."

"You did?" She sank back against the pillow. "Thanks." Her eyes lit up with humor as she stared at him. "Sir, are you smirking at me?"

"Damn straight." He propped his head on his hand and looked at her. "I'm in bed with a hot woman, and she's naked. I'm a guy. Of course I'm smirking."

She tucked the hair behind her ear. "What am I gonna do with you?"

He wiggled his eyebrows. "Taking suggestions?"

She giggled, and he loved that sound. He leaned over and kissed her.

Her lips clung to his as her fingers speared into his hair, and a certain part of his body stirred. He pulled away.

"I'm breaking all my rules with you."

"And that's a problem, why?" She nipped at his bottom lip, and he groaned, sliding further away from her.

"I'm supposed to be protecting you."

She relaxed against the pillow, devouring him with her eyes. "You can protect my body anytime you want, Mr. Collins."

She was killing him here. Shaking his head, he grabbed his shirt off the floor and tugged it on. "I need to check in and see if anyone has made any headway on your case. No more distractions." He watched the disappointment flitter across her face. "For a while, anyway."

She pretended to pout. "Will you at least move into the bedroom with me?"

She was still flirting, but he heard the vulnerability in her voice too. "I insist on it, Miss Dawson. For your protection, of course."

Her smile could have lit up the room. "Of course."

"Get dressed and stop distracting me, woman. I wanna get this case solved."

"Bossy," she grumbled, but she was smiling as she slid out of bed and picked up her clothes.

Zach went in search of his phone and grimaced when he saw he had three missed calls—one from E.J. and two from Kellan. He rang Kellan back first.

"Where the hell have you been? I'm headed there to check on you."

Zach blew out a breath. "I fell asleep. Alarm didn't go off." Hannah padded past him barefoot in those shorts and that tight shirt again, turning his mind to mush. Man, he had it bad. He must have been drooling because she rolled her eyes at him and moved into the kitchen. When she stretched up to look into a cabinet, exposing a tiny strip of bare skin at her waist, he forced himself to turn away.

"How far away are you?"

"Not too far. What's the word?"

"Wilma," Zach murmured, reciting the code they had agreed upon with Hannah for "everything is fine." "Wally" was their code for "I'm in trouble and can't talk on the phone."

"Alright. I'm turning around."

Good. They couldn't have E.J. or Kellan or anyone connected with the office coming here for risk they were being watched or followed to get to Hannah. That had been their agreement.

He swore, cursing himself for compromising her location. Not to mention making his partners worry.

After Zach ended the call, Hannah slid her arms around his waist from behind and kissed his shoulder, causing some of the tension Kellan's words had triggered to melt away. "Everything okay?"

"Yeah, fine." He turned and slid an arm around her. "Interpol is sending someone to look at the jewel. We'll have to go back Tuesday to meet with them for that. It's almost over, Hannah."

She lowered her head to his chest and nodded.

He used his fingers to lift her gaze back up to his. "What's wrong?"

A sad expression played at the corners of her mouth. "I only worry what it will do to Ellie's reputation. As mad as I am at her right now, I don't want it to come out in the press that she was the Fox. She worked so hard to put that all behind her and start over."

He'd assumed she was worried about her inheritance being affected. He should have known. "Want some good news?"

She pretended to consider it. "If you insist."

He smiled. "Statute of limitations has run out. Ellie's money is safe. Even if Interpol wanted to pursue charges against Ellie or try to reclaim any of her money, they wouldn't be able to."

She blinked. "So Ellie's name won't be dragged through the mud?"

"Not likely." He kissed her softly and then tugged her toward the kitchen. "Come on. Let's eat. For some reason, I'm famished."

He did everything he could to distract himself from his internal promise to tell her about his psychic abilities. She was so happy— hell, he was so happy, he didn't want to ruin the moment.

Spending time, doing simple things like chatting about classic cinema over deviled egg sandwiches with Hannah felt like a novelty to Zach. Had he ever been so easy around another woman? He couldn't remember it if he had. They tidied up the kitchen then Zach checked his email account while she called Sarah for her promised daily check-in. Afterward, they settled on the sofa together to go through more of Ellie's papers. She snuggled into the curve of his arm as if her body was made for his. He loved the feeling. Loved having her so close to him.

"Zach?"

"Hmm?" He was skimming a copy of the deed to Ellie's former house.

She gave up all pretense of studying the documents she held and slid her arms around his waist. "Why did you say I deserved better than you? Cause I gotta tell you, you're pretty darn good."

Damn. He'd wanted her to forget. He'd wanted more time with her.

He'd have rather chewed nails than talk about this now. She couldn't hide that glimpse of vulnerability from her beautiful green eyes. That was his undoing. "I haven't always been the best person, Hannah. My past is—" How did he say this?

She lowered her head to his chest and tightened her arms around him. "Everyone has a past, Zach. I care about who you are now."

God, he hoped so.

"Tell me about your brother." Her voice was soft. "What happened to him?"

His body tensed. How the hell did she know about Dylan?

She turned her face up to his again and whispered, "You showed me his picture when you were out of it—after you got hit by that tranquilizer."

He wondered again what else he'd said or done. "I don't know what happened to him."

Her eyebrows furrowed.

"I haven't seen him in years." He sighed, thinking *this is it. This is where it ends, after she finds out what a bastard I am.* "I ran away from home when I was seventeen—a few months shy of graduation."

Her breathing quickened. He looked away. "My mom married a real asshole when I was fourteen. He had it out for me from day one, knocked me around, wouldn't get off my back. My mom either didn't notice or didn't care. He never touched Dylan. Only me."

"I'm so sorry." She slid a reassuring hand across his chest, resting it over his heart.

Her support was like a balm. The rest of the story spilled out without any more encouragement.

"One day my mom gave me her keys and asked me to pick

Dylan up from baseball practice. We were sitting at a red light when a truck rear-ended us. Nothing major. We weren't hurt, but it left a dent in the bumper. When the asshole saw it, he beat me until I could hardly walk. Told me I had wrecked the car on purpose for attention, as if anyone would be so stupid. That was it. I packed my bags, stole some money from my mom's purse. Never looked back."

Her arms tightened around him again. "Why didn't you report him?"

"Didn't see a point." He rested his chin on the top of her head. "He never messed with Dylan. He *loved* Dylan. He never touched my mom. Guess I figured no one cared, if she didn't." He sighed. "I'd always planned to go back for Dylan, but things weren't that easy."

She lifted her head and looked at him. Her eyes were wide. "You kept in touch with him though. Didn't you?"

He'd sent his kid brother a postcard when he'd made it to San Diego for basic training. He'd wanted Dylan to know he'd joined the Marines. Wanted him to be proud his big brother was trying to do something noble.

Dylan never responded. He had no idea if his brother had gotten the card or not.

"After I got discharged from the Marines, I tried calling him, just to let him know I was okay. He wasn't home. Ray answered, so I hung up."

"You didn't try again?"

Sure, he had. "After I became a P.I. in L.A., I tried again. I thought he might want to come visit."

Her arms tightened around his middle. "Did he?"

"I never got the chance to ask."

"You said you were working as a P.I. when a producer offered you the TV show, right?" Hannah's voice was on the teasing side of curious.

His mind went back to those days. Brian had been shipped to Camp Pendleton for more training and was headed to Afghanistan after that. Zach had been alone. Lonely. Desperate. How the hell he hadn't fallen into depression, he had no idea. His arm injury had killed his chances of being a cop like his father, but one day, he'd seen an employment ad in the classifieds for a well-known private investigations agency in Los Angeles. He couldn't be a cop. He couldn't be a Marine. Maybe he could go another route?

He'd been good at it, too. So good, his boss had taken a chance and given him some high profile cases within his first year.

Then, TV producer Connor Pruitt had read a report Zach had typed up—Pruitt's intern had not only been selling spoilers to a magazine, the young woman had also been stealing props from the set and selling them on an Internet auction site—and asked, "How'd you figure this out so fast?"

Zach had shrugged. Nothing major. He'd made some calls. Followed the girl to the post office a few more times than seemed normal. Played a hunch.

"You ever do any acting?" Connor had studied Zach's features closer. "You've got a great look. You know that? I might could use you for a project I'm doing."

The last thing Zach had wanted was to fall into Hollywood's traps. "Not an actor. Sorry."

But the guy had called again, a few days later. He'd explained that the show was meant to be a reality show featuring a real private investigator. "You don't have to be an actor. Could be a lot of money in it for you. Great exposure. Sure you're not interested?"

Zach had turned him down again. He didn't have much, but he'd be damned if he'd lose his integrity.

"Why don't you think about it and give me a call if you change your mind," the producer had persuaded. "I have a good feeling about you, kid. An I-could-make-a-shitload-of-money good feeling."

Him, a TV star? Ridiculous thought. Still, Zach'd wondered if his brother would get a kick out of the idea. Figured it would be a fun ice-breaker.

He'd tried to call Dylan again and froze when his mother had answered instead. He'd finally managed a strangled, "Hi, mama." She'd cried and begged him to come home. He'd been tempted, but—"Is Ray still there?"

"Yes. Zach, please give him another chance." She'd sobbed. "I lost my job. We're about to lose the house. I can't kick him out. We need him too much. Oh, Zach, I wish you would come home!"

Those words had weighed heavy on his conscience for days, until he'd finally called Connor Pruitt and asked if the producer was still interested.

"Sure, kid, but my partner wants us to find a psychic detective now. I don't suppose you're psychic?"

He'd actually thought of saying he was. He wanted, *needed*, the money to keep a roof over his family's head. Maybe then his mother would ditch the loser and they could be a family again.

He'd made some asinine joke about psychics that had left the producer guffawing.

"Tell you what, Zach. You come down to our office tomorrow, and we'll see what happens."

Hannah lifted her hand and touched his face, bringing him back to the present and reminding him of her question. How much of this did he want her to know?

"Your show?" Her gaze radiated concern.

"Yeah, a producer was a client." He forced a smile he didn't feel. "Sometimes when you're young you make really bad decisions. I needed the money, so I signed on to do the show." Connor's partner had liked him enough to put Zach through a series of tests to judge whether or not he could pass for psychic.

"If I didn't know better, I'd say you really had some abilities." Connor had chortled after slapping Zach on the shoulder and congratulating him on winning the role, because that's exactly how Zach had viewed it. As a role.

He'd sent his mother enough money to pay off the mortgage. When she'd called to thank him, he'd said, "You don't need Ray anymore, mama. I'll take care of you and Dylan."

His mother's hesitation had hurt almost as much as one of his stepfather's beatings. "Zach, he's a different man now. I…I love him. I don't want him to leave. Please—"

He'd slammed down the phone and never spoken to her again. Every few months he sent her some money to put toward a college fund for Dylan, but he never answered her calls. Never responded to her letters.

She'd made her choice, and he'd made his.

Regret and remorse settled in the pit of his stomach, sending ripples of nausea through him. He supposed if he had to do it all again, he'd do the same—but he wouldn't have let pride cut his mother out of his life. Now that she was gone…god, he felt sick.

Abbott jumped onto the sofa and plopped against Zach's hip. Zach eyed the cat warily.

*This doesn't mean I like you. It just means I'm cold, and you're warm. Get over it.* The cat stretched out against his leg and went to sleep after delivering that haughty remark.

Costello stirred against Zach's feet, and Zach had to admit, he felt cocooned by the woman and her pets. It was a comforting feeling, but he was supposed to be the one protecting, cocooning, her.

Alexandra King's words from their encounter haunted him. They'd supposedly been his mother's words. Hell, it was probably true, all of it, all of what she'd told him. Alexandra had known things …

*Why haven't you contacted Dylan?*

The only time he'd reached Dylan on the phone, his brother had slammed the phone down as soon as Zach had said "Hey, kiddo."

Why hadn't he tried again? *Because you know he'll want nothing to do with you. Because you abandoned him. Because you're a coward.* He knew it was wrong, but he didn't want Hannah to know how big of a coward he still was.

Damn Alexandra for reminding him of it.

"I'm still listening," Hannah reminded him quietly. "Why don't you like to talk about it?" He felt her muscles tense beneath his touch. "Sorry. Forget I said that. You don't have to tell me."

His mind was still with Alexandra back at the Marriot Marquis. Absently, he said, "It's all in the past, Hannah. I just want to forget about it."

*Why haven't you contacted Dylan?*

How had Alexandra known about his brother? She had to be the real deal, as he'd suspected her of being all along.

His mind caught an idea. Ran with it.

Hannah was oblivious to his inner turmoil. "Okay. Tell me about your psychic abilities. When did—?"

He leaned forward, interrupting her question, grateful to have a reason to distract her. Maybe he didn't have to tell her he'd been pretending to be psychic when he met her and that she'd hired him on false pretenses. He'd do everything he could to make it up to her.

He gently shifted her away from him. Gripping her shoulders and meeting her gaze, he asked, "Who is the one person who could answer all of our questions about Ellie's past, and probably about Roglitz too?"

Hannah shook her head, confused. "I don't know. No one, I guess."

"Ellie."

"*Ellie?*"

He nodded. "I think we should try and talk to Ellie."

# Chapter Seventeen

The gorgeous blonde standing on the other side of the door looked vaguely familiar to Hannah, but Zach had already explained she'd been featured on his show. Not that she looked like much of a star, dressed in leggings and a baggy t-shirt with her hair pulled back into a girlish ponytail. Even in the glow of the porch light, she looked beautiful and natural without any makeup.

Hannah ran a hand over her own hair, hoping she looked half as presentable but feeling anything but.

"Thank God you came," Zach said in a rush, as if he was thrilled to see the other woman.

Hannah tried not to be jealous, much, and it helped when Zach reached across the threshold to—what?—hug Alexandra King in greeting and she immediately shoved him away.

"Try that again, Collins, and you'll be walking funny for a week." She held her hand up in warning.

"I was only going to look behind you and make sure you weren't followed. Geez." He shifted her aside and stepped toward her car.

The blonde sighed and held her hand out to Hannah. They'd finished introductions by the time Zach returned. "Why would I have been followed? What are you mixed up in, Collins?"

"Nothing." He directed the other woman farther into the entryway and shut the door behind them. He stepped behind

Hannah and wrapped his arms around her middle. "I didn't see any headlights," he whispered for her benefit.

Alexandra's eyebrows shot up. "Nothing, huh?" She shook her head and stepped into the living room. Costello whined for the woman's attention, and she looked happy to oblige. "You caught me in time. My flight leaves in the morning. What's so urgent that we couldn't do this on the phone?"

"I need your help."

"No kidding."

"I need you to contact someone."

The blonde pursed her lips. "Zach." She sighed, but her eyes softened. "Who is it? You want me to talk to your mom some more?"

Zach's arms tightened and his voice was firm as he said, "No." He moved around Hannah, nudging her behind him with one arm, and she felt cold without his body against hers. "A friend of Hannah's."

His mom? Zach hadn't mentioned that his mother had died, but she'd gotten the feeling he'd left a lot out of his story earlier. She'd hoped he trusted her enough to share it all, but she could see they still had a lot of work to do in that matter.

She needed to be patient, even if it nearly killed her.

How could he have thought she'd hate him once she'd learned of his past? He'd been young. Stuff happened. She admired the honorable man he was now. Didn't he understand that?

Now that she'd seen a glimpse of the man behind the façade Zach liked to present, she felt confident she could handle the rest. He, apparently, also had a few more things to learn about her.

"Ellie was like a grandmother to me," Hannah said, moving closer to the other woman. "She passed recently, and there are some things I really need to know. Please, can you help? I'm willing to pay whatever your rate is."

She held her breath, waiting for Alexandra's response. Would she ever get used to being able to tell people "I can pay you whatever you charge" without her mind racing to check the balance in her mental checkbook? She doubted it.

Nodding after a brief hesitation, Alexandra took a deep breath and threw up her hands. She sounded much kinder when she said, "Let's do this then. You do want to do this now?"

"Please," Hannah agreed.

Zach was standing quietly with his hands on his hips, intently focused on Alexandra as she gingerly stepped around Costello to find a seat on the sofa. Abbott decided to come out from his evening sleeping spot, his tail twitching straight in the air as he approached their visitor.

"These were her animals," Alexandra declared matter-of-factly, rubbing Costello with one hand while stroking Abbott with the other.

Hannah heard Zach swallow, even as she thought, *holy crap, how did she know that?*

Alexandra peeked up from beneath her lashes as she bent to pet the cat generously. "She visits with them. At least, there's a lady here now. She told me they were hers. 'They're my animals, my babies,' she's saying. It's funny because I see her younger with lots of animals around her, too. She always had at least one pet."

Hannah's eyes darted around the room. She saw nothing and heard no one. Alexandra sat back and patted the cushion beside her. Not bothering to glance at Zach, Hannah accepted the invitation, relieved when the cat decided to jump into her lap, too. Abbott's presence eased her nerves as she caressed his silky fur and she waited for—well, she had no idea. The other woman bit her lip and closed her eyes. Every so often, Alexandra would give a little shake of her head and murmur something unintelligible, as if she were confused and speaking gibberish.

"She wants me to thank you." Alexandra's warm hand settled on Hannah's knee, but she didn't open her eyes. "She says you took care of her. She thought of you as the daughter she never had but always wanted. She's saying she's sorry over and over again. I feel so much remorse from her for some reason. It's so strong it's almost choking me."

*Oh, Ellie.* Hannah fought the tears that burned her eyes.

Alexandra whispered more gibberish. "Okay, she's showing me something. I think it's a bag, but there's something in the bag. It's like a rock, but it's not? I don't know what she's showing me. Hmmm."

"It's probably a—" Hannah began to say. But Alexandra's fingernails dug into her skin, and the other woman murmured, "I don't want to know details. Please, just listen now." Her fingers loosened their grip.

The sofa cushion sank to Hannah's left as Zach lowered himself to the small space on the other side of her, settling his hand on her back as he leaned forward to listen.

Alexandra waved a hand in front of her chest. "She's talking so fast. It's like she feels a sense of urgency about something—like she's worried about something."

"Can we ask her specific questions?" Zach asked.

Alexandra gave a quick shake of her head and squeezed her eyes even tighter. "She's showing me a picture of a man. He's not the one—that's what she's saying now. I think she's trying to tell me he's innocent of something."

"What does the man look like?" Hannah asked softly.

"Glasses. Short hair. Well-dressed."

Hannah searched for Zach's eyes. Was Alexandra describing Roglitz? It was a close enough description of the picture they'd seen of him in Ellie's things.

"Ask her who's responsible for what's been happening," Zach

demanded in a quiet, but firm voice.

Alexandra's lips thinned. Her eyes opened and she looked toward the ceiling. "A younger man. Someone she doesn't know." Alexandra moved to her feet and began pacing. "She's getting kind of pushy now. She keeps getting in my face. I don't like it." She rubbed her palms against the front of her thighs and turned suddenly in the opposite direction. "I think she was used to always getting her way. Did she have a lot of money? I'm getting the impression she did."

"Yes, she did." Hannah sat forward and brought her thumb to her lips. Her nail felt thick as her teeth nibbled it. Damn. She hadn't bitten her nails in years. She jerked her hand away, slid it between her thighs, and sighed.

What was this accomplishing, anyway?

"More than one person, she's saying. She wants Hannah to be careful." Alexandra stopped moving and speared Hannah with a dark look. "You know one of them."

"What?" Hannah barely managed to form the question.

Alexandra aimed a quick look toward the man at her side. "Your mom is here too, Zach."

The sofa squeaked as he shifted away from Hannah. She risked a glance at his face—which had suddenly paled.

"Right now, we need to communicate with Ellie." His knuckles popped as he tightened his fingers into a fist. "Who does Hannah know? Ask her for a name."

"I'll try, but your mother wants to talk to you. She's pushing Ellie away." Alexandra waved a hand in front of her face. "The younger man—he has lots of faces, she's saying. He's dangerous. Very dangerous. He killed Rollins, she says. No, not Rollins. Ral—" She shook her head. "Something with an R. A name. She knew him."

Alexandra's comments were starting to make no sense to

Hannah. She looked at Zach to gauge his comprehension.

"Roglitz," he murmured, and Alexandra stopped pacing and nodded.

"Yes. She's saying yes. Roglitz is the man he killed. He's dangerous." Alexandra closed her eyes and squeezed them as if in pain. "Zach, your brother needs you. Your mother is asking you to please go to him."

Zach sprang to his feet. "Tell her to leave me the hell alone." He grabbed Alexandra by the shoulders and forced her to look at him. "Focus on Ellie, dammit."

Alexandra gasped and shoved him away. "Back off, Collins." She shook her head, looking dazed. "I think we're done here."

"Like hell we are." He reached for her again, and Hannah moved to her feet, in case she needed to put herself between them. "Zach!"

He stilled, but his chest rose and fell with harsh breaths. So did Alexandra's.

"I'm sorry," he said. "I didn't mean to—"

Alexandra stuck a hand in the air. "Save it. It's okay. I want to get out of here. I feel stifled. It's too much."

Hannah placed a hand on the other woman's arm and tried not to take offense when she flinched. "I'm really sorry. Thank you. If you wait one minute, I'll go get some money to pay you."

Alexandra murmured an amount then nodded and stepped back, hugging herself with her arms. Hannah narrowed her eyes in warning at Zach, silently telling him to back off the other woman, and hurried to find her purse in the other room.

Zach's head felt tight with the pressure of too much anger. *Calm down. Compose yourself. You're scaring Hannah—and yourself.*

He took a deep breath, anchoring his hands on his hips so he didn't punch something the way he wanted to.

Even in death, it seemed, his mother riled him to emotion like no other.

"*Zach, your brother needs you. Your mother is asking you to please go to him.*"

Was Dylan in some kind of danger, or was their mother only trying to reconcile them from the grave? Hell if he knew, but he couldn't think about it. He *wouldn't* think about it. Hannah was his priority right now, and until she was out of danger, Dylan would have to wait.

"Why are you so angry at her?"

Alexandra's whispered question took him by surprise.

"She really loves you, Zach. I can feel it. Whatever she did to you, you need to let it go. For your sake—and hers." With a snort, she added, "And mine, apparently."

"I know." He crossed his arms and glanced to see what was keeping Hannah. She was still upstairs. Turning back, he shook his head. "I'm not angry at her. I'm pissed at myself. I'm sorry."

Alexandra's eyebrows shot up. "Yourself? Why?"

Again, he shook his head, not wanting to rehash his feelings with a woman he barely knew. It had been hard enough sharing even part of it with the woman he loved. He was done for the night.

She visibly relaxed. "Does it have anything to do with the whole psychic thing?"

"What?"

"I imagine it's messing with your brain, and your emotions." She shrugged. "You're a guy who's only been pretending to be psychic for, like, forever and now—"

"*What?*"

Alexandra's eyes went wide as she looked behind him. *Hannah.* Shit.

Zach squeezed his eyes shut, wishing he didn't understand what she'd overheard and assumed, but knowing his time had come to pay a long overdue bill to the karma department.

Opening his eyes, he met Alexandra's apologetic gaze and whispered, "It's okay." He turned and saw Hannah standing there, looking like she already had one foot out the door of their fragile relationship. Her eyes flashed with confusion, hurt and anger, but mostly hurt.

"You're not really psychic? You've been *lying* to me about that?" She moved her focus to Alexandra. "Are either of you? Have you been playing me?"

"No, Hannah." He moved toward her, but she jerked up a hand to ward him off. "You misunderstood."

She took a step back, away from him. "So you *are* psychic?" Her tone was skeptical.

Damn, this was so frustrating. How did he explain any of this? "Yes, but I wasn't—" He stopped himself, not certain what to say. Instead, he gestured to Alexandra. "She is the real deal. I promise."

Hannah darted a glance between the two of them, shaking her head. "There's nothing she said that you couldn't have told her beforehand." She touched her forehead. "I'm such an idiot. You followed me three years ago. You had lots of information to use to convince me you were psychic." She flapped the dollars in her other hand. "Is this why? Because of the money? What—you're a couple of con artists working together or something? Are you—" She swallowed. "Are you lovers too?"

"No!" His voice and Alexandra's answered in unison, and he wasn't sure which of them sounded more outraged by that idea.

The mobile phone on the table beside her began belting out a ringtone. She barely spared it a glance, but it was enough to give him an opening. Zach swore and moved fast, grabbing Hannah before she could get farther away from him. His hands cradled her precious face, forcing her to look at him. "I love you, Hannah. No matter what you believe, that is the truth."

He couldn't stand the overwhelming hurt he saw in her eyes.

She didn't move away. "Then explain to me what she meant." She seemed to relax some. "Please."

He gasped, not expecting her to be so willing to let him explain, and he knew by her reaction to his expression that he must have looked as guilty as hell again. "You heard her correctly." He nodded. "Until I started working this case, I didn't know I was psychic. I faked it. I was acting on the TV show. I was acting when you came into my office to hire me. I was—"

A tear slid down her cheek as she jerked away from him again. "You were *acting*?"

"Hannah—"

Her damn phone began belting out a ringtone again. Wiping her face, Hannah reached for it, glanced at the caller ID and turned away from him to answer. "Sarah," she said. After listening for a few seconds, she returned, "Okay. Hold on a minute."

Pressing the phone to her chest, she told him, "We'll talk about this when I get finished talking to my friend."

He watched, feeling gutted and helpless, as she disappeared into his room and shut the door. How was he going to dig himself out of this one?

"Hannah, please listen to me," Sarah said.

There was something about the sound of her best friend's voice that was off. Panicked, even. She'd asked Hannah if she was alone—and if she wasn't, to find privacy because it was "really, really important."

Hannah felt disoriented with racing thoughts—had she fallen for some elaborate con Zach and his associates had set up to get her money? She could have sworn he'd been sincere when he'd said he'd loved her, but she'd thought the same of Eric once. Her judgment was awful. She'd actually believed he was psychic, too.

She wanted to trust him, but…

But first, she had to find out what was so urgent with Sarah. Was it Sarah's mother? Had the last chemo treatment not gone well?

"I'm alone." She moved to the bed. "Sarah, what's wrong?"

There was the sound of muffled movement.

The voice of a man she didn't recognize greeted her. "Hello Hannah. How are you this evening?"

# Chapter Eighteen

"I'm sorry. Who is this?"

A lazy, menacing chuckle raised goosebumps along Hannah's arms. "I'm the man who has your little friend, and if you want to see her alive again, you'll do exactly as I tell you. Understand?"

Hannah's heart quickened its beat. "What?"

"Are you alone?"

"Yes. Where's Sarah. Who is this?"

"Do you know where Oakland Cemetery is?"

Instinct told her not to question him or argue. "I've heard of it. I've never been there."

"Find it," the voice growled. "Nine a.m. tomorrow. There will be a note with directions for you at the Bell Tower Ridge, at the observation point of Confederate Commander John B. Hood. Repeat it back to me."

She did. "How will I find it? I've never been there."

"You're a smart girl. You'll figure it out. Follow those directions if you want to save your friend." He paused and there was a whimpering sound in the distance. Was that Sarah crying? "Oh and Miss Dawson?"

"Yes."

"Come alone. Tell no one. I'll know if you're being shadowed. Understand?"

"Yes, but—"

"Nine o'clock. Don't be late."

"I want to talk to Sarah. Please."

Hearing no response, Hannah glanced at the phone. The call had already ended.

Someone had Sarah.

A wave of panic threatened Hannah's air supply, but she quelled it with deep breaths. What should she do? Should she risk telling someone? This was that awful scenario in books and movies where Hannah always wanted to scream "Don't listen to the kidnapper. Tell the freaking police, for Pete's sake!" because the characters on the page or screen always tried to handle it on their own with disastrous results.

Who could help her? Zach? She wasn't even certain at this point that he wasn't involved. A pang of hurt stabbed into her chest at that truth. She could call Detective Ryan, but the man had done nothing to instill confidence in her so far.

*Think, you idiot. Think.*

Who should she tell?

Maybe Sarah's brothers, get their input on what to do. And then what? The Taylor men would charge off, fueled by rage and emotion, without thinking of the consequences.

Bad idea.

Hannah lifted her phone with trembling hands to scroll through the contact list, desperate for someone, anyone, to call that she could trust with this. By the time she neared the Qs she wasn't even seeing the names anymore. The sinking realization that she had absolutely no one in her life to count on besides Sarah weighed down on her heart. How pathetic was she?

No.

She squared her shoulders as she concentrated on the contact list in her phone. She could count on herself, which meant she needed to make smart decisions. This was about more than her pride. This was about saving her best friend's life.

Finding the detective's name and number, she pressed Call.

She reached his voicemail, so she began by reminding him who she was. "I need your help. It's urgent. Please call me back immediately." She listed her number before hanging up.

Now she had to wait.

And figure out what to do about the man in the next room.

Abbott had had enough of being carried around and petted, and with a hiss and a swipe of his claw, let Zach know he wanted out of his hold—immediately. That, and his forceful *Put me down now, you idiot, or I'll kill you* did the trick.

Dammit.

Zach let the cat drop to the floor before he swung back toward the closed bedroom. It was well after midnight now, and Hannah still hadn't so much as peeked out the door. Alexandra had left hours ago, and Zach had been reciting in his mind ways to explain everything to Hannah to convince her he was a different man than he'd once been and she could trust him.

Metal jiggled, and he turned to see the bedroom door slowly open. Finally.

Hannah wouldn't meet his eyes when she stepped forward and into the living room. She bent and stroked Abbott's back when the cat brushed against her legs and gave Costello a ferocious head rub when the dog bounced over to where she stood.

"Have you taken him for a walk?"

That wasn't the first question he'd been expecting. "Yeah, not too long ago."

"A walk, or did you let him do a quick pee?" she asked doubtfully.

Dammit. She must have been listening to his movements, just as he'd been trying to listen to hers. She'd been quiet. The only sound he'd heard had been her hushed murmuring a couple of times, and he'd suspected she'd been talking to Sarah again.

"Will you take him for a longer walk please? I don't feel up to it."

Her polite coolness was almost worse than the hurt he'd seen in her expression earlier. Almost. He took a careful step toward her. "I will, but I'd like the chance to explain some things first."

She opened her mouth to speak and hesitated. She finally looked at him for the first time since entering the room. With dark and guarded eyes, she gave him a small nod and moved toward the sofa. "I suppose that's fair."

He followed her, perching onto the seat opposite her. *Here's your shot. Make it count, Collins.*

"A long time ago, I taught myself how to survive by being dishonest with people. I'm not proud of that, but it's part of a past I can't deny." She sat, arms crossed, without looking at him, so he could only hope she was actually listening to what he said. "I pretended to be psychic because I needed the money. My family's home was being foreclosed."

Her shocked gaze lifted to his, but she said nothing.

"I'm telling the truth." He reached for her hand, but she jerked it away. "When we started the agency, I wasn't above using my minor fame to establish the business. It was like a gimmick to let people think I was psychic. But I've never accepted a job from anyone expecting me to use my psychic abilities to solve a case. Never, Hannah."

Her eyebrows perked up. "Oh really?"

"Yes."

"Not true, Zach. You took my case. Mine." She bit the word out between clenched teeth.

Dammit. "Never *until* you—and if you remember, I tried hard to discourage you on that front. I don't recall you hiring me for my psychic abilities. I thought you hired me for protection."

"You pretended to know what Abbott and Costello are thinking. You lied to me, Zach—just like everyone else I've ever cared about, except Sarah." Her voice trembled a little at the end, and tears caused her expression to glaze over. She quickly wiped them away. Her voice was raw when she spoke. "I'm sorry. Lying to that extent is the one thing I can't forgive."

She still refused to look at him. Tough, cause he wasn't done yet. He slid forward until he was on the edge of his seat. "Remember how I got hit on the head at your house?"

Reluctantly, she nodded.

"I don't know what the hell happened to me after that, but since then, I *can* communicate with your animals. Hell, I'm hearing and feeling all kinds of things when I'm around different animals and people. I thought I was going crazy at first. Took me a while to figure out the thing I've been pretending to be for so long might not be so off base."

Her lips and brow turned downward. "You mean, suddenly you think you're psychic?" She shook her head. Her tone was harsh, but her beautiful face looked like it would crumble at any second. It broke his heart. "Nice try, Zach. I'm not buying it."

He swore and searched his mind for a way to convince her. "It's true. I called Alexandra for help because she's the only legit psychic I know. She helped me figure some things out."

"I'm sure." She snorted.

"Hannah, I barely know the woman, but I promise you we're not trying to scam you. None of us are."

One of her shoulders lifted in a weak shrug. "I'll admit, I can't figure out how you knew some things, but I'm sure I probably give away some info without realizing it. Everyone does, don't they? That's how you did the show?"

He sighed. "Yes, but—"

"You could've told me you weren't really psychic, Zach. It

wouldn't have mattered to me. I get that a lot of TV shows are staged. We could have laughed about it. I probably would have still hired you because of your agency's reputation." She tore her gaze away again. "That's what I'm having trouble with—that you lied to me from day one. You continued to lie to me after I thought we had a connection. How do I know I can trust you?"

"Give me a chance to prove it to you."

"How?"

He'd decided to use the cat and dog to perform a show-and-tell to convince her he could read their damn thoughts, maybe ask them some questions he couldn't possibly know the answer to. Glancing around, he wondered where the hell the cat had gone. Costello was lounging between them on the floor. The dog would have to do.

Zach whistled and patted his leg. "Come 'ere, boy." The dog's ears perked up and he ambled over. "Let's ask him some questions only he knows the answer to. Okay?"

She said nothing, looking down at the cushions beside her.

"First question, Hannah. What is it?" *Please. Give me a chance.*

With a heaving sigh, she glanced toward the ceiling. "I don't know. Ask him … ask him what day of the week Ellie and I brought him home from the shelter."

Damn. Would a dog even understand that question? Zach lifted Costello's muzzle, looked the mutt in the eye, and repeated it aloud.

*Huh?* Costello opened his mouth and panted.

Zach repeated the question.

*I saw a squirrel today. Can we eat now? Can I eat the squirrel if I see it again?*

"Can't you think of something easier?" Zach scanned the room for the cat. The cat might understand. The cat was scary intelligent in a diabolical kind of way. "Something more recent? I don't think he understands the question."

"Of course he doesn't." She reached up a hand and wiped away a tear. She was *crying*?

"Hannah—"

She scooted off the sofa. "Forget it, Zach. Just give me some time to think. I want to believe you, but I don't know." Pushing her hair back with one hand, she looked composed and unaffected. Maybe he'd imagined the tears. "Will you please take Costello out for a walk, or do I have to do it?"

Her tone implied she was a powder keg about to explode if he said no. He held up his hands in surrender. "I'll take him."

"Thank you. I'm going to bed. I need to think about some things." Her voice broke on the last word, and she turned away quickly.

The hours had ticked by at an unbearably slow rate.

Double checking her bag that she had everything she needed—her ID, her phone, the directions she'd scribbled down—Hannah rubbed at her tired eyes and reached for the keys to the SUV she'd swiped from Zach's room last night while he'd been walking Costello.

She'd been as nervous as a kitten in a dog pound all night, expecting him to barge into the room and demand to know why she'd taken them, but he'd remained in the other room, making little noise, oblivious to her devious planning.

She'd also borrowed his laptop to look up information about Oakland Cemetery and to email Detective Ryan, who had yet to return her two phone calls and messages. Her fingers had wanted to type *Why the hell haven't you been returning my freaking phone calls?* but her mind had reined in the panic and kept it cordial. She was hoping and praying he was waiting until the morning to call her back, because she didn't know what to do if she didn't hear from him. Her plan was to proceed with the kidnappers' instructions until the detective told her otherwise. It might not be the smartest thing she'd ever done, but what was she supposed to do? Ignore the call? Not show? Those weren't options. Sarah had always been there for her, and she sure as hell wasn't going to leave her best friend in the hands of a maniac when Hannah was the reason Sarah was there in the first place.

She'd also spent most of the night debating telling Zach what was happening. In the end, she didn't know if she could trust him, especially after that ridiculous scene with Costello last night. Why was he trying so hard to convince her he was psychic when he'd already admitted he wasn't? He was trying to con her again, but why?

Abbott jumped onto the bed and sat on her bag, demanding attention. The cat had been in her hair all night, walking across the computer keyboard while she used it, rubbing against her elbows seeking adoration as she typed. Hannah picked him up and cuddled him now, finding comfort in his vibrating purr against her chest. "I love you so much, kitty. I'm sorry I have to leave you here, but it's the only way."

The cat pushed his head against her neck and nuzzled her. He was being unusually affectionate. She really did hate to leave him, and Costello too. She hadn't heard the dog all night pawing at her door to get in, so she knew he'd stayed with Zach. *Traitor.*

At six-thirty, she quietly made her way out of the room, pausing to listen for any movement from Zach. All was quiet. She half expected Costello to come bouncing at her in early-morning greeting, but he didn't. She hated not telling the dog goodbye, but she couldn't risk searching him out. She had to stick to her plan, or everything would fall apart. Hurrying to the front door, she reached into her bag for the note she'd written and slid it onto the entryway table. She steeled her nerves and refused to look back as she slipped outside, shutting the door behind her as softly as she could manage.

*Stay calm. You can do this. Zach is still asleep. You're good.*

She slid into the driver's seat of the SUV, adjusted the seats and mirrors and turned the ignition over. It wasn't until she was on the highway that she stopped glancing in the rearview, expecting Zach to be behind her.

The air was cool and refreshing as Zach took Costello for an early-morning walk along a trail he'd discovered yesterday behind the building. He'd barely slept, battling memories of Dylan and his mother alongside more recent ones of all the sins he'd committed against Hannah. It had been hell, resisting the urge to demand that she listen to his arguments. He was much clearer now on what he wanted to say to her, and dammit, he would force her to listen this morning.

He'd start with letting her know he was voiding her contract with the agency. He would never take a dime from her. Surely that would make a dent in the wall she'd put up between them last night. He might lose the agency, but it was worth it if he had her.

In the distance, the hum of a vehicle's engine kicking over mingled with the chirp of birds and crickets. That was odd. Maybe one of their neighbors was heading back to the city for work this morning.

The sound made him uneasy for a reason he couldn't describe.

"Come on, boy." He steered Costello back in the direction of the condo. He decided to walk around the building to make certain it was secure before going inside and froze when he saw the SUV was missing from the driveway.

Hell.

His feet pounded the dirt and the dog struggled to keep up with him as he rushed inside to verify Hannah was missing and someone hadn't only stolen their vehicle. She wasn't in her room.

She was nowhere to be seen.

"Meow." The cat jumped onto the back of the sofa.

*She's gone, you idiot. You gotta go after her. She's in trouble. Understand what I'm saying?*

"What? What kind of trouble?"

*Check the message she left you.* The cat jumped down and hurried over to the table near the door. *Over here. Hurry up.*

There was a note, and Zach skimmed it.

*Zach, I had to get away to clear my head. Be back later. Please take care of the boys while I'm gone. I'll be fine.*

Shit. Why the hell would she risk leaving when there was still a madman somewhere out there, stalking her? Did the woman have no common sense? His fist crumpled the note and tossed it across the room along with a loud growl of frustration.

The cat brushed against his legs.

*She had me locked in the room with her last night. I couldn't get out to warn you what she was planning. You gotta help her.*

Zach picked the cat up. "How long has she been gone?"

*Not long.*

Zach found his phone and dialed Kellan. The other man answered on the third ring, sounding grumpy and half asleep. Zach explained the situation.

Kellan sounded much more alert when he said, "I'm on it. Any idea where she was going?"

Zach looked at the cat.

*She was looking at the glowy square thing a lot, and kept writing stuff down.*

Glowy square thing?

An image of Hannah typing on his computer flashed into his mind. The picture was so clear he could even see the screen.

"Oakland Cemetery." Zach raced toward the room she'd been using, clutching the cat safely to his chest with one hand while the dog chased on his heels. He found his laptop on the bed and opened it. Checking the history, sure enough, she'd been viewing the website for the famous landmark. "That's definitely where she's headed."

Why the hell was she going to a cemetery at this hour?

"Want me to send E.J. after you?" Kellan asked.

"That depends."

"On what?"

"On whether or not I can remember how to hotwire a car."

# Chapter Nineteen

The gates of Oakland Cemetery weren't even open for the day when Hannah cruised up to the main entrance.

After parking at a business near the cemetery, she reached for her phone. No missed calls from Detective Ryan, but at least a dozen each from Zach, Kellan and E.J. She refrained from listening to their messages, knowing they'd fill her mind with doubt that she was doing the right thing.

What the hell was she supposed to do now?

Dialing the detective's number again, she reached his voice mail—which an automated message now informed her was full. She did a quick Internet search on her phone for the front desk number of the Atlanta Police Department. The lady who answered did not sound like a morning person.

Hannah sucked in a breath. "I've been trying to reach Detective Jacob Ryan. Can you please tell me if he's working today?"

"What zone?"

"Zone 2. Um, he's with the Criminal Investigation Division." She'd memorized his business card.

There was a long pause filled with the sound of shuffling papers and a couple of computer clicks. "Detective Ryan had a family emergency. Detective Flannery is handling his cases in the meantime."

She almost laughed hysterically. Of course he was. Of course.

"Can you please transfer me to Detective Flannery?"

Hannah waited while she was connected to a new person. She rubbed at the bridge of her eyes, trying to alleviate the dull ache forming there. Why the hell did everything always have to be so damn complicated?

A gruff, masculine voice answered, only to inform her she'd reached the desk of Detective Martin Flannery and he was unavailable to take her call. She almost pressed END, frustrated as hell, but reminded herself that Sarah's life was at stake. She rambled off another frantic message and left her number. Hopefully this detective would check his voicemail soon.

Around eight o'clock, Hannah watched a school bus enter the cemetery and realized the gates had opened. The caller had told her nine o'clock, but if she could find his note now, she might have time to somehow relay its contents to the police.

It took her much longer than expected to figure out how to get to the Bell Tower Ridge and find the right marker. As she followed the walking paths past tombstone after tombstone and crypt after crypt using the visitor's map she'd snagged at the entrance, Hannah felt a chill creep down her spine. She had the strangest feeling she was being watched, but this section of the graveyard was empty except for a lone lawnkeeper raking leaves.

A business-sized white envelope was propped against a brown package sitting on the ground where a marker proclaimed "Where Hood Watched The Battle of Atlanta."

She tore open the envelope with surprisingly steady hands and read the small note inside.

*Open the package.*

Glancing around, she saw no one. She picked up the small cardboard box and lifted the lid. A mobile phone sat beside a key taped to the inside back. No sooner had Hannah lifted the phone from the box than it started vibrating.

It wasn't nine o'clock yet.

He was watching her. This was it.

"Hello?" she answered, spinning in her spot to scan the area around her.

"Take your phone and toss it into the bushes. Do it now."

"My phone?"

"Yes, your phone. The one you came here with."

She grasped her phone out of her bag and threw it into some shrubbery beside a nearby tomb.

"Good girl. There's a car parked on the next street over. A silver Chevy. Take that key and get in the driver's seat."

"Wh-what?"

"You'd better hurry. Your friend is waiting."

Zach swore as he wove in and out of early morning traffic in the ridiculous car he'd stolen from one of the cabin's neighbors.

He'd had to walk a couple of miles to find an older model he could lift, and then he'd raced back to the cabin to pick up the animals—Hannah would have never forgiven him if he'd left them there alone. Stealing a car, maybe, but not abandoning her boys. Besides, he'd needed to grill the cat for more information.

"Come on. Come on." He slammed his fist against the dashboard as he slowed the lime-green colored Volkswagen Beetle to a stop at a red light.

He felt like a freaking giant in the small car, and crowded with the dog standing in the passenger seat with his front paws on the dashboard looking out, thinking *We're going for a ride. Yeah, we are riding fast, too! Oh, we're stopping. Is the ride over?* Zach had left Abbott out of the bag, and about ten miles back, the cat had decided to hop into his lap and stand with his front feet on the steering wheel. The cat hissed. *Why did you stop? Go faster! Move this heap!*

"Shut the hell up and let me drive," Zach muttered, shoving the finicky feline aside.

His phone rang and he had to move Costello aside to dig it out from under the dog's back feet.

"Talk to me," he told Kellan.

"She's on the move."

"Where?"

"On foot. She threw her phone into some bushes and is walking toward the exit."

"Dammit, I'm almost there. Don't let her out of your sight."

What the hell was Hannah doing? The cat had told him she'd gotten a phone call and then left messages for what Zach had determined was the police. From what the cat had overheard it sounded like Sarah had been taken hostage. That was the only reason Kellan was keeping his distance. They'd assumed the police must be keeping their distance too, trying to trap the suspect without risking Hannah's best friend in the process.

Costello wiggled backward into his seat and then tried to climb over the gear shift and into Zach's lap. The car was an older automatic without safety features, and his fat paw knocked it back into a slower gear. The car lurched and sputtered for a second before Zach pushed it back into Drive.

"Stop that." Zach yelled and pressed the dog away. Costello tilted his head and looked down at the gear shift as if he'd discovered a new friend.

*The stick moves. Is that a toy? Is there a treat if I move the stick?*

He reached to paw the gear again. Zach flicked a finger against his nose. "No. Bad boy."

"What the hell are you saying?" Kellan asked.

"Uh, nothing. Not to *you.*" He shook his head. "Any sign of the cops?"

"No, man. If they're out here, they're really keeping things on the down low."

"Make sure you do the same. If these people have been watching Hannah for a while, they'll know what you look like."

"I slipped one of the groundskeepers twenty bucks to borrow his shirt and rake when I came in." Kellan was starting to sound a little short of breath. How fast was Kellan walking? "You forget I do this for a living."

"Stay with her. I'm going to try to check in with Detective Ryan again. Call me the second anything happens."

"Done."

Zach struggled to find the detective's number in his phone as he swung the car around a turn, sending Costello and Abbott both sliding toward the door.

"Sorry," he mumbled and pressed the phone to his ear. He swore when he got the detective's voicemail.

Abbott's furry head pushed between his arm and body, demanding back in the driver's seat. Zach glanced between the two animals in his care.

He was coming up on the cemetery now.

What the hell was he going to do with *them* when he got there?

Hannah's skin was still crawling with the knowledge she was being watched by a psychopath as she hurried to find the silver Chevy parked on the side street. Seeing one in the distance, she hesitated. What if it was the wrong car?

The phone in her right hand vibrated again.

"You're almost there. A few more steps. Get in."

She used the key to unlock the door and slipped into the driver's seat. Shutting the door behind her, she put the key in the ignition. "What next?"

"Sit there a few minutes. I'll tell you when to start driving."

She took a deep breath and glanced around. Where the hell was this guy?

"Are you wearing a wire?"

She swallowed. "No."

"Do you have a weapon?"

"No, I don't have anything."

His voice was a quiet snarl. "If you're lying, you'll never see your friend alive again."

The passenger car door suddenly jerked open and a man slid into the seat beside her, the scent of stale cigarette smoke assaulting her nostrils. A flash of the sun against silver drew her attention to the gun in his hand—aimed straight at her. The black leather gloves on his hands looked odd considering it was seasonably warm outside.

"Eyes on the road, Miss Dawson."

She briefly risked a look at his face before turning her head and grasping the steering wheel with both hands. He was well dressed in a dark suit and tie with sunglasses covering his eyes and shielding most of his expression from her.

She didn't recognize him from Adam.

"Start the car and drive."

Swallowing, she did, moving into the line of traffic with much more ease than she would have expected. Several school buses had pulled up and were parked along the street around them, causing the road to become slightly congested.

"Where's Sarah? How do I know she's still alive?"

"Quiet." His eyes were trained on the cars around them. He must have deduced they weren't being followed because his shoulders relaxed, but he never lowered the gun. "We're going to the bank to retrieve a certain precious jewel. Once it's in my possession and I'm safely far away, I'll tell you where to find your friend."

"How do I know I can trust that?"

His breath blew through his nose as he made a sound of laughter. "Do you have a choice at this point?" His hand waved the gun slightly for emphasis.

Hannah's fingers tightened around the wheel.

*Try to find out as much as you can. Maybe you can at least leave clues for the police.*

"You're not Roglitz, are you?" She skimmed her glance quickly over him. "You're too young."

His lips twitched. "Please. You thought the old man had orchestrated this?" He chuckled. "Hardly. He was a decent teacher, but I was a much better student. He would have never made it this far if he was still alive."

Then Alexandra had been telling the truth? Roglitz was dead? The medium had also warned her that the person after her was a dangerous man. A killer.

*Keep him talking.*

"Did you know Ellie?"

"What's with the twenty questions? I told you to be quiet."

"I'm sorry. I'm nervous. I talk a lot when I get nervous."

"Don't. I don't like it."

She sucked in a breath for courage. "What does it matter? You're not going to let me live, are you?"

He didn't answer right away. "Maybe. I haven't decided yet."

"I don't believe you. I've seen you." She darted another glance at him.

His smile practically engulfed his entire face, and she felt her insides cringe. He sounded amused when he finally responded. "You must think I'm incredibly stupid, if you think this is really my face." He snorted. "Relax, Miss Dawson. Do as I tell you, and I'll have no reason to harm you."

Zach's muscles were as tight as a coil as he struggled to keep his distance from the silver Chevy.

He'd been circling the cemetery, trying to get around the damn buses full of schoolchildren, when he'd seen Hannah duck into the unfamiliar car. He'd pulled over, watched, and nearly lost his cool when a man dressed in dark clothes had slipped into the seat beside her.

Costello whined, staring straight ahead, focused on the silver Chevy, too. The dog had seen Hannah first. That ear-piercing whine had alerted Zach to her proximity, as had the dog's pathetic inner turmoil as he'd scrambled to get her attention. *I'm here! Oh, I love you so much! Where are you going? I'm right here! Pleaaase!*

"Are you still on their tail?" Kellan asked through the phone. Zach had put it on speaker so he'd have better control of the car.

"Yes. I'm keeping a good distance."

"Any idea where you're headed?"

Zach took the same turn as the Chevy. "The bank. Bastard is taking her there to get the jewel."

"I'll let the others know and try again to get through to Detective Ryan. I'll head to the bank. What's the plan?"

The plan? Hell if he knew. If they tried intervening at the bank, the guy could pull a gun and end up taking multiple hostages, or worse. Besides, if they took him down prematurely, they might never locate Sarah. "Let him get the jewel. We stay glued to them like white on rice, and if it looks like Hannah is in immediate danger, we move in."

"You sure that's the way you want to play it?"

No, but he was choosing to trust that Hannah could handle herself, and that the police hadn't let her go into this without some kind of contingency plan. He'd never forgive himself if something he did put Sarah's life at greater risk. Neither would Hannah.

"That's the way we're gonna play it."

No sooner had Kellan ended the call than Zach's phone began

chiming. He glanced at the caller ID. *Detective Ryan.* About damn time.

"This is Collins."

"Please tell me Hannah Dawson is with you right now."

"What?"

"I checked my messages from the past day. I'm out of town. My father's funeral. Look, she left messages saying some whack job kidnapped her friend and demanded she meet him this morning, wanted to know what to do. Please tell me she isn't that stupid that she actually went without talking to us first."

The police weren't involved. That meant—

Zach swore and pressed his foot harder on the gas. Like it or not, he was the only help she had coming. No way in hell was he going to let her down again.

# Chapter Twenty

"Do you have new security personnel, Miss Dawson?"

The bank manager, the same man she and Zach had gone through a couple of days ago, refused to take his gaze from her companion.

The question threw her, but Hannah recovered fast. "Um, yes, I do. This is Mr.—" Crap, what did she call him? "—James."

The manager didn't blink. As she repeated the security code to him, he typed something into the computer. "Very good then."

He led them to a private room and disappeared to retrieve her box from the vault. Once they were alone, her kidnapper swept a curious look over her. "Well done, Miss Dawson. You might get to see your friend soon after all."

She lifted her chin. "How did you know Ellie had left the security code on her pets' collars?"

His right eyelid twitched as his lips tightened. The man she'd named Mr. James shrugged as he appeared to come to an internal decision on how much he was willing to reveal. "Roglitz. He shared all of the Fox's old tricks with me. Taught me everything he knew."

"That's why you broke into my house and tried to take my cat and dog."

"I didn't want the cat and dog. I only wanted their collars." He shrugged in a what-the-hell kind of gesture. "Roglitz knew

235

the old woman had held onto the LeBeau Diamond and he was going to use that to get back on his feet. Stupid man had a devil of a time finding her. When he saw her picture in the paper with those two rats after she died, he suspected she'd stored the jewel in a vault somewhere here in Atlanta. I thought it would be an easy job, in and out, but that damn dog of hers is more aggressive than it looks."

A swell of pride for Costello lifted her shoulders.

"You would have never been able to get inside the vault without me. I don't understand."

"So naïve." He tsked. "We could've gotten into this vault if we'd known the jewel was here."

"Then why didn't you?" Lord, she was going to get herself killed. Then again, her chances for survival were pretty slim. Might as well keep him talking while she could.

The man's mouth quirked into a half smile as he considered her. "We're on a bit of a deadline. Roglitz got cocky and promised our buyer we'd turn over the LeBeau Diamond within a month. They're not the type of people who give extensions, and, well, we never expected you to give us so much trouble."

"Partners?" So there were others involved? "I thought you said Roglitz was dead?"

The man smirked. "Now he is."

Hannah instinctively took a step back. "Why?" Her voice was barely a whisper, but he heard it.

He shrugged one shoulder. "I did him a favor. He spent most of his life plotting revenge, trying to find Ellie Nichols, so when she died, he didn't have much purpose left. All those years in prison, cluttering up our cell with notes and plans and newspaper clippings—" He suddenly stopped speaking and looked at her with widened eyes. Just as fast, he regained his composure. "Well, let's just say that when he botched our first attempt to get the collars from you, my patience had run thin."

*Our cell.* This man had been a cellmate of Roglitz. There had to be records indicating his identity. And he must have realized that.

"Considering you and I agreed to no questions earlier, you're good at getting answers, aren't you?" His eyes gleamed dangerously as they pierced into hers across the small space.

There was a knock and then the manager opened the door and slid the box onto the table.

"I'll give you some privacy, Miss Dawson." With a curt nod at her captor, the older man disappeared again.

"Get the jewel," the stranger told her. "Hand it to me."

This was it. The moment of truth. She handed him the diamond, and he would kill her and Sarah both. What the hell did she do now?

She removed the bag containing the heavy gem and reluctantly passed it to him, an idea swimming around her head. Could she pull it off?

Probably not, but she had to try.

"I've lived up to my end. Where's Sarah?"

Tugging the diamond out of the bag, Mr. James examined it closely. Then he gave a slow shake of his head. "Not yet. Not until I'm safely away from here, remember?" His fingers pressed into her arm and shoved her toward the door. The creep must think she was dense to believe him.

He kept his grip on her as she spoke again to the bank manager and as they exited the building.

Hannah could have sworn she heard a bark in the distance that sounded like Costello, but that was crazy, wasn't it? Cars whizzed past them on the busy street, and the only people in sight were all scurrying in opposite directions.

Oh, Costello. And Abbott, too. Would Zach make sure they found a good home as she'd asked, or would he throw them aside now that his paycheck had been cancelled? She hoped she made it out of this, for their sakes alone, but the doubts were crowding her mind.

She had to think fast. No way was she going down without a fight.

The WALK sign came on and, still gripping her arm, the man shoved her forward across the street and snarled, "Pick up the pace. This is almost over."

As they entered the parking garage, her gaze caught sight of a lime-green Beetle parked a few rows behind the Chevy. The dog she'd just been thinking about stood with his front paws on the dashboard, his toothy smile big and his fluffy tail wagging like crazy as he watched her pass.

Sweet heavens, was that Zach in the driver's seat, struggling to haul Costello back and out of sight? A surge of hope lifted her chest.

She felt the man at her side turn to follow her gaze, so she deliberately stumbled against him. This was her chance. Her fingers slid into the man's pocket the way E.J. had showed her. He swore and tugged her hard against his side. "Do that again, and I will get very angry. Understand?"

She nodded, holding her breath, but he didn't glance toward the Beetle again. He kept walking fast.

He had no idea she now had the diamond. Bloody hell, she'd done it!

"Driver's seat," he instructed and watched her as she circled the car. They both opened their doors and slid into the vehicle in sync. "Very good, Miss Dawson." He settled comfortably in his seat. He gestured to his right. "Head that way. Let's go see your friend, shall we?"

Hannah glanced in the rear view and started the car, feeling comforted now that she knew Zach would be following her.

She should have trusted him.

She hoped she'd get the chance to tell him that.

Zach herded the animals into the tan car Kellan was driving as soon as Hannah and her captor were out of sight. At least Kellan's ancient Toyota was a hell of lot less conspicuous than the damn Beetle.

Zach saw a single police car turn into the parking lot and creep past the first row of cars, scanning the area with a light. "You've got to be kidding me." He reached for his phone and dialed Detective Ryan's replacement—Detective Flannery—as Kellan drove. "They're already leaving the damn bank. I've known snails who move faster than the APD."

"We had units on the way to the bank when someone reported a fire four blocks over. Some of our guys had to reroute because it was a public building."

Zach swore, and a weird thought popped into his head. *Deliberate arson. Probably meant as a distraction. This guy's good. Knows what he's doing. Must have a partner.*

"You think it was meant as a distraction," Zach asked, wondering if he'd actually picked up on the detective's mindset.

"Hard to tell. Where are they headed now?"

"Northeast on Peachtree."

"I'll have a car pull them over. Stay out of the way, Collins. Do you hear me?"

Zach pressed END without answering.

They tailed the silver Chevy as it drove through the commercial district of downtown. After zigzagging through several streets, it pulled into the parking lot of some kind of industrial building. They kept a healthy distance, but never saw a police car approach.

What the hell was going on with the cops in this city?

Parking on the street, Kellan reached for his phone as Zach pushed to open his door. Kellan grabbed his arm. "We should wait for the police." With a nod toward the dog and cat in the back seat, he added, "Besides, what about them?"

"Stay with them. Wait a few minutes and then pull in behind the Chevy. Block it in. No way am I letting this guy get outta here."

Costello whined when Zach shut the door behind him, but he didn't look back.

The building was obviously abandoned, judging by the broken windows and lack of people around. One of the doors was cracked open, making it easy for him to slip inside. The crunch of broken glass beneath his feet stopped Zach from moving further, praying the sound hadn't carried far.

A feeling of déjà vu overcame him, and his mind yanked back to six months ago and another warehouse similar to this one. The man Zach had been hired to find evidence against in a white-collar Ponzi scheme had worked in an office inside a warehouse like this in the neighboring suburb of Kirkwood. Three people had ended up dead because of Zach's carelessness.

He couldn't let something like that happen again.

Voices echoed in the distance. Hannah. He thought she asked, "Where are we going?" but he wasn't sure.

Carefully, he followed the muffled conversation, playing closer attention to the debris on the floor.

He finally reached a point where he could understand them clearly. He was close. Real close.

"Hannah? I've never been so glad to see someone in my life." Sarah's broken sob tugged at his insides. "Untie me, please."

"Are you okay?" Hannah asked.

"I've been better. I've been worse. You?"

"I'm fine." There was a brief pause. "You've got what you wanted. You brought me to my friend. We're even now."

Zach pressed himself to the wall and waited, close to the entrance of one of the old offices inside the building. He listened for a fourth voice or more, but all he heard was Sarah, Hannah and the one man.

"Come on, Sarah. Let's get out of here." Hannah's footsteps were loud and easy to follow.

"Not so fast, Miss Dawson." The unmistakable sound of a gun being readied to fire filled the space. "I'm afraid we have a problem."

"W-what kind of p-problem?" Hannah whispered.

"Oh, I'm sure you can figure it out." More movement, but from who, Zach had no idea. "Perhaps if you had listened and not pried for information, I would've allowed you and your friend to walk out of here. As it is, I'm afraid you'll run straight to the police with what you know, and I can't have that, now, can I?"

"We won't tell anyone." Sarah sounded frantic.

"Shut up." The man yelled.

There was no sound, no movement, as Zach held his breath, his muscles tight and ready to spring into action.

"On your knees. Both of you."

"Please." Sarah whimpered.

"Do it!"

"Wait," Hannah pleaded. "Maybe you want to think about this. If you kill us now, you'll never find out where I hid the diamond."

Zach froze. What was she talking about?

The sound of clothes being shuffled echoed in the space. The man growled, "How did you—?" Zach edged closer to the door and risked a peek inside. Her captor was padding down his coat. With a growl, he grabbed Hannah by the hair and jerked her close. "Where is it?"

This was it. If he could draw the man's gunfire away from them, it might give the women a chance to run. The man stood with his back to him. It was now or never.

The solid impact of his body colliding with the gunman's was teeth-rattling. The weapon fired, the sound deafening in the small room, but Zach couldn't allow that to distract him. His ears hummed as he slammed the man into the wall and delivered a heavy punch that elicited a huff of breath from his opponent.

"Zach!"

He felt a moment's relief hearing Hannah screaming his name, knowing she was unharmed enough to call out. Had she been hit? Had Sarah?

With a roar, the other man elbowed Zach in the rib and rounded with a right hook that caught him in the jaw. He staggered back as red and white stars flashed in his vision.

A glimpse of movement to his left confirmed that the man was running for the door.

"Zach!" Both women screamed as he gave chase.

The man rammed through the outside door and stumbled over something, falling to the ground, scrambling to regain his feet. Zach blinked until he could see clearly again, sidestepping the body that lay outside the door.

Shit.

Kellan lay sprawled on the ground, and his associate made no sound as Hannah's attacker fell almost on top of him and kicked away from the body.

The man lifted his gun, aimed it right at Zach. A loud pop sounded and searing pain lanced through Zach's left side like nothing he'd ever felt before.

He instinctively hunched over and grabbed his middle. Behind him, footsteps crunched toward the doorway.

"No!" Hannah stumbled forward. Sarah grabbed her arm, tugging her back.

"Stay back, Hannah." Zach held a hand up to the women. He took a step closer to the man, trying to put some cover between them and the gun.

"If you shoot him again, I'll never tell you where the jewel is,"

Hannah warned.

The man stood, keeping the weapon trained on Zach, and struggled to catch his breath. His eyes darted toward the Chevy, which Kellan had blocked with his car, and back to Hannah. Zach saw that both Abbott and Costello were standing on the back seat of the old-model Toyota, watching them. Costello gave a ferocious bark that sent Abbott scattering for cover.

Zach met the man's eyes. *What are you gonna do now, pal?*

The sound of police sirens in the distance were both a relief and an irritation. What the hell had taken them so long?

Zach and the madman seemed to have the same realization at once. Kellan had left his car running, probably so the animals could have air conditioning.

The man took a step back, sideways, moving toward the vehicle.

Shit. They couldn't let him take the animals. If he did, he'd have something to ransom. This would never end.

Zach swallowed and felt the pain in his side intensify. He staggered, almost to his knees, and his vision blurred. Dammit. He was in no shape to take this man down, but he had to try.

*I wanna kill the bad man. Grrrrrr. Bad man.* Costello barked again, and Zach heard his thoughts loud and clear, repeating over and over.

The bad man continued stepping back, not taking his eyes off the humans. Zach realized he was almost standing directly behind Kellan's car.

The asshole wanted to shoot but was hesitating. He didn't want to leave without the diamond. Zach sensed it as if the man had spoken the words to him. He was thinking, trying to figure out a way to snatch Hannah, but Zach was in his way.

*He's going to shoot me again, get me down, and then threaten Sarah to make Hannah talk. That's his plan.*

Zach looked at the dog and urgently willed him to listen to

his thoughts.

*Costello, good boy. Good boy! Want a treat? Does Costello want a treat?*

The dog stopped barking and tilted his head at Zach.

Yes. This worked.

*Move the stick, Costello. Find treats under the stick. Remember the stick?* He imagined an image of the gearshift in Kellan's older car—one he knew didn't have the safety features to prevent a child, or pet, from accidentally slipping gears.

Costello turned and looked toward the front seat. *The stick?*

Zach nodded, feeling sweat bead on his forehead, and struggled to keep his balance. Man, he wanted to sit down for a few minutes. The sirens grew closer. He felt an arm slide under his from behind and recognized the feel of Hannah's body as she used herself as a crutch to keep him standing. Smart move, but she didn't know it. The guy would hesitate before shooting Zach now, not wanting to hit the only woman who could tell him what he wanted to know.

"The stick, Costello. Press the stick forward," he whispered. "Lots of treats."

*Treats. Ohmygod, treats!*

Zach saw the dog scramble toward the front of the car. If Costello managed to push the gearshift forward—please, let him press it forward into reverse and not backward into a drive gear— they might actually catch this guy.

Suddenly the car jerked and began rolling back, and fast too.

"Ah!" The man's grip released the gun. It fell to the ground as he struggled to keep the vehicle from pressing him under it. After walking backwards, pushing against the trunk, he finally lunged sideways away from the car, but not far enough. The Toyota kept rolling, rolling past Zach and the women, and blocking the man from view. Without the sound of the sickening crunch of bone and ear-piercing scream that followed, they might have wondered if he'd made it free.

"Stop…the car." Zach gritted his teeth and moved to go do exactly that. His limbs were like jelly. "The animals…"

Right on cue, a police car rolled into the gate, followed by another and another. One of the officers parked in the path of the Toyota. The man got out, drew his gun and then leapt out of the way as the Toyota showed no signs of stopping.

Zach struggled to focus and noticed Costello standing with his front feet on the steering wheel, his tongue lolling out of his mouth.

*Get down, boy. Down. Lay down!*

Costello disappeared from view seconds before metal impacted with metal, and Kellan's car screeched to a halt.

A groan nearby was one clue that Kellan had regained consciousness. His muttered "What the hell did you do to my car?" was another.

Hannah helped lower Zach to the ground, her beautiful face swimming above his as she looked at Sarah. "Put your hands here and press."

Kellan shifted, then groaned. Hannah's head whipped in his direction. "Don't move. Paramedics will be here in a minute."

"Someone came up from behind. Clobbered me good." Kellan swore. Unfamiliar voices demanded answers to questions as anonymous officers gathered around.

"Oh my God, Zach, you've lost a lot of blood." Hannah pressed her fingers against his abdomen. "We need an ambulance."

Sarah hovered over him too, her hands on top of Hannah's. One of the officers stood above Hannah, talking into his walkie and requesting aid.

Zach opened his mouth to say "I love you," but no words came out. He reached a hand toward her, but nothing happened.

His lids closed as a sea of darkness engulfed him, body and mind. He'd tell her after he slept. Sleep was good.

# Chapter Twenty-One

"Miss Dawson, can I have a word with you?"

Hannah clasped her fifth cup of coffee a little tighter and nodded, standing when the detective she'd only met a few hours ago gestured in the direction of the door. Both Brian and Sarah sprang to their feet, too, but Hannah shook her head, placing a hand on Sarah's shoulder to keep her down. "Stay and rest. You've been through a lot."

"But—"

"Stay here in case the doctor comes back while I'm gone. Please? One of you come and get me if he does?"

Brian nodded, and sinking back into the waiting room chair, Sarah gave in easily too, which had to mean she felt like hell. She'd been checked over by the emergency room staff and deemed healthy enough to be released an hour ago, but Hannah knew her friend. Sarah was still shaken up by her experience, and who could blame her?

Hannah was shaken up as well, mainly because Zach had been in surgery longer than she'd expected. Almost three hours after they'd rolled him into an OR, she'd heard nothing. Had something gone wrong? She'd worried the bullet had pierced a kidney, ruptured a major artery, or worse. There had been so much blood, but she refused to let herself dwell on the worst possibilities. She'd find out what was taking so long as soon as she was done with the officer's questions. Harriet, one of the nurses on duty, was an old friend from nursing school.

"We're still piecing some things together, but I wanted you to know we've IDed the guy that took you," Detective Flannery said. "Name's Tim Polanski. You were right. He served time for armed robbery in the same prison as Roglitz before being released on good behavior. He has a history of stealing cars and robbing businesses going back to his teens, and apparently he was known for using some pretty clever disguises to evade capture. We think he and Roglitz might be responsible for a number of high-profile thefts across the country."

"Has he confessed to anything?"

"Nah, he's not talking yet. Then again, he's gotta be feeling some hurt with that shattered leg." He reached into his jacket and grabbed his phone. A mugshot type of picture of a young man was displayed on the screen when he held it out to her. "Do you recognize this person?"

She shook her head.

He sighed. "Guy was driving the exact make and model of Chevy headed Northeast on Peachtree when your security alerted us to be on the lookout for that vehicle. Our men stopped him, thinking he was the suspect, which is why it took us so long to find you." The detective wiped a hand over his face.

He was right. There was no telling what would have happened to her if Zach hadn't followed her from the bank. She'd love to know how he'd found her to begin with, but so far she'd only heard bits and pieces of it from Kellan before he'd been admitted to the hospital for observation.

"Do you think he's Polanski's accomplice—the one who knocked out Kellan at the warehouse?"

"Nah, I think he's some poor kid who got caught in the middle of this. I wouldn't worry too much. The diamond is in our possession, and Polanski strikes me as the ringleader of this operation. You should be a hell of lot safer now, Miss Dawson. Keep alert and maintain your private security, and you'll be fine."

She relaxed a little at that reassurance.

The detective started to walk away, but hesitated. "There's a matter of a stolen car. Volkswagen Beetle. It's out of my jurisdiction, but I'll talk to the owner, try to explain things, see if we can't get those charges dropped. No promises, but I'll try. Let him know I'll be in touch, will ya?"

"Thank you."

Tossing her empty cup into the trash, Hannah was hurrying to the nurse's station when she spotted Harriet walking in the opposite direction to the waiting room. She reached her old friend as Harriet called for Zach's family. Brian stepped forward eagerly, sliding his hand along Hannah's back.

"That's us."

"Me, too," Sarah said, squeezing between them.

They were led to a private room, and Hannah felt her stomach sink, remembering the handful of times she'd showed a family to a similar room knowing they would hear devastating news. She searched Harriet's face for reassurance but found nothing that gave away the outcome. Harriet excused herself quickly, but not before giving Hannah's arm a quick squeeze in passing.

The doctor came in, rubbing the back of his neck, his shirtfront stained with blood. Zach's blood.

"He's out of surgery and stable. The bullet passed through the muscles of the abdomen but didn't enter the abdominal cavity. He lost a helluva lot of blood, but we got the bullet out and I think he's going to be fine. Best case scenario, he'll be up and around again in a matter of weeks."

Brian asked several questions, but Hannah remained quiet,

absorbing all that had happened over the last twenty-four hours. Zach was going to be all right. In the end, that was all that mattered.

"Can I see him?" she asked when Brian seemed satisfied with the doctor's answers. She touched Brian's arm, adding, "I mean, if that's okay with you."

He gave her a crooked smile. "I'm sure he would rather see your face than mine when he wakes up."

She hoped so.

Zach was in recovery when she slipped her hand in his and began taking inventory. She couldn't help it. She needed to know his pulse was normal and his breathing steady.

"I must have died and gone to heaven to have an angel as beautiful as you come greet me." His voice was raspy, but his mouth was curved in a smile. "Are you okay?"

He was awfully alert for someone who'd spent almost three hours under the knife.

Nodding, she gently touched his face. A line of stubble scraped her fingers. "Hi. How are you feeling?"

"Not bad for a guy who just took his first bullet."

He sounded proud, and she frowned down at him. "Don't make jokes, Zach. This is serious."

He settled his other hand on top of hers. His smile vanished. "How are the boys? Are they okay?"

She was happy he seemed to care for her pets as much as she did—or, well, at least he was getting there. "E.J. took them to the vet for me to be checked out. They're fine. I'll pick them up later."

"Good. I was worried."

She was grateful to feel the warmth of his skin beneath her fingers. "Zach, I heard what you told Costello to do…and he did it. How—?"

"Long story. I'll tell it to you sometime."

A nurse Hannah didn't recognize gave Zach some medicine

through the IV and asked him how his pain level was. Adjusting his covers, she told Hannah, "We're getting ready to move him. We'll need you to head back to the waiting room now."

"Wait," Zach interjected, clasping Hannah's hand. His grip was weak, but still strong enough to make a point. "Give us a few more minutes. Please?"

The nurse rolled her eyes. "Alright. Three more minutes, then you'll have plenty of time to visit later." She scurried off to tend to another patient.

Zach wasted no time. "Hannah, I love you. I know things are screwed up right now, but please, give me a chance to prove it to you when I get out of here."

"Oh, Zach." Hot tears swelled behind her eyelids. "You already have." She leaned down and kissed him, gently. "I love you, too."

"Really?"

She nodded and kissed him again. "I'd better go." She sniffed. "The nurse is right. We'll have plenty of time to talk later. Right now, you need to rest."

He tightened his grip on her hand. "Did the police catch him?"

"Yes. Well, sort of. He's somewhere in the hospital under police guard."

"His accomplice?"

She didn't want him to worry. "The police are tracking down some hot leads now." She moved his hand to his side and pried her fingers away, reluctantly. "Don't worry. I'm not going anywhere, Zach."

His eyes looked more bleary than they had a few minutes ago. The meds were kicking in, pulling him under. "Get someone to go home with you. Get some rest. I'm the one who's not going anywhere." His throat moved beneath a big swallow. "Take the boys home and give them lots of treats. Those critters sure as hell deserve it."

"Zach—"

"Promise me." He gestured to her chest even as his eyelids drooped. "Freaks me out seeing you with blood all over you. Go home and change. I'll be…fine."

And he was out.

Hannah pressed another kiss to his forehead and stepped away, eager to find Brian and put him at ease. Odds were Zach was going to be fine. The heaviness that had been weighing down her heart lifted. He loved her. Everything was going to be okay.

"You should go home and rest for a while," Brian encouraged, and Hannah gave in. She was worried about Abbott and Costello. She wanted to get them home and love on them a bit.

When Brian offered to take her, she stopped him. She could see how badly Brian wanted to stay and see his friend. She wouldn't interfere with that.

"I should be fine. Maybe you can ask E.J. to drive by every now and then if it makes you feel better, but I really want to be alone for a while with my cat and dog."

Not fifteen minutes later, E.J. arrived to drive her and Sarah to their respective homes. He chattered a mile a minute, asking questions, thrilled that Hannah had used his lessons in pickpocketing to gain an upper-hand in the situation, but frustrated because he'd missed most of the action. Hannah was grateful, though. His enthusiasm brought Sarah out of her shell and had both women laughing by the time Sarah got out of the car.

When they arrived at Hannah's doorstep so she could change clothes, E.J. followed her inside and did a quick inspection of the house. "All clear. You sure you don't want me to hang out on the couch?"

She shook her head. "I love you, E.J., but I will love you even more if you can find a way to get Zach's car. I left it at the cemetery."

"You want me to do that before or after we go get the animals?"

She considered the question. She looked like a hot mess. "Before. It'll give me a chance to take a quick shower and rest for a few minutes."

"No problem." He took another glance around. "I'll get my cousin to drop me off at the cemetery. I'll try to hurry. Lock up behind me."

After doing that, Hannah stripped and headed for the shower, moaning when the hot water washed away the sweat and blood and grime from the past day. She lingered until her fingers began to turn to prunes, slid into a t-shirt and yoga pants and headed to the kitchen for a snack. It felt strange and lonely in the house without the animals or Zach or his friends. The quiet was almost unsettling. She realized it had been a long time since she'd been this alone. She turned the TV on for company.

A glance at the time on the screen surprised her. It was almost four. She quickly called the vet's office and assured them she'd try to be there by closing.

She couldn't wait to cuddle with her brave little boys.

A knock at the door startled her. She hesitated then shook her head. Sooner or later, she'd have to get back to normal and stop being so paranoid. Sighing, she looked through the peephole and recognized her neighbor—what was her name? Carolyn?

Hannah kept the door on the chain but cracked it open. "I'm sorry. I'm getting out of the shower. Did you need something?"

The woman lifted a casserole dish. Through the opening, Hannah caught a scent of something mouth-watering and enticing. She almost drooled she was so hungry.

"Oh, I'm sorry, Hannah. I wanted to bring this over. I made it especially for you."

Should she?

Peeking at the middle-aged woman who looked like she belonged on one of those real housewives shows, Hannah couldn't imagine any harm coming from this lady. Besides, it would help pass the time until E.J. returned.

Unchaining the door, she gestured Carolyn inside. "Like I said, I just got out of the shower. I'm sorry for the way I'm dress—" She lifted her eyes and saw the gun pointed at her. Again.

"Lock the door, please."

Hannah turned and slid both locks into place. Her hands trembled as she touched the chain, but she willed them to steady.

She was going to kick this woman's ass as soon as she could figure out the safest way to do it.

She took a deep breath and turned around, calm. The casserole dish had been placed on the table, too far out of reach to grab and throw as a potential weapon. "What do you want? The diamond? I don't have it. The police do. Sorry."

Carolyn looked her up and down, a twinkling of disgust in her gaze. "I want the other ones."

"Other ones, what?"

"Don't play dumb. Ellie had to leave them to you. They weren't in the vault. If they were, I would have heard you talk about them, too." She backed up to the island separating the kitchen and living room and reached a hand under the edge. Lifting it, she held a small round thing in between her fingers.

Was that a listening bug?

Hannah mentally slapped her forehead in a D'oh moment. Carolyn, if that was really her name, must have put it there the day she'd played the nosy neighbor.

"Peter told me about them. He knew that asshole Polanski would try to doublecross us with such a big payday on the line, so he told only me about it." She lifted the gun higher. Her hand was a little shaky. "Just tell me where they are, and you'll never see me again. That's all I want."

Hannah held her hands up. "If I knew what you were talking

about, I'd give it to you. Believe me, I want nothing to do with that part of Ellie's life." *Them. Tell me where they are.* Who was *they?* Hannah struggled to comprehend the strange request. She was tired. Mind-numbing, bone-heavy tired. She wanted this over, and she would have gladly cooperated if she understood. "Do you want money? Is that it?"

"You know damn well what I want." The older woman's eyes bulged as she screamed the declaration. Lifting her free hand to cover her mouth, Carolyn's entire body seemed to be trembling now. The woman was obviously out of her element. Lowering her hand, in a much softer voice, she pleaded, "Please tell me where they are."

Hannah almost felt sorry for her. "I swear. I don't know what you want."

Carolyn shook the gun at her. "The cats." She yelled the word as if it was supposed to explain everything. "Where are the cats?"

"What?" Hannah shook her head. The woman was coming unhinged. "He's at the vet." Hannah was grateful for that fact. If this lunatic wanted her animals, she wouldn't get them without a fight.

"You really don't have a clue, do you?" She lifted her hand again and pounded her palm against her forehead. "I thought—" She mumbled something incoherent.

Hannah lifted her hands in a calming gesture. The other woman's nerves seemed to be getting the better of her. Call her crazy, but Hannah didn't sense that Carolyn had it in her to pull that trigger. That didn't mean she wouldn't by accident or if provoked.

"Listen to me, Carolyn—or whatever your name is." Hannah took a slow step to her left. "You didn't kill anyone. None of this was your idea, was it?" Another step. "If you hand me that gun and leave, I won't say a word. How can I? I don't even know who you really are."

Hannah kept moving, slowly, until she was standing in front of the entryway table Sarah's mother had given her. Stepping back, she pretended to bump into it by accident, gasping and dropping her hands behind her, feeling along the edge until she found what she wanted.

"Stop moving. I can't think with you moving around." Carolyn stepped closer. Her gaze shifted to the door. "You won't tell anyone? How can I be certain?"

"I promise." Hannah's fingers brushed then gripped the ceramic vase behind her.

Carolyn seemed to consider the idea, and Hannah relaxed a fraction. Maybe this would go in her favor after all. Maybe she wouldn't have to go on the offensive. But then the gun lifted. "I'm sorry. I really am, but I can't—"

The vase was small, but heavy. It flew across the short space separating them and missed its target—Carolyn's head. *Dammit.* Carolyn's cry of frustration mingled with the sound of ceramic shattering against the wall as Hannah ran straight for the patio doors. The other woman dodged it clumsily and stumbled sideways into the sofa. A deafening blast ripped the air as the glass in the door in front of Hannah exploded in a spray of splintered glass.

Bloody hell. The woman had shot at her. *I'm glad her aim is as bad as mine.*

Hannah leapt over the glass, landing on the cold concrete outside, ignoring the stinging prick of pain in her bare right foot as she ran for the gate. She needed a weapon—something she could wield rather than throw, but her yard tools were scattered between the garage and the shed.

"Come back here!"

Hannah bent and grabbed the small garden stone that read LOVE and tossed it wildly behind her, hoping to hit Carolyn somewhere debilitating or, at least, distracting. She kept running for the gate, flinching when the sound of glass shattering warned her the rock had sailed through a window instead of into her attacker. As she came to an abrupt halt at the gate, a stabbing pain shot through her foot and up her leg.

"Come on. Come on." Hannah jiggled the wooden gate door, trying to get the damn thing open.

Carolyn's loud grunt and a muffled thud followed by metal clanging against concrete drew her attention back to the house.

Alexandra King stood, chest heaving, hands fisted in a fighting stance over Carolyn's prone body.

With a self-satisfied smile, the blonde took a deep breath and met Hannah's confused gaze. "Kickboxing class. That crap *really* works." She sounded almost astonished.

Hannah lifted her eyebrows and sagged against the gate in relief. "What are you doing here?" She winced as the pain in her foot won the battle over adrenaline.

"Ellie." Reaching down to pick up the gun between her thumb and index finger, Alexandra stepped around Carolyn to help Hannah stand straight. "Your foot's bleeding like crazy. Oh, hell. I've been known to pass out at the sight of blood."

Hannah lifted the foot and examined it. "I stepped on glass. I need tweezers." She was more interested in what Alexandra had said. "Ellie?"

Alexandra slid her arm around Hannah and helped her hop around the glass and back into the house. "Damn woman has been pestering me since yesterday. I missed my flight this morning, and I'm pretty sure it's because she screwed with my alarm clock. She led me here, insisted you were in danger. Guess she was right."

"How did you get in?"

"I heard the shot, and uh—" She pointed at Hannah's front door, which was hanging off its hinges. "Kickboxing. You should try it."

Hannah sighed, not caring about the damage in the least. "I

think I will." She sank onto the sofa. "I need to call the police." Hannah nodded toward the patio. "What if she comes to before the police arrive?"

"Um." Alexandra looked around the room. "Do you have rope?"

Hannah bit her bottom lip. She pointed toward her bedroom. "We could use belts. I have some in my closet."

"Sit tight. I'll take care of it."

After Alexandra left the other woman bound to the table in the yard, Hannah instructed her where to find her first aid kit. Alexandra used her mobile to call the police while she searched. Hannah listened to her calmly explaining the situation as drawers were yanked open and slammed shut in the other room. Alexandra finally returned with everything she needed.

"I was right. The police were already on their way. Should be here any minute."

Hannah cried out as she plucked the two tiny shards of glass from her flesh. Relief immediately followed. She noticed Alexandra was looking away.

"Thank you—for everything." She could hardly believe Ellie had led Alexandra here, but she didn't doubt it. Trusting Zach meant she had to trust that what he'd told her about this woman had been true, too. She glanced around at the disaster that was suddenly her house and was comforted by the thought of it. Sweet, dear Ellie. The woman truly had cared for her. "Is Ellie still with you?"

Alexandra pursed her lips. "Yes. Take her back, please. She's been driving me nuts."

Hannah smiled. "Tell her thank you."

"She heard you." Alexandra stood back and glanced around. "It's rare for one to follow me home, but this old gal has been something else. Zach's mom is almost as bad. Geez."

Hannah explained what had happened—to Sarah, to Zach, to her—while Alexandra helped apply ointment to her cuts. "I don't even know what Carolyn wanted from me. All of this, for what?"

Alexandra looked quickly to the left. She held up a finger, stood and backed away. "Can you walk?"

Hannah nodded, moving gingerly to her feet. The pain was nothing compared to what it had been.

"This way." Alexandra led her into the garage and looked around. She pointed at the stack of boxes in the corner. "Do you mind?"

Hannah shrugged, fascinated.

Alexandra shifted some boxes around, focused on one and ripped the lid open. She lifted one of the cat figurines Hannah had packed up—there had been so many.

"She wanted these."

"Those?" Realization hit her fast. *The cats. Where are the cats?* But why? They were ugly as hell and probably worthless. Hannah still hadn't figured out what to do with them.

"Stand back." Alexandra smashed it against the ground. When the pieces settled, a tiny black bag stood out from the white debris. Alexandra lifted it and dangled the bag in front of her. "This is what she really wanted. Some kind of diamonds, I think. You'll find others in here too." She tossed the bag to Hannah. "The old woman is saying sorry. She never meant to cause you trouble. Um, these were the only ones she kept besides the one you already have. She's showing me Paris. The Eiffel Tower. A museum…maybe in France? I think she wants you to return them for her. She says it's over now. Holy hell, does any of that make sense to you?"

Hannah nodded.

"Good, cause I still don't know what the hell Collins got me mixed up in here." Sighing, she placed her hands on her hips. "I could totally use a drink right about now. You?"

Hannah laughed. "I could probably use a couple." She had a feeling she was really going to like this woman. "I think I have a bottle of wine somewhere in the kitchen. That's the strongest I've got."

"It'll do. While we wait for the cops to get here, you can explain to me why you've got a box full of diamonds stashed in your garage and the skank who tried to kill you tied up in your back yard. Seriously, I've got to hear this."

Chuckling at the absurdity that was her life, Hannah didn't protest when the beautiful blonde slid a supportive arm around her waist and urged her forward. Police sirens were already approaching in the distance.

"What happens to Ellie now?" Hannah whispered. "Will she— you know—hang around here forever?"

"No, I don't think so." Alexandra sighed. "She had unfinished business. Now she can find peace and finally cross over."

The thought of it was both sad and wonderful. Sad because Hannah would miss her all over again. Wonderful because, despite her faults, Ellie deserved peace. "I miss her."

"I know." Alexandra snorted. "Although I'm not sure why. She can be a real pain in the ass." The raised tone of her voice implied she wasn't directing the comment to Hannah.

"Yes, she could be." Hannah snickered. "Oh no."

"What?"

"I'm supposed to pick up my pets from the vet. I can't bring them home now. Not with this mess."

Alexandra shrugged. "We'd better call and have them kenneled for the night. Then you can crash at Collins' place while he's in the hospital. Something tells me he'll be thrilled."

"Where are you staying?" Hannah asked.

"Probably in my rental car. I'm totally zapped out on the money front."

"I'll book us a suite for the night at the Ritz Carlton and help you get a first-class flight home tomorrow. It's the least I can do."

One of Alexandra's brows arched high. "Woman, exactly how rich are you?"

Oh yeah, Hannah decided. She and Alexandra King were going to be good friends.

# Epilogue

"I don't know, Zach. Do you think it's too soon for us to be making this big of a commitment?" Hannah toyed with her fingers like an anxious schoolgirl.

Zach's hands tightened around her waist from behind. "You aren't trying to back out already, are you?"

He couldn't see her face, but he was pretty sure she rolled her eyes, based on the haughty way she huffed in response. "It was my idea, remember?"

"It was a great idea."

"I don't want you to feel, you know, overwhelmed or pressured. It's only been a few weeks since you got out of the hospital."

He kissed the top of her head and chuckled. "Stop worrying. I'm fine. The boys are fine. See? Everyone's getting along."

He gestured to the annoyed cat sprawled on the cushion of his sofa, watching Costello run rings around his coffee table faster than he'd ever imagined the dog could run. A gangly pup, leaner and taller than Costello, chased him energetically, only occasionally bumping into furniture in his pursuit.

*I love it here. I love to run and play in my new home. Run. Run. Run.* The dog that the shelter had informed them was a retriever mix, and blind because of a former abusive owner, skidded up to the sofa, sniffed furiously around Abbott and then jerked his head back. *You smell kinda funny.*

Abbott bristled. *I do NOT smell funny. Get away from me unless you want to taste claws for lunch.*

The excitable young canine launched forward and gave the cat a fast and sloppy tongue lick, right across the cat's face. *We're family now. I won't ever let anyone hurt you, 'kay? Love you. Gotta run.* And then the dog sprinted sideways, chasing a visibly winded Costello who kept thinking *I am the leader. I am the leader. Can't let him get in front of me. No, can't let him.*

Abbott heaved a sigh and turned his kitty eyes up at Zach for a mere second. *Well, maybe the new one won't be so bad. We'll see.*

Zach laughed, pleased the three animals were falling in together. Yesterday, Hannah had gone to the local Humane Society to meet with its director about building a new wing in memory of Ellie. She'd been meeting some of the animals too when the cutest, clumsiest mutt had come prancing right up to her in a walk that had reminded her of Charlie Chaplin—and instantly won her heart. She and Zach had rounded up Abbott and Costello and taken them to the shelter this morning to see if they'd all mesh, and now Charlie was an official part of their family.

*Family.* Zach liked the sound of that. His family. So what if the cat still threatened to kill him sometimes? They were working it out. At least the cat talked to him—which was more than he could say about his own brother.

"I've got to go meet with the contractor about the repairs and do a final walk through the house." Hannah turned and gave him a quick kiss. "You'll be okay while I'm gone?"

He nodded. "I don't understand why you won't move in with me."

Zach was sure he sounded as petulant as a twelve-year-old who'd been refused his favorite gadget, but dammit, he didn't want Hannah—or her annoying cat and two dogs—to leave. She'd been staying at his place, and it felt right. Like she belonged here.

"I told you, Zach. I don't want to rush things too fast. I'm starting my new job at the free clinic on Monday, and maybe we can, I don't know, go on a date sometime, like a normal couple before we start talking about moving in. Maybe after the trial."

They'd been warned it might be a year or more before the separate cases against Carolyn Heckler and Polanski ever came before a jury. Best case scenario, Heckler would accept a plea deal for a lesser sentence and help them see to it the more dangerous Polanski spent the rest of his life beyond bars.

Zach blew out a breath. He shouldn't complain about the wait. Things were finally falling into place for him. Hannah had encouraged him to claim the one hundred thousand in euro reward from a French museum for aiding in the return of the famous LeBeau Diamond. One hundred thirty-three thousand American dollars had been wired to the firm's business account. Instead of being in the red, Collins Security Firm was back in black. Zach sure as hell planned to keep it that way.

They'd hired some computer hacking genius with purple hair and an unnatural fondness for licorice to set up a suitable computer network for the agency's new cyber-security initiative. Hannah had smirked and cracked a joke about the young woman fitting right in with the other misfits at the office, and Spider—who the hell called themselves Spider anyway?—had managed to hack into a state agency's website before his own eyes during her initial interview. Since that agency was now a client, who was he to question anything about the girl? Heaven help them all, Alexandra had also accepted a position with the firm. If anyone wanted to hire them for psychic investigation services, that option was now on the table. The lady's credentials were already luring in business. Why the hell hadn't he thought of hiring *her* sooner?

He owed it all to the beautiful, stubborn woman he now held

in his arms.

Hannah arched a brow as her fingers drew a circle over his heart. "I'm not opposed to spending the night every now and then, if you want."

If he wanted. Was she kidding?

It had killed him to keep his hands off her these last few weeks, but she had insisted on no funny business while he healed.

He leaned down and nuzzled her neck. "I like the sound of that."

A part of him was always going to be scared to death she was going to wise up and leave him, but he planned to give her every reason he could think of to stay. He didn't have to be psychic to know one thing.

Someday she was going to marry him. She just didn't know it yet.

# *BONUS MATERIAL*

**And here's an exclusive sneak peek of book two...**

# Something Wicked

# Chapter One

She'd only been at the restaurant five minutes and already a freaking ghost had zeroed in on her.

Crap. Crap. Crap.

Alexandra King jerked her gaze away from the tall man in the corner near the bar—the one wearing a double-breasted black coat with a gray vest underneath—and drummed her fingers against the table top as she waited for her waitress to bring her a bowl of she-crab soup and Caesar salad. The white cotton shirt the man wore was too long for his arms and erupted in ruffles at his wrists. His hair curled below a low Derby hat, and he looked as real as any flesh-and-blood man in this place.

Except for the bloody gash at his throat.

She couldn't help it. She risked another glimpse in his direction. Still watching her, the dead man tipped his hat and winked at her.

Pushing out of her chair, Alexandra shoved her way through the small crowd of people gathered for a Wednesday evening outing at the Southend Brewery and Smokehouse in historic Charleston, South Carolina, and headed toward the sign marked Restrooms.

This stylish specter made about the tenth dead person she'd seen since checking into her room at the inn forty minutes ago. Thankfully none had shown more than a passing interest in her... so far.

She glanced over her shoulder to see if this ghost was going to make a pest of himself. He didn't seem to be following. Good.

Derby Hat Guy was behind the bar now, pouring himself a draft, unseen by the bartender shuffling around him. Stifling a chuckle, she ducked her head and pretended to find the floor interesting. She'd learned long ago that if she ignored dead people, nine times out of ten, they would do the same. It was the ones who didn't that gave her headaches as they chipped away at her mental barrier, made her lose sleep, and do stupid stuff like fly hundreds of miles to hunt down a person she didn't know.

A vibration against her right hip distracted her, and she dug her phone out of her pocket. Glancing at the caller ID, a smile tugged at her lips as she saw her newest—and possibly closest—friend's picture on the display. She leaned against the wall outside the ladies room and focused on the call.

"Hey, Hannah. Did you get my text?" She'd sent a quick one as soon as she'd landed to let her friend know she had arrived safely.

"Yep. You made it there okay? No problems with the flight or getting checked into the hotel?"

"The flight was surprisingly easy, and the place you chose for me to stay at is incredible. More like an apartment than a hotel." Much better than the dumps where she usually stayed anyway. It had been her fortune, meeting Hannah Dawson three months ago. Not only was the woman richer than sin but she had a generous heart that extended to her friends and anyone she assessed had a dire need.

In this case, that had included Alexandra on both counts.

"Good. I wish I'd been able to come with you. You're doing me as much of a favor as yourself." Hannah's voice lowered a notch. "Zach is still being stubborn."

Alexandra resisted the urge to roll her eyes. When wasn't Zachary Collins stubborn?

She'd come to appreciate just how pigheaded the man was when she accepted a job working for him at his private security and investigations agency a few months ago.

The steady paycheck was hella nice, and she loved using her gifts as a psychic medium to help people. Already she'd assisted a family in finding their runaway daughter and helped a desperate single mother locate the good-for-nothing ex-husband who owed her thousands in child support.

Dead people could be so full of useful information.

But she and Zach had butted heads more than once—usually over the fact he refused to use their resources to track down his younger brother and make amends for something—what, she had no idea.

None of her business. She got that. She was *fine* with that. She would've stayed fine with it, but Zach's dead mother had taken up residence in Alexandra's new apartment and refused to leave until her two sons had been reunited. Every time Alexandra lowered her guard, oh look, there was Rebecca Collins again, harping on about her sons. Zachary this. Dylan that. Nag, nag, nag.

Stupid ghost was driving her *insane*.

"Yeah, well, tenacity must run in the Collins family," Alexandra told Hannah. "I've been trying for weeks to get his mom to cross over, or at least get the heck outta my apartment. She doesn't listen either."

Hannah snorted. "I'd believe it. Once Zach gets an idea in his head, he doesn't let go."

"Still pestering you to move in with him, huh?"

"Yes." Hannah drew the word out on a long-suffering sigh. "It's not even that I don't want to. It's like I've told you before. I am crazy about the man, but we need to get to know each other better before we both dive into the deep end. Plus, I'd feel better if he patched things up with his brother first. I know it's important to him, even if he won't admit it."

"Hopefully, the lead that Spider got for us will pan out." Alexandra twirled the ends of her long blonde hair between two fingers. Two guys at the bar hadn't even noticed yet that the bar's friendly spirit had switched their drinks while they'd been distracted checking out the female bartender. Oh my. This was a mischievous ole fellow. "If Dylan Collins is in Charleston like Spider thinks, I'll find him."

The young female hacker Zach had hired to bring his security firm into the twenty-first century had become everyone on the team's "little sister." She was wicked smart and had tracked Zach's brother from Baton Rouge, Louisiana, to Charleston, South Carolina, in under ten minutes. Spider would have probably given them a phone number and address if Alexandra hadn't opened her mouth to ask what the heck that weird action figure was on Spider's desk. It looked like a demonic wild boar on steroids, wearing spikes and armor. Creepy.

Alexandra rolled her eyes at the memory. After a lecture about how awesome the Guild Wars online game was, Spider had been offended enough not to offer any more help in the matter.

Annoying little sister, more like it.

So here Alexandra was, voluntarily in one of the most haunted cities in America, surrounded by freaking dead people, with no idea where to start looking for Zach's little brother.

"Is, um, Rebecca with you?" Hannah's question about Zach's mother drew her back to their conversation.

Alexandra sighed. "Haven't seen her since I boarded the plane. She'll pop up. She always does. Hopefully she'll point me in the right direction so I can get this over and done with."

She'd kind of been counting on Zach's mother to manifest and lead her the rest of the way to the mysterious Dylan Collins. The fact it hadn't happened yet was pissing her off. She'd left herself open to communication with Rebecca, which also left her vulnerable to any ghost, spirit or whatever in search of a conduit between dimensions.

If she didn't show soon, Alexandra was flipping her mental Open sign over to Closed.

After promising to check in with Hannah with frequent updates, Alexandra ended the call and washed her hands to give herself an excuse for visiting the ladies room. She was a little hungry and a lot tired after her evening flight.

She hadn't mentioned it to Hannah, but she'd also been uneasy since touching ground in Charleston. The feeling had intensified the closer she'd gotten to her hotel. She'd never seen anything like the spiral gray beams whirling up toward the skyline from what she assumed was the city's historic district. She'd never encountered so many ghosts so quickly in such a small area either. Not even when she'd lived in Germany, where ghosts were *everywhere*. A heavy, sick weight had sunk into her stomach, manifesting a mild headache as she'd watched the beams wave and shimmer against the setting sun. This city felt...unhealthy.

Or she could be feeling ill because she'd skipped lunch. She hoped that was the reason. Hopefully a decent meal and a good night's sleep would right things.

This place had been highly recommended by the desk clerk at the inn, or she might have opted for junk food out of a machine and called it an early night. She rubbed her eyes and blinked them open again, only to see the man in the Derby hat standing directly behind her, grinning like the Cheshire cat. He lifted a finger and pointed at her in the mirror.

"Ya can see me, can't ya?"

Crap.

A woman came out of the stall behind her, so Alexandra kept her mouth shut and made a quick escape. Maybe if she kept ignoring him —

"I don't mean ya any harm." The Derby Hat Guy followed her back to her table and took the seat opposite her just as the waitress appeared with her food. "I hear the food here is delicious. I know the brew is!" He lifted his mug and chugged back several gulps. The bloody gash at his neck shifted with every swallow. Since the mug gave off a slight orange glow, Alexandra knew it wasn't visible to anyone else. Ghost mug. "Tell me, miss." Reluctantly, she looked his way. "How can a pretty little thing like yer'self see me when no'un else can?"

Alexandra kept her mouth busy, pushing spoonful after spoonful of soup between her lips, avoiding eye contact as best she could. Sometimes she forgot she was in public and launched into a full-fledged conversation with her unseen visitors, but she had no plans of doing so now. Nuh uh. No way. The place wasn't overly crowded, but there were enough people around to notice if she suddenly started talking to The Invisible Man.

But maybe this guy didn't know he was dead. Maybe he needed her help crossing over.

Maybe —

*Stop it! Don't engage him. He's not the reason you're here.*

As the man rambled about the dress of the men and women around them—"Woo-wee! Ain't ever seen the likes! She's practically wearin' nothin'! Would ya look at that?"—Alexandra finished her salad, quietly amused by his observations. He was a chatty fellow, and if she had spoken, she doubted she could get a word in edgewise. Seeing he wasn't going away, she began to study him as he yakked. She'd guess he was in his late thirties, maybe early forties. Lanky. Not overly handsome, but not a dog either. Kind of reminded her of that guy who'd played the Doctor on that British show Hannah had been making her watch. Oh, what was his name? David Tennant. That was it. Except this guy wasn't the least bit British.

Where was Zachery's mom, Rebecca? She might get on quite well with this character—being that they were both highly obnoxious and all. Perhaps she could hook them up in the afterlife and give the dead woman someone else to nag for a change.

"It must be your lucky night, hon." A woman's voice drew her attention.

Alexandra blinked up at her waitress as the young woman slid a mug of beer in front of her. Did the girl seriously just call her hon?

The redhead nodded over her shoulder. "The hunk at the pool tables bought you a drink." She winked. "Enjoy."

Oh, no. Not only were the dead people around here clamoring for her attention, so was some a-hole on the prowl. She bit back a groan and lifted her gaze to give the man a polite shake of her head, a silent thanks but no thanks and –

Hello, Mr. Delicious.

He was hands-down the most criminally sexy man she'd ever laid eyes on, and for a woman who worked with some serious man candy these days that was saying a lot. He studied her from the billiards area as he chalked up one of the cues. He was the only person over there, playing a solitary game while most people congregated at the bar. A slight smile teased his mouth as she managed to lift the mug and nod. So what if she hated beer? She'd gulp the whole thing in one go if that sex god wanted to watch. He nodded back, gestured to the pool table beside him, and—

Oh, yeah. She was tempted to saunter over there and see what happened. Beyond tempted. She'd never had a one-night stand in her life, but maybe this was as good a time as any.

"Well, I'll be! He sure seems to have struck yer fancy."

Oh, no. She scrunched her brows and shook her head. She had a bad feeling about this.

The ghost wooped. "Oh, but I think he has." He glanced toward the billiards. "And I dare say he has taken quite a fancy to you, miss. Comes in here a lot that one does. Never been able to spook 'em though." Derby Hat Guy abruptly stood and started walking toward the other man, saying, "Let's give 'em a game. Have a bit of fun with the rascal." He rubbed his hands together.

"Wait! Uh," Alexandra jumped to her feet and realized a few seconds later she was practically on top of the pool table when Mr. Delicious said, amused, "Whoa now. I'm guessing you like a good game of pool?"

Among other things.

She bit her lip and tried to ignore the ghost bent over the other end of the table, reaching for two of the balls that had been scattered near a corner pocket. She'd made this poor, delicious man a target of the ghost's tomfoolery. Oh dear. She needed to fix this.

"Pool?" Her eyes widened when Derby Hat Guy picked up the white ball behind Mr. Delicious and moved it clearway across the table. There was no orange glow to it, which meant the ball had actually moved. Had anyone else seen that? This ghost was an old and smart one. Not many could move objects like that. "Yeah. Yeah, I love pool. Game on." Leaning over, she slapped the green felt and flicked her fingers a few times toward the wall, trying to convey the message to Derby Hat Guy to get lost.

Mr. Delicious held out a cue stick to her in offering, distracting her from the ghost past his shoulder. "Great. We'll start a new game. I was getting tired of losing to myself." He looked her up and down where she leaned against the table and seemed to like what he saw. His smoldering blue eyes burned with heat so intense, she felt her insides ignite. He wriggled the cue in his hand. "You know how to use this thing?" His smile was kicked up to full charge on the suggestive meter.

Oh, my, he was flirting, and that was a game best played by two. Accepting the cue from him, Alexandra arched a brow and slowly ran a finger along its length. "I can handle a stick pretty good." She pursed her lips, blew at the chalk on the end, and slowly batted her lashes when she looked at him again. "Besides, what woman doesn't love to bust some balls every now and then?"

He gave an appreciative chuckle. "Alright." He began setting up a new game and she sighed, watching his taut backside move deliciously against his faded jeans as he bent over. Whew. Levis should pay him a royalty. Who looked that good in jeans, besides Calvin Klein models? No one, except this guy. Maybe he *was* a Calvin Klein model. He definitely had the face and body for it.

And maybe she should offer to buy him a drink or something—you know, to apologize for making him a target of the resident ghost.

"Can I get you a beer?"

"Nah. I'm good." His back muscles stretched against his black t-shirt when he rested his elbows on the table, highlighting some serious muscle definition beneath.

"Something else? Whiskey?" She tilted her head at him. Me?

"No thanks." His eyes twinkled with amusement as he straightened and moved closer. "Girls take advantage of me when I drink. I can see I'll need to keep my wits around you."

"Is that so?" She cast a meaningful glance over her shoulder at the beer he'd ordered for her. "Crap. You've obviously found me out. Whatever will I do now?" She sent him a pointed look that she hoped said *I know your game. Trying to take advantage of me, eh?*

He selected a stick from the cue rack and sauntered over to her, not looking the least bit remorseful.

"I was hoping if you drank enough, I'd start looking good enough for you to come talk to me. Since you didn't even take a sip before rushing right over, I'm flattered."

She snorted, but yeah, she was as embarrassed as heck about the way that must have looked. "Maybe I thought you were someone else."

"Who?"

She said the first name that came to mind. "Robert Pattinson." And then winced.

His eyebrows squeezed together. He looked almost offended. "Really?"

No, not at all, but what was she supposed to say—oh, there was a ghost coming to play with your balls? She shrugged.

"I won't hold that against you." He winked. "And I should probably warn you." He leaned in close, the tantalizing scent of raw masculine energy exciting her nostrils and causing her inner siren to sit up and sing. "The guy I've been playing against tonight is pretty tough. He might not go easy on you."

"You mean, the guy you were playing pool with earlier?" She glanced around, spotted only Derby Hat Guy leaning against the table, drumming his fingers impatiently, sending her a bored look. "Who is he, Casper the friendly pool player?"

He grinned. "He's the guy who sent you the beer—the one who thought to himself, 'I think the most beautiful woman in the world is in this room, and I'd like to talk to her.'"

Oh, mercy, that was both the best and the worst pickup line she'd ever heard. He had a sense of humor as well as being sexy. She liked that.

She tilted her head and feigned concern. "Have you seen a doctor?"

His eyes widened. "For what?"

"Multiple personality disorder. I think you have it." She smiled to let him know she was only teasing. And she gripped the cue tighter to keep from doing something ridiculous like ripping his shirt off. "Here's a hint, Casanova. Guys who talk about themselves in third person tend to come off as a little bit crazy."

He leaned so close his hot breath teased her face as he tried to stifle a laugh. "Good point. And I'm a jackass. I haven't even asked your name."

"Alexandra." She held out her hand. "And who will I be crushing in this game tonight?"

The warmth of his fingers against hers was stimulating. "Name's—"

The sound of wood knocking against wood startled them both, and Alexandra sprang away. Derby Hat Guy had moved to the cue rack and was purposefully knocking the sticks against one another. He stopped when Mr. Delicious turned around to inspect the noise.

"I thought we were gonna have some fun with the rascal!" complained her newest dead friend. "Come on, already. Let's play!"

Ghosts. They could be so annoying.

***

"You know, they claim this place is haunted."

Dylan Collins leaned against his pool cue and watched as his enticing opponent lined up her shot perfectly—and abruptly banged the white ball against the left side when the words left his mouth.

She swore softly and sighed. "You don't say."

He shrugged and moved to take his first shot, regretful he no longer had a good view of her cleavage as she bent over the table. She'd already sunk a number of the balls. The woman knew her way around a billiard table. "I don't believe in that stuff, personally. If that's your thing, Charleston has a ton of ghost tours."

"Hmm." Her concentration seemed off as she frowned slightly, gazing toward the wall. Maybe she was like him and thought the whole Haunted Charleston spiel was just a gimmick to attract tourists.

Change the topic, dumbass. He didn't want to scare her away

or make her think he was a paranormal freak when he wasn't.

He couldn't believe his luck in luring a beauty like her over here. He circled the pool table and lined up his cue with the ball.

His favorite way to unwind from a bad day at work was to come to the Southend Brewery for a beer, a game of pool, and a game on one of the TVs above the third-floor bar, but he'd never seen a woman like this one here. Usually the women he attracted at bars were young, more than a little tipsy, and as sexually aggressive as sailors turned loose in a whorehouse.

His partner on the force liked to think of them as cop groupies, although Dylan never advertised the fact he was with the North Charleston PD before he decided to take one home. Besides, Reedus was wrong. Usually in this part of the city they were either co-eds or tourists looking for a little naughty fun before returning home to their mundane lives or boyfriends or husbands or whatever. Didn't matter a bit to them that he wore a badge. They were more interested in what he *didn't* wear.

But this one, there was something different about her.

Older than his usual pick up, definitely. He'd guess early 30s.

Lifting his gaze from the end of his cue and toward the blonde across from him, he drank in the sight of her curvy figure. The ball soared forward and clanged against two others that drifted into the corner pocket. He wouldn't stretch his credibility by saying she was the most beautiful woman he'd ever laid eyes on, but she was close. She had something else too that had caught his attention from across the room before he'd ever glimpsed her pretty face. The way she carried herself. Confident. Classy, even in jeans. Two traits he found sexy as hell, and then to come to learn she was smart *and* funny, too? Hot damn.

Normally he went for petite brunettes, but he wouldn't mind a change of taste sampling this leggy blonde for a night or two. Especially tonight, when he needed to erase thoughts of the case that had been eating him up all day.

Was she willing to help him with that?

*Let's find out.*

First, he had to sink the rest of these balls to impress her. He took his time finding the right angle—oh yeah, he could nail three in one shot from here—and made a show of leaning over, sliding the stick through his fingers, oh so slowly, and then snapping forward with just enough finesse to hit his target in the right spot. The white ball clanged against the orange No. 5, sending it into a corner pocket, then spiraled toward both the green No. 6 and purple No.4.

The white ball abruptly took a sharp detour to the left, missing his remaining targets completely.

What the-?

Alexandra's eyes and mouth were wide open, probably a match to his own expression. She blinked and shook her head. "That was…a little weird, huh?" Red began spreading from her neck up through her face.

He scratched at the hair on his head. "Yeah, weird."

"You sank the five though. Uh, good job. Still your turn."

"Right." He bent to find his next shot, narrowed his eyes and spotted three balls clumped together near the middle pocket. That might get him at least two scores. He slid the cue forward then jerked it back when the white ball began slowly rolling toward the left.

He straightened and grabbed the white ball, picked it up and felt its weight in his hand. Damn thing felt normal. He glanced at the woman standing on the other side of the table, her hand now covering her mouth and her eyes glistening with amusement.

She lowered her hand and placed it on her hip. "Are you trying to cheat?"

"What? No. Hell, no. Didn't you see that? The ball moved—"

He bit back a curse and put it where it was before.

He sat his bridge hand on the table, kept his angle smooth, and struck it this time.

Almost every ball on the table rolled out of its way as it bowled forward. It banked off the corner pocket and fell in.

*What the—?*

He reached a hand out over the table. Had someone turned the air conditioning on full blast? Was there a vent he couldn't see?

He didn't feel anything abnormal.

Instead of the impressed cheer he'd been soliciting, he was rewarded with feminine snickering. "Smooth," Alexandra said, pushing him out of the way. "Let me show you how it's done, hot stuff."

She backed her ass up, spread her legs, set up her shot and sent the white ball sailing. She clinked one into the middle pocket, then three more she hadn't even touched flew into other pockets, one after the other.

"How the hell did you do that?"

She held up her cue and blew the tip. "Guess I'm just better at this than you."

Something weird was going on here, but hell, that was okay. She wore amusement well. It lit up her face and looked damn attractive on her. He leaned closer. "Still your turn."

She moved around him to find her next position. He waited until she had leaned down with her cue arranged to follow. He curved over her, resting his hands on the table edge on each side of her, and breathed in the intoxicating scent of strawberries. Mmm. Nice.

Her back lifted slightly, pressing against his chest. "What do you think you're doing?"

He nuzzled his mouth close to her ear. "Making sure you don't cheat. Got a problem with that?"

Judging by the way she wiggled her backside against him, he didn't think so. "You're in my way."

He eased up, but didn't move away completely. He left his right hand resting on the spot above her belt.

She pulled her elbow back, slowly, and sank two more balls. He thought she did, anyway. He wasn't really paying attention to the table anymore. His mind was distracted by the strip of bare skin his fingers had discovered between her jeans and shirt. Smooth, silky smooth. And hot, so hot to the touch.

She turned her head back to glance at his hand before lifting her gaze to his. "Well go on, then. Keep fondling me. I'm still gonna win despite your little distractions."

"Oh, really?"

"Yep."

And then she sank the eight ball.

Game over.

He liked this woman, liked that she gave him a lil bit of hell. "Where are you staying?"

Straightening, she curled both hands around her cue and considered him. "Why?"

"Cause I'd like to know where I'll be spending the night."

She laughed. "Presumptuous, aren't we?"

"Mmm-hmmm. And cocky too."

"No kidding."

He couldn't resist touching the strip of skin still visible between her belt and shirt. Her breath hitched at the contact, so he knew she wasn't as unaffected as she played. "I live just around the corner. We could be there in less than ten minutes."

She said nothing for so long, he started to think he'd overshot this one. Handing him her cue, she arched a brow. "My hotel sounds closer."

They made it there in eight, and if his steps slowed a little when he realized she was leading him to the Lodge Alley Inn, she either didn't notice or didn't care.

Too weird.

His place was on the next street over.

But he kept his mouth quiet about the irony of her stay and put it to better use, nibbling her earlobe as she struggled to open the door to her room. He liked hearing her breathing quicken and turn raspy as his hands had fun, too, sliding around and beneath the hem of her t-shirt. He trailed his fingers along the silky smooth skin of her stomach as he pressed his front against her backside. He couldn't remember the last time he'd wanted a woman this much.

Pushing inside, she didn't turn on the lights, just pulled him in after her, reaching up to devour his mouth like a woman starved for kisses. Man, she was hot.

She tore away from him. "Bed is upstairs." She toed off her shoes and hurried up the spiral staircase inside the entryway of her room. He was right behind her.

***

Dylan must have fallen asleep because the alarm clock read three o'clock when a sound awoke him from a pleasant dream hours later. Alexandra grumbled and snuggled deeper into the sheets as he maneuvered his way to the end of the bed and found his phone.

Speaking quietly, he answered, "Collins."

"Sorry to interrupt your beauty sleep, but we've got another one," his partner's voice was brisk. "Same calling card as the one last month. Pretty sure we've officially got a serial on our hands."

Dylan swore and glanced at the woman sleeping peacefully behind him. It had been nice while it lasted. Reedus gave him a few details and the address while he tugged on his pants.

Picking up the rest of his clothes, he ended the call and moved quietly to the stairs. He hesitated, glancing back toward the bed. A smile tugged at his lips as he walked over, knelt beside the mattress and just looked at her for a minute.

He leaned and kissed her lips softly, quickly, so as not to disturb her.

"See ya later, beautiful."

And he had every intention of doing so.

www.ingramcontent.com/pod-product-compliance
Lightning Source LLC
Chambersburg PA
CBHW010857130726

47900CB00017B/2806